Corina sat in her car for a moment, trying to decide what to do next.

Skin had claimed Eugene Belmont murdered Tina Kellog. He had abruptly ended their phone conversation. Was that reason enough to call the police? Would she look foolish if she did? What if Skin had just been in a hurry? What if he were with his fiancée somewhere? She had to take a look around so that she didn't appear a total neophyte to Henderson and J.T.

She got out of the car and headed toward the blaze of lights in the back. The yard was empty, shadows swallowing the fruit trees and flower beds.

"Skin?" Corina felt silly calling out to anyone in this obviously uninhabited place.

The gray enamel patio furniture was huddled in ghostly clusters around a black-bottom swimming pool. Skin had never set foot in it, though, was terrified of water.

Next to it something glittered in the moonlight. Glass, a broken bottle of some kind. She willed the pool to be as empty as the yard, but already the fear crawled up her arms, constricting her throat. She moved closer to it and forced herself to look, confirming what the silent part of her had already suspected. Pale, chalky-white flesh, the texture of chicken meat, caught the light and shimmered in the black water.

She recognized the bald head and knew it was Skin, his body unmoving, floating, with limbs splayed as though over a barrel facedown.

BONNIE HEARN HILL

IF IT BLEEDS

ISBN-13: 978-0-7783-2339-6
ISBN-10:   0-7783-2339-0

IF IT BLEEDS

Copyright © 2004 by Bonnie Hearn Hill.

www.MIRABooks.com

For Harold Zinkin
1922–2004

ACKNOWLEDGMENTS

My thanks to the team for their
contributions to this book:

Amy Moore-Benson, editor and friend;

Tania Charzewski, Donna Hayes, Loriana Sacilotto,
Alex Osuszek, Gordy Goihl, Ken Foy and
Fritz Servatius, the MIRA team;

Nené Casares, for sharing her culture,
her friendship and her fabulous mind;

Genevieve Choate, for taking me inside
her world—cool beans!;

My friends at the *Fresno Bee,* who kept telling me
I should write this book;

Sheila Stephens, for all of the good gun stuff;

Harold Zinkin, the king of West Shaw Avenue, for the
conversations and the insights;

Larry Hill, Meg Bertini, Pat Smith, Cindy Wathen,
Linda Nielsen, Sheree Petree and Hazel Dixon Cooper,
for their input and encouragement, even when
Mercury was in retrograde;

The Tuesday Night Writers;

Mona Lisa Badasci, for the yellow-cat stuff;

Dianne Moggy and MIRA Books, for their support,
And to my amazing agent, Laura Dail,
who is always, always right.

Prologue

Ensenada, Saturday, June 2, 7:25 p.m.

Even before she finished the Tecate, Roxene knew the informant wasn't going to show. She could almost always sense the ones who would pan out and the ones who wouldn't. She placed the beer on the bar and looked at big Norm Flannigan next to her, his smug smile wet with tequila, still wanting to believe they'd luck out twice in one week.

In his bunched, bulky jeans, his sandy hair covered by a baseball cap similar to hers, he seemed to fade into the smoky room. She was sure she did, too. Invisible came from attitude as well as attire, something she had learned back at Quantico and practiced every day since.

They'd picked a public place, not a tourist hive like Hussong's, but with enough Americans that they wouldn't attract attention. Sepia sketches of former patrons covered an entire wall. What kind of person, she wondered, would pay to leave a portrait behind?

The sad-faced bartender reappeared, as if he'd been waiting for her to take the last swallow, but, like a true macho man, he directed his question to Norm. *"¿Una más?"*

"Por favor."

She cringed at Norm's sucky Spanish. "Why bother?" she asked as the dreary fat man returned to his cooler. "I told you it was a dog call. A guy knows a guy who knows a guy who has a boat. Decides to be a hero, calls DEA, then has second thoughts."

"Last time I checked, this was still Mexico." Norm downed the rest of his shot with a swallow, then, with the glass still grazing his lips, gave her the senior agent smirk she hated. "Because *you* go at full throttle doesn't mean the rest of the world does. Why not try to slow down a little?"

She decided to let the remark pass. This wasn't the time nor the place to discuss their differences.

In the corner behind them, a guy with a guitar sang "Paloma Querida," doing a pretty fair impression of Pedro Infante and a less-than-fair job of accompanying himself. In spite of a couple of college-age girls at a back table taking a fast tequila ride to the nastiest hangovers of their lives, the air was tense with too much smoke and too little light. Something about the place—the music, the bartender with his mournful expression, the portraits left behind—unnerved her. It was too textbook Ensenada, too safe, on the surface, at least. The Glock pressing against the small of her back no longer felt uncomfortable.

"I think we should go."

The bartender put another can of beer before her, then refilled Norm's shot glass from the Sauza bottle. Norm swept coins across the bar to him as if they were poker chips. Then he turned back to her. "One more *cerveza* won't kill you. Then, if the guy doesn't show, we can grab a late dinner."

She pushed away the can. "Now," she said.

Norm pulled himself up from the bar stool. "Whatever works," he said, then downed the tequila without as much as a squint.

He'd read the meaning in her words, and she knew he'd respect her request, even if he thought this were just one of her crazy whims. They left as anonymously as they'd entered. Norm pulled open the door of peeling wood, and she stepped out. The air smelled of ocean, of the deep-fried shrimp the taco vendors had been selling all day. But it didn't revive her.

She leaned close to Norm, trying to shake the confusion out of her head. "Did that place creep you out as much as it did me?"

"No more than any of the others." He took a deep breath. "Must have been the cigarettes. I think you're right about our guy, though. He's not going to show. Want to get something to eat?"

She shook her head again and walked around the building to the car. "I need to sleep." The feeling wouldn't let go of her. She tried to think, but even in the fresh air, she could still smell the smoke. What was wrong? What had changed? *The music.*

"That guitar player," she said.

"What about him?"

"He stopped playing the minute I stood. But it was more than that. I couldn't put my finger on the feeling, but that's what it was. He was watching us."

"You think—?"

Before he could finish, she heard a rush of footsteps behind them, the deadly metal-on-metal *chuchunk* of a shotgun being rechambered. She whirled around. A shotgun, all right, aimed at her. The guitar player faced them.

"You left before we could talk," he said in precise English. "Over there." He motioned toward the alley less than a couple of feet away.

"We can talk out here." Norm ignored the command and edged closer to him. "You're the one who called in the tip, aren't you?"

"*Sí*, but you left too quickly. Back there, *por favor.*"

Roxene scanned the street. Empty. Riddled with alleys where anything, anyone, could be waiting. Their only hope was that someone saw them. She caught Norm's eye in the moonlight, told him in that quick glint of connection to distract the bastard.

Norm moved a little closer. She stepped to the side. The moon seemed too intense, a vivid splash of light, almost blinding her. She jerked away from its glare. She had to focus on the man before them, try to get at the gun tucked into the waistband of her jeans.

"You son of a bitch." Something was wrong with Norm's voice. "What kind of games are you playing? What'd you put in my drink back there?"

His tequila, her too-bitter Tecate. Damn. The moon found her again, played games with her vision, her equilibrium.

"Won't do you any good." The man motioned toward the alley. "I don't want to hurt you, but we have to talk. Let's go."

Norm rushed him. Roxene flew into combat mode, knocking the shotgun from his grasp, going for her own gun. Variegated colors danced before her eyes. She ignored the light show, steadied the gun.

Someone grabbed her from behind. There were two of them. She hadn't counted on that. The man struggling with her felt larger, stronger, more dangerous than the other. Her strength ebbing, she kicked, jerked, tried to twist free, to connect with any part of the one who pinned her hands behind her back. In the jagged moonlight, she saw Norm's big body fall before her like a bolt of fabric flung to the ground. Another blur of a man, as large, larger than Norm, knelt beside him.

Then, Norm disappeared.

Fight it. She had to fight it. If she gave into the lights, to whatever they'd used to drug her, it could mean their lives.

Hoisted in a heavy grip, her body began to float toward the shadows. Somewhere she heard laughter, a faint humming, a song, Pedro Infante. She tried to hold on to the song as long as she could, but already it faded, softer, softer, more distant, as the silence and the darkness descended.

One

The San Joaquin Valley in summer was hotter than Mexico and hell put together, Corina Vasquez's father always said. At that moment she would have settled for either locale, anywhere but the *Valley Voice* cafeteria, where, thanks to the new management's cost-saving measures, the heat was almost as stifling indoors as out.

Nothing warm about the way her co-workers were treating her, though. Corina bought a glass of Chai tea, paid the cashier and looked around. If the studied lack of interest of the others in the café were any indication, nobody was going to invite her to share their table. Might as well take the tea back to her desk. At least she could get some work done without Matthew Henderson breathing down her neck.

She'd just started back down the hall when J. T. Malone, the metro editor, dashed out of the elevator.

He put on the brakes when he saw her. "Where the hell's Henderson?" he asked. Dressed down by his standards, in a white shirt and chocolate-brown slacks a shade darker than his skin, J.T. was the only person in the building who looked untouched by the heat. They'd been easy with each other once, almost friends, but that had all stopped when Ivy Dieser, the new managing editor, had promoted Corina to Matthew Henderson's assistant.

"He's off today," she said. "It is Sunday, you know."

"Where'd he go? He's not at home, not answering his phone nor his e-mail."

"He'll be in tomorrow. What's so urgent?"

J.T. hesitated, then said, as if she'd forced it out of him, "Got a lead on something big. A body's been uncovered outside of town. PD source says it's the mayor."

For a moment, Corina was taken aback. Wes Shaw, her Wes, was mayor now, but J.T. wasn't talking about him. Her brain processed the scant information, and in doing so, reminded her that Wes Shaw was no longer hers and hadn't been for almost a year.

"You mean Tina Kellogg?"

"That's what I said. The mayor."

Shock gave way to emotion. Tina Kellogg dead. It wasn't right, but it was what everyone suspected after she hadn't returned from a trip to the coast, hadn't made her house payment, hadn't contacted any of her friends. Corina fought the tears that came with the realization. "That's so awful. She was such a decent woman."

"Yeah." J.T. studied her with even more intensity than usual. "If we can't find Henderson, I guess I'm going to have to send you out there."

I guess?

"We don't have time to look for him." She began walking as she spoke, heading for the stairs, adrenaline building. "Just tell me where they found her. I'm on my way."

"Wait." J.T. reached for the cell phone on his belt. "Let me try Henderson one more time."

Corina whirled to confront him, seeing it all there in his face: the suspicion, the distrust, the damned, rotten doubt. It was the way all the old-timers looked at her since the promotion, as if she were after their jobs.

"Your call, J.T. You want me to cover this, or you want to stand here talking about it while the TV stations grab the story?"

Moisture glistened on his forehead. He glanced at his watch, then at her, a man without choices, she thought, an editor who knew that, live or die, the only real enemy was time. "Okay," he said. "Get going."

Even as she rushed for the door, she silently cursed him—he, who should know better than anyone—for how she felt trying to prove herself in this world, that regardless of what anyone said or pretended, was still run by white males.

Two

The smell hit her first. Even across the field, it carried like the stench of the stockyards, only more cloying. Standing outside her car, sun hammering down, Corina fought the reflex to gag. She'd been so intent on getting a decent story and proving herself to Henderson and the rest of the staff that she hadn't stopped to think about how she'd react to the grim reality of murder. And now here it was, in a decomposed heap, just across the yellow tape a few hundred feet ahead.

A company station wagon pulled up beside her car, and Wally Lorenzo, the photographer, stepped out. He nodded to her on his way to unload his equipment, an old guy with a permanent frown that seemed to deepen when he looked at her. Talented photographer, though, in spite of his dandruff-flaked thick glasses that didn't stop him from seeing the story behind a shot. The editors always said you didn't have to crop Lorenzo's photos; he cropped them himself when he took them.

"How'd they get you out here?" she asked.

"Changed my hours a few weeks back. Needed

one more person on weekends.'' He ran his free hand through salt-and-pepper hair that was more salt than pepper these days.

''I'm sorry,'' she said, then wondered if that were the right response.

''Doesn't matter. A job's a job. Better get to work.'' He trudged ahead in the direction of the taped-off area, humming softly.

That smell. God, he must be faking his nonchalance. This couldn't be something one learned to tolerate. How many of these scenes had he photographed? How many bodies that used to be human, mutilated and decaying in any number of unsavory locations?

Even the officers beyond the yellow tape wore masks. A group of them scribbled notes and clicked photos of something at the bottom of a dried-out canal. Corina watched them, not sure whether or not she was relieved she couldn't see the body, as she followed in Wally's path through the vacant field.

Who the hell was she trying to kid? She was a business reporter. The closest she'd been to death was fleeting glances at the waxy replicas of her grandparents in the relative safety of a funeral home. She hadn't asked for this promotion, but she had to prove herself, especially with old-timers like J.T., Wally and Henderson, her own supervisor, waiting for her to fail.

She would prove herself, too. She just had to learn the ropes, and the sandy-haired officer guarding the site where Tina's body was being unearthed was as good a place as any to start.

He looked up from his clipboard when Corina approached. His unlined face set his age at thirty,

thirty-five maybe. His experienced eyes of appraisal told a different story.

"Hot enough for you?"

It was the usual greeting of two strangers meeting in the middle of a San Joaquin Valley summer, even two strangers meeting over murder.

"I hear tomorrow will be worse," she said.

"We can count on more rolling blackouts, that's for sure." He did not appear bothered by either the weather or the nature of his job. He had the demeanor of a mortician—a smile, a friendly attempt at empathy—then once the pleasantries were exchanged, a voracious return to business. "I'll need to get your name."

"Corina Casares Vasquez," she replied, in a precise voice that just barely hid her distaste of the activity near the freshly dug earth a few hundred feet from where they stood. "*Valley Voice* newspaper."

"That's a mouthful." He flashed her a perfunctory smile, then returned to his clipboard and the job at hand. "Corina," he began. "You spell that with a *C* or a *K*?"

"*C.*" She walked him through the rest of the drill, explaining that, yes, both names were her last name, no hyphen, thank you very much.

"New to the *Voice*, are you?"

"Just to this beat."

He glanced at the clipped-on ID that jutted out from her vest. His eyes darted back and forth as he compared the image there to the real thing.

"I guess it's you, all right." He studied her feature by feature, from straight hair to her jeans and vest, both of which suddenly felt too tight.

"Our security supervisor takes new photos once

a year,'' she explained. The solemn, swollen face on the laminated strip of plastic reminded her of how, for weeks after Wes left her, she'd cried every day— to work, from work, sometimes sitting at her desk, staring at her computer while trying to squeeze back tears. She thought she'd hidden it, but looking at her ID, she realized how obvious her pain had been, and how far she'd come. She looked away, vowing to ask Verna to take a new photo at once. ''What can you tell me about what happened here?''

''There's not a whole lot to tell. Two kids making out in the vineyard spotted the victim's shoe sticking up from the dirt in the canal. They investigated and discovered the remains.''

Corina shuddered silently. ''Man's shoe or woman's shoe?''

He swallowed noisily, as if she'd glanced up and caught him chewing gum. ''You know I can't talk about that. You guys been hounding me around the damned clock, and we haven't even taken the body to the morgue yet.''

To cops, all reporters were guys. She considered pointing out the fact but thought better of challenging him. Forcing the image of the skeletal foot from her mind, she cut to the chase. ''We heard it was the former mayor.''

''Lots of former mayors in Pleasant View.''

''Last I checked, Tina Kellogg was the only one missing for three months. We heard belongings of hers were found at the scene.''

''I know what you heard,'' he said. ''That's what happens when officers talk off the record. There's no such thing. You guys don't respect it.''

''We do respect it. It's your *guys* who run their

mouths and then try to change the rules on us." His jaw stiffened, and she wished she'd kept quiet.

"I can't tell you anything else right now," he said. "You want any more information, you check with the coroner. Better get out of the sun, too. You ask me, you're not cut out for this beat."

The foul air closed in, threatening to prove him right. "I'll get used to it."

Something akin to sympathy crept into his pale eyes. "Takes a while."

"I guess so. Thanks for your help."

"Sorry I couldn't give you more information. You know how it is."

"I understand, but it would help a lot if you could just tell me why they're withholding her name. Is it because they have to notify family members?"

He nodded. "Part of it. But in the case of a public figure, we have to take more precautions, even when we're sure."

"I didn't mean to hound you," she said, as if the interrogation were over and she were leaving. "It's just that our source told us there'd been an absolute ID."

"It's not absolute until the coroner does it," he said, as if lecturing a criminology class. "We still have to go through the motions, even in a case like this where we find ID on the victim."

She jumped on it. "But if you have personal items of hers, a purse, say, a driver's license—"

"Takes more than that."

"So," she said, as if playing a game of speculation, "who do you think killed her?"

He shrugged. "Pissed-off boyfriend? Who knows? I hear she had a few."

She thanked him again and left. An ornate For Sale sign stood next to the entrance to the main road. The poor farmer who owned this vineyard wouldn't be selling it any time soon. On the road, she passed a Channel 5 van driving in. It didn't matter. She'd learned what she was sent here to find out. She could go back to the paper and tell J.T. his source had been confirmed. The body in the field was their missing former mayor's. But first she needed a shower. And she needed to shampoo the smell of death from her hair.

A few minutes past five, she parked her Corolla in the *Voice* parking lot. The sun-baked asphalt still radiated heat. She tried not to think about the source of her excitement, but it was there like a shadow she glimpsed from the corner of her eye. A woman was dead, a public servant who, despite her flaws, had done a damned fine job as their backward city's first woman mayor.

A security guard on a bicycle stopped and walked Corina to the ramp leading to the side door. She lifted her ID to another young, uniformed man at the guard station, then followed the long, polished hall past the executive offices on her left, through the art and features departments.

Metro buzzed like a single engine made up of countless coordinated parts. The staff moved in sync, each a segment of that miraculous twenty-four-hour machine called a newspaper. The front page was a last-minute job.

The above-the-fold piece covered the disappearance of two DEA agents, a man and a woman, in Ensenada. Norman Flannigan and Roxene Waite had uncovered a scheme by the drug cartels earlier in the week. No one knew if the kidnappings were related.

That's all they needed. War hawks, including and especially Governor Craig Menlo, were demanding military intervention, claiming the Mexican government was involved. This would worsen an already volatile situation.

Metro staff members had made last-minute phone calls to highway patrol and fire department sources, checking to see if there were any stories grisly enough for the front page.

"If it bleeds, it leads," they always said. For the first time, the meaning of the mantra hit home with Corina. Find a really gruesome story, and you'll lead on A-1, above the fold, as she'd be doing tomorrow, unless something bloodier occurred somewhere else. Because a public figure was dead, she was getting a break. It was that simple and that complicated.

J.T. looked up when she passed his office, then waved her over. His closely cropped hair and expansive forehead exaggerated the arch of his eyebrows, giving him a cynical look he worked a little too hard to live up to. It was impossible to relax around him. She suspected Henderson maligned her abilities at every opportunity, and she had neither the talent nor the taste for sucking up to management, even when the management person in question was someone she had once liked and respected.

It was Ivy Dieser who had engineered her promotion a few months after stepping into the managing editor job, vacated when her predecessor made one of those convenient "lateral moves" that were so prevalent with new management. So clueless was Ivy that when she informed Corina of her new position, she immediately asked whether she wanted to be called Hispanic or Latina.

"Mexican," Corina had told her, stunned that Poison Ivy, as they called her, could be so blatant as to the reason for her good fortune. "I'm Mexican."

J.T. met her at the doorway to his office, a sparse room except for the numerous photos of his vacations to Jamaica. "You get it?" he asked as if he'd sent her to Starbucks for a latte.

She nodded. "Cop wouldn't confirm anything on the record, but he made it clear."

"Same here, but we can still say our sources believe the body is hers. Where the hell is Henderson, anyway?"

"I can write the story by myself, J.T."

"I'm sure you can. Matthew knew her is all. You never even met the woman."

"Sure I did, right after I first came here. Remember that Hispanic Scholarship thing? You and I went together, in fact. I was still in the business department."

He nodded and gave her a cryptic smile. "That's right. Janie sent her entire minority editorial staff, you, yours truly and Linda Woo in features."

Finally common ground. "Minority quotas, that's all we are to them," she blurted.

"And twenty years ago, when I started, we'd play hell getting a job here at all." His eyebrow arched even higher, and he enunciated carefully. "I have been the first black at every paper I worked for, lady. It hasn't changed that much. Dieser'd have me out on my ass right now if it weren't for those minority quotas."

"I just meant—"

"I know what you meant. Now, stop feeling sorry for yourself and write that story. Henderson can fill you in on everything he has on Tina Kellogg later. For now, just cover the basics. Widow takes over husband's construction business, forges a career in politics, leads the city at a time of unprecedented growth. What took her from there to—where'd they find her?"

"A vineyard," **she said,** still stinging from his reproach.

"What took her from there to the dusty vineyard, her body unclaimed? **Something** like that."

"You sound a little television, if you don't mind my saying so."

"That's why I'm the editor and you're the reporter. Now go write it."

"What about Henderson?"

He shrugged as if unaware of the silent war raging right under his nose these past two months. "He's not here," he said.

Three

In spite of what he said, Corina knew J.T. wished Henderson were here. He didn't like her, maybe just didn't trust her. But he didn't know her, either; Henderson had made sure of that.

The incandescent ceiling lights illuminated the L-shaped desk butted up against the outside wall of Henderson's office. The *Associated Press Stylebook*, thick with yellow sticky notepapers, stood sandwiched between the dictionary and Strunk and White on Corina's desk. She ignored the blinking red light indicating phone messages, pulled up her chair to the computer and called up the archives.

Tina had disappeared in March, a week before her forty-fourth birthday, leaving behind everything but her cell phone and the clothes she was wearing. When her son couldn't reach his mother on the phone, he reported her missing, and although no one said the word, let alone printed it, Corina knew they all suspected murder—another woman who ended up the loser in some weirdo's version of Get Even.

The city council held an emergency election and filled her position with mayor pro tem Wes Shaw.

Don't, Corina warned herself. *Don't even think about him.*

She forced herself to concentrate on Tina Kellogg. Every image she called up on her computer screen looked vibrant, alive. Tina at election headquarters, winning by a landslide, hugging a supporter. Tina in a pair of jeans and cap hammering nails at a Habitat For Humanity project. Tina standing next to Skin Burke at the ribbon cutting for Vineyard Estates, her smile radiant. Tina after September 11, leading the city's memorial service, her head bent in prayer. Corina took notes as she went through the archives. Widowed mother, one son. She scrawled a question. "Where is the son?" Another note: "Husband?"

She focused the story down to a summary lead and the facts, tacked on a working head. Body In Field Believed To Be Former Mayor's.

As she waited for her computer to shut down, she pressed the button next to the red, blinking light on her phone. Probably nothing, but she couldn't turn her back on unheard voice mail any more than she could leave a letter unopened.

The first two were guilt calls from her mother that Corina star-sixed before they had a chance to do their intended job. The third was an announcement from her younger sister, Guadalupe, that she was coming to spend a night next week with her. Oh, great.

No immediate action required. Her mother's calls were beyond her control. And Lupita came and went, using her condo as a motel whenever she and their mother fought. Corina pressed the star button, then the number six to delete the message, then went on to the last one.

"Hey, Corina. This is Skin. Got to talk to you ASAP about that story you're working on, the mayor. Call me as soon as you hear this." He repeated his phone number twice, his voice tense, unrecognizable from the one on his radio commercials for Vineyard Estates.

How could Skin Burke know what she was working on? He'd been a source when she worked in the business department, and she hadn't talked to him since her promotion. She called his office and house, leaving messages at both. No luck. She would have to try again on the way home. The strangled quality in his voice troubled her. Skin was not easily rattled. He'd come up the hard way, from a manufacturer of security systems to one of the city's most successful developers. What was it about Tina Kellogg's probable murder that could make him sound so agitated, maybe even scared?

Four

Ivy Dieser stood outside J.T.'s door, trying to look patient. It was good form to show respect for lower management, to wait for an invitation, or at least a notice. When he finally looked up, he gave her a frown.

"Trying to sneak up on me?" he asked.

"Not at all. Just wanted to talk, if you have a minute."

He gave her a look that said she had to be kidding. "On a Sunday night? You came down here for a chat?"

"I have a dinner date later on and thought I'd drop in on the way." She leaned against the door to his office, and when the expected invitation wasn't proffered, entered, anyway, and sat. "I wanted to see what came down with the body they found."

He surveyed her with narrowed eyes. "Looks like it's Mayor Kellogg. I sent Corina to cover it."

That surprised her. Cooperation was the one word sorely lacking in his extensive vocabulary. "A fine choice. That pleases me, J.T."

"Don't be too pleased. I sent her because I couldn't find Henderson."

"You snooze, you lose, as Chenault always says."

"When you tell him about it, please point out that Henderson didn't snooze. He just took a Sunday off."

"Of course." She stretched out in the chair and studied the smudge on the leg of her pants. She should have known better than to wear white down here. Unconcerned as J.T. pretended to be, she knew he'd watched her stretch out in the chair. She knew that, in spite of his hostility, he'd give two inches off his dick to have her. It would never happen, though, not that he wasn't cute, not that she wasn't totally without prejudice where men were concerned. He just wasn't management material, and he wouldn't be managing anything around here for long.

"How'd Corina do?" she asked.

"So far, so good. Of course she doesn't have Henderson's experience."

"Neither did Henderson when he was twenty-eight. You need to give her more assignments like this."

"Dead bodies in fields?"

Although he kept his voice clipped and polite, she'd have to be blind to miss the disdain he telegraphed. Well, she knew how to deal with disdain, and so did their publisher, Brandon Chenault.

"I'm saying that I want to see more than one by-line coming out of Matthew Henderson's department."

"I know what you're saying."

"You have a problem with that?"

He glanced down at the brochure he'd been holding, then leaned across the desk, dropping the pretense, as she knew he would if she pushed him far enough. "I have a problem with taking a promising reporter out of the business department when they're so shorthanded there already."

"We're shorthanded all over. I don't have to explain the economy to you. We have to work harder and smarter, that's all."

"But we don't have to get rid of good employees just because they're earning more than the new ones."

Ivy leaned back in the chair, letting him consider what he'd just said. "Is that what you think I'm trying to do? Get rid of good employees?"

He wadded up the brochure and tossed it in the trash can. The famous J.T. temper. Good. She'd come back later, retrieve the remains of the brochure. One never knew when something so apparently meaningless might come in handy. She had a whole drawer with neatly labeled exhibits just like this.

"I don't know what you're trying to do. In the six months you've been in this job, my whole damn staff's been rearranged."

"It happens that way sometimes," she explained calmly, "especially with the economy so uncertain. What's happening in Mexico could launch another war."

"Let's hope not."

"Not that they'll call it a war. Broke as the state is, California is one of the top ten economies in the world. They'll say we're restoring political stability or something, but it will be a war, and our financial picture will get even worse."

"I know. I know. The economy sucks, and everyone is being sacrificed because of it." He spoke without emotion, secure, she thought. Black and over forty and not really giving a damn about anything but planning his next vacation.

"We want to keep you, J.T." she said.

"I'm sure you do."

"Even though we know you're looking."

He paused just a moment, but the surprise lingered in his eyes. "Everyone's looking."

"But as you so eloquently put it, the economy sucks." She smoothed her slacks against the curve of her legs, letting him get a glimpse of what he was missing for being such an insufferable asshole. "Take care of Corina, okay?"

He, of course, pretended not to notice her little display. "I'll do that anyway. It's my job."

"Yes," she said, rising. "It is."

Five

Corina tried to call Skin's office two more times from her car on the way home. On the second try, he answered.

"Corina? It's about time." He sounded breathless.

"I've been trying to reach you since I got your message."

"I was rounding up some stuff I want to show you. Just walked in the door. We need to talk right away. You're the only one down there I trust."

His voice began to fade, and she pulled to the side of the street to keep from losing the signal. "What's so urgent? You know I'm covering hard news now."

"This is hard news and hard ball, lady. That body they found today? It's Tina Kellogg. That bastard Belmont killed her."

A chill zigzagged through her. "Why would Eugene Belmont kill Tina?"

"Because she wanted me out of Vineyard Estates. Because she found out what was really going on."

"What is going on?"

"Something too big for us to stop. Believe me, I tried. Bastards won't be happy till they start a war."

He paused. "What the hell? There's someone out there. Hang on for a minute, will you?"

"Skin?" She heard a sharp noise, as if he'd dropped the phone, then it went dead.

"Skin, are you there?"

Nothing. She turned her car around. Maybe she was blowing his phone call out of proportion. Maybe one of his old cronies had just stopped by for a visit. Either way, Corina knew she couldn't just sit there.

Sunday, June 3, 9:22 p.m.
Skin

It was never supposed to be this way. Not like this, on all fours, in front of my own swimming pool, trying to keep from passing out as the black water shimmies closer, and wave after wave of chlorine hits my burning nostrils. Got to breathe. Got to explain while I still can, before it's too late.

"Security," I say, but the albino bastard shoves my face into the pool again. I choke on the words, and he yanks me out. I turn my head, retching, focus on the blur of his face in the moonlight, swear I see a smile.

"I won't tell." The words spill out in snotty sobs. Can't even talk, the throbbing gash on my head drizzling blood into my eyes, down onto my arm.

"Where is it?"

I can breathe. He's holding me up from the water, his hot breath on my face. He's letting me go, finally. I'm safe. Air fills my flooded lungs. I gulp it in.

"Where?" The voice is whisper harsh.

I peer up through the blood, and spit out the only thing I know will save me. "Corina Vasquez."

"The reporter?" But it's not a question.

"I'll never tell," I say. "Never tell, never. She won't use it unless—"

The words burst out of me in bubbles. I'm pushed down, down again, eyes exploding into a burst of light, then nothing but searing pain. I can no longer hear my screams, not even in my head now, where the roar of the water drowns out everything else. Drowns. Shit. No.

Six

The Vineyard Estates complex was located in a new industrial park in the northwest area of town. She found Skin's office easily. It was the only one with a light on. The door stood open, a beige wash of carpet reflecting the overhead light. She hesitated. Janitors, tending to the trash of the day, went about their business without taking notice of her.

"Skin?" Her voice sounded high-pitched in the empty room. Maybe she should call the police, or at least J.T. No. She needed to find Skin. When she stepped inside, she saw only empty desks, magazines squared into perfect symmetrical piles on glass-topped tables. "Skin, are you here?" No answer. Well, was she going to be a coward, or was she going the rest of the way in? Her feet made the decision for her, carrying her unwilling body into the small reception area and the darkened office beyond.

She flipped on a light switch, illuminating the dark wood of his L-shaped desk. A notebook lay open in the middle of the desk, perfectly aligned as Skin liked everything in his life. She walked closer to it, picked it up. A single phone number was printed on

the page, a name above it. Hers. She recognized
Skin's boxy handwriting. He always wrote in pencil
as if he didn't trust the permanence of ink. The thick
strokes on the pad looked almost violent. Where the
hell was he?

She tried calling his home but got only his answering machine. Maybe he was with his fiancée.
No, he'd been at the office less than an hour ago,
and he'd spoken with too much urgency to have decided to put off their meeting.

She stepped outside and called to the janitors.
They exchanged glances, and the youngest-looking
of the group came over. He asked her in broken
English what she needed.

Corina answered in Spanish that she was looking
for her friend, who was supposed to meet her at this
office.

He grinned at her use of their shared language and
answered eagerly. "Does he drive a gold Mercedes?
Really nice car?"

She nodded. "Yes. Have you seen him?"

"I think so. Hair about this long?" He touched
his shoulders. "Head over to the side like this?"

"No," she said. "This man is short, and he's
bald."

"Oh, the other man, not the driver."

"There was somebody with him?" she asked, trying to hide her frustration. "Two men in the car?"

"Two men?" he replied. "A tall man, his head
like this, and a short, bald man. He looked sick."

"Sick, how?"

"The other man, his friend, had to help him in
the car."

Corina thanked him and drove to Skin's house. If

he weren't home, maybe someone would be. The place was lit as if for a party, the rainwater-scent of the river making the air feel cooler than it really was. She pulled into the long driveway and sat in her car for a moment, trying to decide what to do next.

Skin had claimed Eugene Belmont murdered Tina Kellogg. He had abruptly ended their phone conversation. Was that reason enough to call the police? Would she look foolish if she did? What if Skin had just been in a hurry? What if he were with his fiancée somewhere? She had to take a look around so that she didn't appear a total neophyte to Henderson and J.T.

She got out of the car and headed toward the blaze of lights in the back. The yard was empty, shadows swallowing the fruit trees and flower beds.

"Skin?" She felt silly calling out to anyone in this obviously uninhabited place.

The gray-enamel patio furniture was huddled in ghostly clusters around a black-bottom swimming pool Skin kept for show. Always looking for an edge, he had worked out a deal with a pool contractor, who had put it in for nothing in return for Skin's referring business to him. He never set foot in it, though, because he was terrified of water.

Next to it something glittered in the moonlight. Glass, a broken bottle of some kind. She willed the pool to be as empty as the yard, but already the fear crawled up her arms, constricted her throat. She moved closer to it, and forced herself to look, confirming what the silent part of her had already suspected. Pale, chalky-white flesh, the texture of chicken meat, caught the light and shimmered in the black water.

She recognized the bald head and knew it was Skin, his body unmoving, floating, with limbs splayed as though over a barrel facedown.

One of the two officers assigned to her call paced patiently in Skin's circular driveway, while Corina finished the conversation with her mother and shut off her cell phone. There'd be hell to pay with Mama later, but she could deal with that. The question was, could she deal with this? The questions, the answers, the image that she knew she'd never forget of Skin's grotesque body?

The officer *du jour,* older than the one guarding Tina Kellogg's remains, had professionally friendly eyes about the same color as his curly gray hair.

"Sorry," Corina said, joining him before his car. "That was my mother. She checks up on me sometimes."

"She live near here? Maybe you ought to have her come over for the night."

"North of Bakersfield," she said. "Forty minutes, give or take. Besides, I don't want to tell her just yet. She worries too much."

"Are you going to be all right?" the cop asked. "You're shaking."

She glanced down at her hands and realized he was right. "I'm fine," she said, "honest."

It was the biggest lie she'd told in a long time, and she could tell by the look on his face, the cop didn't believe a word of it.

Parental guilt call 553

"*Mija,* I didn't like the way you hung up on me. What's going on?"

"I was just running down a story. I'll explain later, when we can talk."

"We can talk now. How many hours those people make you work at that newspaper, anyway?"

"I said we'll talk later. Mama, I've got to go now."

A long sigh. "You don't have to work so hard. You know how much Lydia's boyfriend makes?"

"Pete's an attorney. I'm sure he does well. I earn more than Lydia, though, or more than she did. Before she quit that paralegal job."

"Pete needs her at the office. There's nothing wrong with helping your man find success, *Mija*. That is the one lesson I wish I could teach you."

"You've taught me, Mama. You've taught me."

"Honest? You aren't just mocking again?"

"Honest. Picture me before you. I'm crossing myself as we speak."

"Mija!"

"I'll call you tomorrow and explain everything, okay? Right now, I have to get some rest. Good night."

Seven

Melissa Henson looked even better naked than she did with clothes on. Wes watched her walk in from the bathroom, the towel wrapped around her like a short, lavender dress. She was also a voracious lover; the shower she'd just taken didn't guarantee there wouldn't be a round two.

"Come on, lazy," she said. "You haven't moved the whole time I was in there." Tight wet curls bobbed as she approached her bed. She could go out of the house like that, with her hair still dripping water, and look better than most women who spent hours in a salon. *Most women. Don't go there.* This one was sexy. She was funny. She was bright. That should be enough.

"Show some pity for an old man." He patted the still-warm place beside him.

"I'll show you pity, Mr. Mayor." She flipped off the towel in one quick movement and stood before him with both arms up, as if she'd just jumped out of a cake. Moisture still glistened on her golden skin, illuminated her pink-tipped breasts.

"Come here," he said, his voice gritting in his

throat. It had been one of those nights, and it was going to be one of those mornings, too. Good.

Melissa put one foot on the bed, then the other. Towering over him, she began to bounce, as if on a trampoline, tantalizing him with the view.

"Where shall I land?" she asked in a breathless voice that sounded nothing like the television Melissa.

Before he could respond, her phone rang, one of those silly cell-phone tunes that took forever to complete.

"Don't answer it," he said.

"I have to. That's the number the station has." As she scurried into the bathroom for it, she said, "It will only hold us up for a moment."

He lay there, listening to the yes-no fragments of her conversation in the next room, hoping the call wouldn't mean she'd have to go down to the station this early.

She returned to the room still holding the cell phone. Stopped in the doorway. The smile on her face was odd, as if she'd put it on in haste to hide her true emotion.

"What is it?"

"Skin Burke, the Vineyard Estates developer."

"I know Skin. What happened?" But he knew, even before she said it.

"He was found dead in his own pool tonight. They think it's murder."

"First Tina, now Skin." Why did it have to be the good ones? "Do they have any idea who did it?" he asked.

She shook her head. "Not yet. There's more, though."

"What?"

"I'm telling you this now because you're going to hear it soon enough, and I know you'll be pissed if I keep it from you just so I can fuck your brains out right now."

"What are you talking about?" Wes rose from the bed, his muscles tensing. Something was really wrong. In the short time they'd been together, he'd never seen anything shake Melissa. "Just tell me. What is it?"

Without moving from the doorway, she said, "Corina Vasquez is the one who discovered his body."

"Corina." The word hit him like a fist. "Is she all right? Where is she?"

"She's fine. That's all I know."

They stood looking at each other for a minute. "I'll keep you posted," she said. "I don't have to go down there."

He looked over at his clothes, tossed in a lump in the chair beside her bed. "I think I'd better get dressed."

She shrugged. "Somehow, I thought you'd say that."

"And you told me, anyway. Thanks for understanding."

"Oh, I didn't say I understood. I just said I didn't want to piss you off." She stood before him, wrapped now in a long, white robe. "You would have been, wouldn't you?"

"Been what?" He could barely concentrate thinking about Corina, wondering if he should phone her.

"Pissed off. If I'd kept it from you and let us have

a nice little time here together, you'd never forgive me, would you?''

"Of course not. How could you even consider doing something like that?'' His clothes seemed to come on faster than they had come off. Now, to get out of here. He gave her a quick kiss on the lips.

Melissa placed her hand on his shoulder and pulled him back to her, a real kiss, all mouth and tongue. He touched her cheek. "I'm sorry,'' he said, then headed for the door.

From behind, he heard her chuckle. "Oh, Wes. You just don't get it, do you?''

He couldn't worry about Melissa's games right now. His priority was Corina.

Eight

Monday, June 4, 5:45 a.m.

Cool beans. Early dawn was the best time to stalk the halls of the building. Geri LaRue did just that. She'd already memorized the story she'd recite if anyone saw her. But no one would.

The key fit the lock of Chenault's office door. She slipped inside and closed the door behind her. For a moment, poised there in the semidark, she felt queasy. Guilt, the rascal, trying to bite her in the butt. One should show more respect to one's bene-factor, it reminded her. One should show gratitude. Without this man and his new management team, she'd probably still be trying to squeak by in a job at Wal-Mart. Now she was going to rat fuck him, plain and simple.

She'd have to deal with the guilt later, she knew. Who'd said the only way out was through? The Bi-ble? Shakespeare? Bob Dylan? She was always get-ting them mixed up.

A shaft of light sat on the window like a quiet bird. No windows in the mausoleum except here in the exec suite. Her ears felt empty and vague, shaken free of sound. Usually they were stuffed with it in this building of too many noises. The big boss's office was different, though, vacuumed free and sweet. She'd rather crawl to Turlock than do what she had to do next, but she'd promised.

Geri reached into her backpack and brought out the first of the cans. She had only an old-fashioned twist opener she used for dog food for Nathan. As she tried to disengage it from the first can, she toppled the whole thing over, and some of the contents ran onto the desk. She looked for something to wipe up the mess, then immediately chided herself. *Stop being the good girl. You're playing with the big kids now.*

So, what would be next? The desk, the lovely leather blotter, the carefully blocked-out calendar, the new gray carpet, the swooping, spotless chair? As good a place as any. Geri picked up the can with both hands, and beginning with the chair, poured the chocolate syrup in gleaming brown ribbons until the container was empty.

By her sixth can, her hands were aching, and the room reeked of chocolate.

''Hey.''

She looked up with a start. Verna stood only a few inches from her. ''You scared the hell out of me.''

''You ought to be scared.'' Verna glanced around at the damage, her dark eyes growing large. Her dreadlocks hung over her security patrol shirt, making her look as if her head had been superimposed on someone else's body. ''You're in big trouble, girl,'' she said. ''You trashed the publisher's whole damn office.'' Then she let go with a wild whoop of laughter.

* * *

About twelve of them stood in prepress behind the coffee area. Anyone walking in on them would think there had been a run on the bitter chicory coffee Sam the printer brewed every day.

Geri wiped her hands with the detergent-soaked rag Verna handed her.

"Beats the smell of chocolate," she said. The others tittered, as nervous as she was, she thought, in spite of their posturing.

"Think Brandon Chenault will get the point?" Verna asked.

"He'll get it, all right. Don't know that it will do any good, though."

"What do you mean?" Verna glared at her as if she were a betrayer. The others moved closer to watch them square off. "He fires people who've been here longer than we've been alive. He tried to bust the union. He promotes kiss-asses who'll work for nothing."

The others joined in, voicing their own grievances. Geri hated this, hated trying to defend herself from the buzzing accusations, the demands of people, most of them older than she, who seemed to be looking to her for guidance.

"Wait," she said, putting up her hand. "I agree with you. I did what you asked me to. I'm just not sure rat fucking management is the answer."

Verna crossed her arms. "Better than them fucking us."

"It won't stop them."

"You got a better way?"

Geri leaned against the wall, trying to fight the nausea brought on by the overdose of chocolate and confrontation. "If we're going to change things around here, we have to catch them doing something wrong. Then we can take it to corporate."

"You think corporate cares?"

"They have to care. There are legal liabilities for everything these days, and the *Voice* certainly doesn't want its precious community image tarnished."

"She's right." Wally, the old photographer standing in the back, spoke up. "There are laws. If we could prove they're breaking them by getting rid of these people, corporate would have to listen or face a lawsuit."

"Look at what happened in Matthew Henderson's department," Geri said. "They put in Corina Vasquez, a business writer not much older than I am, as his assistant. How long before she has Henderson's job?"

"It could happen," the photographer said. "They said Ivy Dieser kept memos of everything Janie Penny did wrong when she was her editor. Corina could be screwing over Henderson the same way."

A smile spread across Verna's broad face. "There's enough of us here to find out," she said, as if it were her idea. "Instead of just F-ing management, let's do what they do, starting with keeping a few files of our own."

"Good idea," the photographer said. "I'll help out with photos."

"I suppose I could go through that file of Poison Ivy's," Verna said.

The others joined in, offering their various skills to the cause.

"What about you?" Verna asked Geri. "You're a researcher, ain't you?"

"Editorial librarian."

"Whatever. Maybe you can get something on Corina Vasquez."

"Cool beans. I could do that."

After the meeting, Verna followed her toward the elevator. "I'm on to you," she said as the elevator ground to a halt.

Geri willed all expression from her face. "On to me, how?"

"I know people. That's why I'm good at my job."

"And?"

"And I'm on to you, girl. You want everyone to think you're out there in la-la land, but you're taking in everything, ain't you? What you are is smart. Scary smart."

The elevator doors slid open, and Geri followed her inside. "Thanks," she said, "I think." Close call, she thought. She'd better watch herself around Verna.

Verna gave her a knowing grin and pushed the button for the first floor. "I'm just glad you're on our side."

Nine

As she sat in front of her computer, Corina couldn't drive the image of Skin's body from her mind. How the hell could anyone do this for a living? She'd never get used to it, and if she did, wouldn't that be worse? Maybe then she'd end up like Matthew Henderson, spending her days smoking, nights drinking and around-the-clock hating the world.

Henderson arrived less than five minutes after she. He hadn't bothered to shave or comb his wispy, receding hair, and he'd forgotten the required tie with his denim shirt.

"You had a busy Sunday night, I see." He leaned over her desk, clutching a cup of coffee he looked too tired to drink.

"J.T. sent me when he couldn't find you." Her voice reminded her of how drained and hollow she felt.

· He gestured toward his office, and she followed him inside. After closing the door, he settled into the old leather chair. The fake wood grain of the metal desk was barely visible beneath piles of paper, telephone books and assorted coffee mugs, at least two of them containing sticky-looking, brown residue.

A file cabinet painted military khaki stood to his right, yellow squares of paper littering its surface. A photo leaned against the mug closest to the file cabinet and lit that part of his darkened desk with the wide smiles and sunny curls of what must be his daughter and ex-wife.

Corina sat across his desk and scooted up as close as she could.

"Okay," Henderson said. "Get yourself together and explain what the hell happened."

"I *am* together. Skin called me when I was writing the Kellogg story. Said Eugene Belmont killed her."

"Shit." He reached for a cigarette and lit it, absolutely against the rules in their nonsmoking building.

"Our conversation was interrupted. He hung up suddenly, and I went to his office, then his house." She stared through the irregular shape of smoke into his eyes.

"What do the cops say?"

"That they're waiting for the coroner's report, and that it could be an accident. There was an open bottle of whiskey by the pool, a glass broken beside it."

He took a final drag and smashed out the cigarette. "So maybe he had a few drinks and decided to take a swim."

"Skin hated water. He never used that pool."

"You were personal friends?"

"He was one of my sources when I worked in business. I wrote a profile on him for a building magazine."

He met her statement with a frown as if to say he'd never get that chummy with his sources. "If he were drunk, he might have slipped and gone in."

"He was a recovering alcoholic, had been for years," she said.

"Maybe he fell off the wagon."

"I don't think so."

"It happens."

"He sounded sober when we talked. Besides, the janitor at his office said he saw him leave with another man. He said Skin looked sick."

The doubt on Henderson's face changed to something she couldn't read. "Are you sure?" he asked, in the careful voice of a seasoned reporter looking for a lie.

"Positive. Skin knew something about the mayor's death, and someone killed him before he could talk about it."

Their meeting was interrupted by Ivy Dieser, who looked as if she'd thrown on her hair along with her turquoise linen dress. She could pass for late maybe midthirties, except for the outdated high heels and that blond-frosted pile of curls, that looked as if it had always been too young for her.

"Are you all right?" she asked Corina. "Have you talked to the police?"

"Yes, of course." She wasn't sure which question she was answering.

"What possessed you to go to Skin Burke's house?"

"I was worried. Our phone call was disconnected."

"That was courageous," she said. "I'd never want you to risk your life, but you've gotten a story that we wouldn't have had any other way."

"Thank you." Corina squirmed in her chair. She could feel the animosity oozing from Henderson.

"I'll let you two get back to work now," Ivy said. And to Corina, "Let me know if you need anything at all."

"We need to check with the cops," Henderson said after Ivy left. "Then, I'll start making calls, see if I can dig up anything."

Wait a minute. He couldn't mean— "What about me?"

Henderson looked as if he'd forgotten she was still in the room. "I've got your story right here. There's a safety-committee meeting at nine," he said. "Someone in the department has to go. Since there are just two of us—"

"Matthew." Her voice grated in spite of her efforts to swallow her fury. "I found the man's body. I'm not walking away from this story now."

He blatantly assessed her, as if trying to measure her anger with his eyes. "I'm not even sure there is a story, at this point."

"Two people are dead, and you're not sure there's a story?"

"I'm not sure they're related, but I plan on finding out."

"And when you do?"

His gaze didn't waver. "I'll let you know. Now, you don't want to be late for the meeting. You know how upset Chenault gets when his employees aren't on time."

She had no choice but to leave him there with her story and head, still dazed, for the conference room on the fourth floor.

* * *

Safety meetings, sexual-harassment workshops, diversity training—Cover-your-ass meetings, as they called them—were part of working for a newspaper in a litigious society. Corina put in her time with the others, eager to get out of there and back to her office. Who had killed Skin? What had he been "rounding up" to show her?

"Vasquez? You paying attention?"

Verna, the supervisor leading the fire inspection, seemed more hostile than she had in the past.

"Sorry. What did you say?"

"This extinguisher," she said, pointing to a small red unit on the wall. "I thought perhaps you might like to know how to use it, in case you're ever around next time the building catches on fire. I just explained it to the others."

"Guess I didn't catch it."

Verna continued in an exasperated voice, demonstrating how to pull the safety tab and point the unit. It wasn't her imagination. Verna had turned on her, too.

Corina looked at the others. Geri LaRue, the weird kid from the editorial library, watched her as though her face were a television set with an intriguing show on its screen. She stared back, expecting to shame Geri into looking away. She didn't. Well, okay, then. It was time they got acquainted, anyway.

As she checked out the editorial librarian, Corina realized that her hair was the same shade of purple as her Doc Martens. Underneath the bulky T-shirt that draped her like a tent, she had a petite frame. Her complexion, creamy as a redhead's, caused Corina to wonder if it might be auburn highlights trying to glint through the purple gel.

Once Verna finished speaking, Corina approached Geri.

"I need some help on a story I'm working on," she said.

"Subject?" Geri replied, as if answering an e-mail instead of talking to a real person.

"The developer, Eugene Belmont. Anything you can find—his background, bio, especially anything questionable."

She blinked behind her narrow rectangular glasses, the same mahogany color as her eyes. "Lawsuits, that kind of thing?"

"Yes."

"In other words, dirt." She gave Corina a straight-lipped smile.

"That, too. I don't really know what I'm looking for."

She processed the information like the computer she seemed to prefer to people. "Understand. I'll get back to you, e-mail." Everyone knew it was her preferred form of communication. You could never reach her on the phone. "This for you and Henderson, or just you?"

"You can send it to me." Corina felt herself flush. Why had she said that? What did she think she was doing? Geri didn't seem to notice.

"Cool beans. You'll have it this afternoon."

With that, Geri LaRue trudged down the hall, heading for the elevator. Weird was an understatement. Her customer-service skills were nonexistent. She could barely converse. And, like Corina, she'd just gotten a promotion. Why?

Although Millie, the editorial librarian Geri had replaced, took early retirement, the result was the same—a step up for Geri, who probably earned less than Corina. Geri, Ivy Dieser, the new printing manager in prepress who'd nudged out Sam, his former boss; inexperienced newcomers in every department from circulation to sales. "The inmates running the asylum," Sam had told her the day he'd been replaced by one of his assistants.

And now she was one of them.

No longer could she kid herself that she'd been promoted because of her abilities. She was a cost-cutting measure, like the cheap ballpoint pens that had replaced the felt-tips. No wonder they hated her.

Monday, May 28, 11:20 a.m.
Skin

*Security, safety. That's what it's all about. I've
known that since I started in business. How did I let
myself forget? Tina is gone, missing. Not with the
boy. Not on a business trip. Missing. And The Trio
is involved. It has to be. It's some kind of fucked-up
blackmail attempt, a scheme to get me to keep my
mouth shut. Or worse. One thing I'm not going to
do is sit on my butt. I'm going to find out. Going to
make Nan Belmont tell me the truth about what's
going on.*

Ten

More trouble with Mexico erupted. During the night police and local soldiers crashed into the homes of Americans living in Baja, rounding up American property owners and herding them to the borders. The local governments claimed the property in the name of Mexico, according to their boisterous leaders. Americans with land in Baja were outraged. The president of Mexico claimed the local government was behind it, but California Governor Craig Menlo proclaimed to all who would listen that he and the great state of California did not believe it for a minute. He demanded military action, threatening to call in the National Guard. He'd do it, too.

Corina was shaken. Her parents had been born in Mexico, but no one could justify what was happening in Baja.

That morning, Henderson was already in his office when she arrived. That was a first. She spread out the paper on her desk. The Mexico news dominated A-1, above the fold. The article about Skin was on the bottom.

Developer's Death Questioned, the headline above Henderson's byline read. Her hands trembled.

An autopsy was underway to determine if developer L. "Skin" Burke's drowning should be treated as a homicide, the article stated. His body was discovered by *Valley Voice* reporter Corina Casares Vasquez, after he telephoned her expressing concern about the murder of former mayor Tina Kellogg. According to family friends, Burke did not swim.

While she had been in the safety meeting, Henderson had been working on this, stealing her story.

She could hear his cigarette cough in the office next to hers. She should wait until she calmed down. She should take a deep breath, plan what she was going to say. Henderson coughed again. Without pausing, Corina clutched her paper and burst through the door.

Henderson hunched over his desk, the newspaper open before him.

"I gave you this story, then you thank me by taking me out of it."

"Settle down." He poked a stubby finger at the page. "You're not out of it. I quoted you."

"As a source, not as a cowriter. You said you weren't even sure there was a story. Then I open the paper and see this."

He glared at her with watery eyes. "Sit down."

She tried, couldn't. "You ripped me off, Matthew."

"Look, I wanted to work with you, but we had a deadline. I had to write it before the TV people beat us to it. Next time it will be different."

"Oh?" His acquiescence took her off guard. "How different?"

He lifted his hand. "Will you sit down? You're making me nervous."

She slid onto the chair. "Okay."

"I did some checking yesterday. Skin was just the front for Vineyard Estates." He pressed his fingers against his temples, as if she'd given him a headache.

"That's not unusual," she said. "But who are the partners, and how do they tie into Tina's murder?"

His guard seemed to drop. "Eugene Belmont's first choice. Skin told you he suspected him."

"What he said was that Eugene killed Tina because she wanted him out of Vineyard Estates."

"Why did she care whether or not he got out? She was a straight shooter, as far as we know. Could she have been a partner, as well?" He stared at her, his forehead glistening with sweat. "I've been covering this beat for almost fifteen years, you know that?"

She nodded once more. "I respect your ability, Matthew. I can learn a lot from you."

He bristled. "This is not Investigative Reporting 1-A, or graduate school, for that matter. If I allow you to blow any aspect of this story, there won't be a second chance."

His words infuriated her. "You think because I'm young, because I'm a woman—"

"Listen." His ruddy cheeks flushed a shade darker. "I don't have a problem with women, and in case you're wondering, I'm not prejudiced, either. If you're thinking of filing a grievance against me, you'll find it pretty tough. I've got a fifteen-year paper trail with 'liberal' written all over it."

He really was a bastard. She lowered her voice,

trying to squeeze out the anger. "All I want is a chance to prove myself to you. Just give me an assignment."

"Okay." He reached for the pack of forbidden cigarettes. "Wednesday night, the governor's speaking. Building Industry Association is sponsoring a reception for him."

"Right."

"Cover it," Henderson said. "The BIA people will all be there, Belmont, his daughter, Senator Nan Belmont, for sure. See if you can figure out Belmont's ties to Vineyard Estates and Tina Kellogg."

"I think we'd be better off talking to Tina's son. Maybe she mentioned something to him."

He waved away her words. "Investigative reporting doesn't work that way. We're not cops who can just go tracking down anyone we want."

"Talking to Tina's son could be important."

"Covering the governor could be more important, at least for now."

"But Skin always said those building-industry functions are nothing but scotch-and-sofa affairs."

He almost smiled. "An apt term, but this will be major with all the shit that's coming down in Mexico."

"You think we'll go to war?"

"If Menlo has his way."

"He still has to convince the president."

"And he's doing it. He's going to convince his supporters here tomorrow night. Every one of the people we want to check out will be there."

"You think so?"

He gave her a look that said he couldn't believe

how naive she was. "You know the first rule of hunting elephants?"

"Suppose you tell me?"

"Go where the elephants are."

Irritating as he was, damned if he wasn't right. "The elephants we're after will be there to hear the governor, whether or not they're with him on the Mexico situation," she said.

"Exactly. There's one elephant in particular I'm interested in."

"Who's that?"

He met her gaze, as if waiting to read a response. "Our illustrious mayor."

"Wes Shaw." Her stomach sank. She tried to keep the cross fire of emotions from showing in her expression.

"He carried on his daddy's partnership with Eugene Belmont, didn't he?"

"That was three, maybe four years ago. Wes dropped Belmont after Wes Senior died last year. They hate each other."

"But Shaw doesn't hate you." Henderson's chapped lips cracked into a smile. "Does he?"

"I have no idea, nor do I care what Wes Shaw thinks about me." Her voice came out weak, thin. Henderson lifted an eyebrow, as if to let her know he noticed.

"Whatever. Try to get him to go on the record about Belmont, Skin Burke, anything he'll discuss. I'd planned on contacting him myself, but I'm sure he'd rather talk to you."

So, he knew about Wes and her, right down to his unceremonious dumping of her, no doubt. Probably expecting her to beg off the assignment on the spot.

"I get your point." She rose from the chair, forcing herself to match his smile. "But we need an understanding. The next byline's mine."

"We'll see."

She waved the paper at him. "I mean it. I could have run to J.T. or Dieser with this. I'm trying to work with you, but you've got to work with me, too."

"Don't threaten me," he said. "You want to go to Dieser, go. You're not getting a byline until you earn one."

"I found a dead man's body. You don't think I earned one for that?"

He looked away, then back at her, his face flushed. "Let's see what you turn up at Menlo's talk," he said. "Help me find out what's going on with Vineyard Estates, and you'll get your byline."

"Fine," she said, rising from the chair. To herself, she said, *I'd better.*

Parental guilt call 591

"*Mija,* I know you're there. Please don't make me talk to this machine."

Can't deal with you tonight, Mama. Promise to make up for it later.

"Lydia's birthday's coming up, you know. It would be nice if you could come to dinner Sunday. We're guessing Pete might ask her something *muy importante,* and we want to show the support of the family. We can't count on Lupita to be there, although as far as I know, she still lives under our roof. Well, I'm sure you're standing right by your telephone, and I just ask you to pick it up and let me hear your sweet voice, *Mija,* so that—''

Bleep, buzz

Sorry, Mama. Times are tough. Talk to you soon.

Eleven

Forty thousand people had filled the stadium for Billy Graham's last appearance a month after September 11, and about half that crowd was expected tonight. It was only war. They could read about it in the paper tomorrow, tune into Channel 5 tonight.

Security was tight, and it took Corina the best part of an hour to move from the sweltering lot of cars through the gates, where Eugene Belmont's white limousine stretched, illegally parked, of course. She paused outside the large tent that had been set up for the media and VIPs. A faint breeze stirred the heat-stilled air, carrying with it a fragrance of expensive perfume and sun-soaked dirt. Her throat felt parched and dry as the land.

She had hurried home after work, fed her cat and changed into a gauzy taupe shirt and matching skirt which wasn't flashy but clung just enough to attest to the fact that she still made time every week for a few hours in the newspaper's employee gym.

The thought of a last-minute rush to buy something new and wonderful did cross her mind, but she knew it wouldn't do any good. She'd already lost

Wes. Besides, she didn't want to look as if she were dressing up for him.

She thought that she was going to be okay until, as she scanned the parking lot, the familiar Saab pulled in. For a moment, she felt like running. But she had an assignment, and Wes was part of it. She forced herself to walk in the direction of the silver automobile. Might as well get it over with right now, she thought.

As Wes approached her, she stared directly into the sun. In the still-harsh light, he looked soft and surreal. It was his imperfections that made him handsome, the high forehead, the thin lips that made a smile seem like a gift.

His hair was a little longer than she remembered, swept straight back, dark brown except for a few scattered strands of gray he'd acquired at his temples the year of his father's slow acquiescence to cancer. The arresting blue eyes hadn't changed. He'd looked like this at twenty-five when he'd starred in his own TV series and probably would at sixty-five.

In spite of her resolve, she was momentarily stunned. His power had nothing to do with his looks or even his short but successful television career. Wes was an original. Everyone from the bartender to the governor tried to dress and talk like him.

Because of the sun in her eyes, because of the memories, she didn't notice, for a moment, that he was not alone. About the same time he saw her, she recognized the woman beside him, Melissa Henson, from Channel 5.

Why hadn't anyone told her? Why hadn't she figured out that only a fool would have remained celibate, not to mention dateless, since their breakup?

How stupid must she possibly look right now? Here was Melissa, silver from toe to crown, from shiny toenails in black wedges to clingy knit dress, to glistening hair and platinum ear hoops. And here she was, wrapped in taupe gauze.

"Hi," she said, with an expansive gesture that she hoped included both of them.

He shifted from the Public Wes smile to something more serious. "I don't believe it," he said. "I'm hallucinating, right?"

"If you are, so am I. How are you, Wes?"

"Much better, all of a sudden."

His short-sleeved shirt was manganese-blue, an expensive yet home-crafted style with a nubby texture. His understated citrus scent enveloped her. She drew back from it. Almost a year, and he hadn't changed. He still looked like her Wes, the man she had not so long ago planned to marry.

"Well." Melissa's voice sounded amplified many times over.

Corina forced herself to study her replacement—damn, don't let this be her replacement. Not this squinty-eyed, ferret-toothed TV anchor with, okay, a great mouth, a wonderful, wide, smiling mouth, actually, in spite of the tiny teeth, and with hair that sprang from her head like music. Rich-girl hair, straight from a chemist, painted from the roots out, pulled through plastic, pressed in foil. Phony, phony, phony. And gorgeous.

Wes looked from her to Melissa, or was it the other way around? "You two know each other, of course."

"Nice to see you," Corina said. How the hell was she going to get out of here with her dignity intact?

Melissa looked down at her silver cuff bracelet as if it were a watch, then wrinkled her nose at Wes in an intimate gesture that excluded Corina. "I need to get ready for my interview. Catch up with you inside," she said, her voice softening. And as an afterthought to Corina, "Take care, honey."

A chilling thought slipped through her numb mind. Could Melissa be the reason for their breakup, the "second thoughts" Wes had refused to share with her when he left last July?

She choked out a laugh. "I feel as if I should apologize for something."

"Don't be silly. I'm just so happy to see you. I was worried when I heard what happened. Let's go inside. May I get you a drink?"

She forced herself to remain cool. She had to talk to him or admit to Henderson that he'd been right about her. "I'm here on assignment, too," she said. "Like your friend."

"I wish I could explain to you about Melissa, but everything that occurs to me sounds so crass, especially now."

She couldn't allow his words to register, just had to keep talking. "What I meant is that I'm not in the business department anymore. I'm an investigative reporter."

His smile remained inquisitive, but wrinkles creased his high forehead, as if he were vaguely displeased he hadn't been notified of the change. "Skin Burke's death?"

She nodded. "And Mayor Kellogg's."

"They're not connected?"

"The police haven't released that information yet. They may be."

They walked inside the tent, where they were assigned their name tags. Waiters wove in and out of the crowd, carrying trays of drinks. Strains of a jazz combo, with a Diana Krall wannabe singer, added more noise to the cacophony of disjointed conversations. The builders had spared no expense to make the governor feel welcome, and they would support him in his call for war against Mexico.

"I still can't believe it," Wes said. "You can't imagine how I felt when I heard you were the one who found Skin. I don't know what I would have done if anything had happened to you."

She looked into his eyes trying to gauge if there were real feelings there. Something *had* happened to her, damn it. He had caused it to happen. No words of concern right now would change that.

"It was a shock," she said. "I didn't agree with Skin's politics, but I would have tried to help him if I'd known what was wrong."

"Why would he call you?"

"He trusted me," she said, "because of other articles I've written about him."

"He always spoke highly of you. And Skin didn't hold women in the highest regard."

"Especially not Latinas."

"Yes, white males should run the world. Just see what a great job we've done." He lowered his voice. "You look wonderful, you know."

The words stirred emotions she thought were dead. "Wes, please."

"How's the little red one?"

Too bold a question. He had been with her when Rojito, then a skinny stray, had wandered into her backyard one morning as they drank coffee on her patio, in a world she would never again visit.

"The same." Her gaze drifted down to his hands, his long fingers. The brushed-gold watch she'd given him caught every light in the room.

"I've never stopped wearing it," he said.

She stepped back from him. "I can't do this, Wes. Not here."

"When then? We need to talk. You never returned my phone calls."

"I do have some pride."

He gave her a rueful smile. "I've never questioned your pride. There's a lot I need to say to you, and I'm in a position to say it now."

"You said it all last July."

Broken July. That's how she'd always thought of it. What he'd done had smashed the month and all the days that followed into pieces, destroying her dreams in the process.

"No, I didn't. I asked for time, space."

And he'd ended their engagement.

"I'm on assignment," she said slowly. "I need your help."

"Well, if it isn't the mayor." Governor Craig Menlo approached from behind, a group trailing him. "You're still looking like a star." He surveyed Wes's attire. "Very nice. Ermenegildo Zegna, right?"

"I don't have any idea," Wes said.

"You wear it well. How's it going? I can see you're still attracting the most beautiful women in the room."

Menlo shook his hand, and Wes introduced them. "Corina's a reporter with the *Valley Voice*," he said.

That stopped Menlo's smile in its tracks. He did

a double take, his smile more solemn. "Oh, you're the one," he said. "I knew Skin Burke well. Such a tragedy."

Something about his mismatched features fascinated rather than repelled her. Tall and pale, with vampire-white skin and black eyes that matched his hair, Menlo was a study in contrasts. His voting record attracted voters, women voters especially, ironic, Corina thought, since in person he demonstrated little regard for women.

Menlo's exuberance earned him the Public Wes smile. "Good to see you, Governor. I'm looking forward to your talk tonight. I'm interested in your opinion on what's happening in Mexico."

"Total disregard of our country, that's what," Menlo said. "Don't get me started." He glanced again at Corina then back at Wes as if he could sense the emotions that still linked them. "You here alone?"

Wes ignored the question. "How's Mary. Did she come along?"

"She's in Sacramento," Menlo said. "I'm staying here for a few days, going to do a little business before I go back." To Corina, he said, "I thought Henderson was covering this meeting."

He looked as if he had brushed his eyebrows to make them slant upward. Bird eyes, Corina thought, all feathers, no lid. "Matthew asked me to fill in for him."

"You taking over the whole Burke story or just doing Matt's legwork?"

She smiled through his bluntness. Nobody on the planet dared to call Matthew Henderson "Matt."

"What makes you think I'm here because of the Burke story?"

"Well, aren't you?" His smile was pleasant, as well.

"Perhaps I'm here, as Wes is, to listen to you."

"You flatter me," he said. "Besides, Matt Henderson already has a copy of my speech."

"He does?"

"Yes. Professional courtesy. Matt and I have worked together for many moons."

"And he told you I'd be here?"

He inclined his head slightly. "I think he mentioned it."

"And he also mentioned I was working on the Skin Burke story?"

"I don't recall. Perhaps he did." He opened the slim leather envelope he carried and took out several single-spaced pages. "Here," he said, "now you have a copy of the speech, too. All you'll find out about Skin here is how much everyone loved him. He had a heart as big as he was. Never turned away from a cause. He believed in this community, this country."

She had the distinct feeling that she was witnessing the dress rehearsal for his speech. Praise Skin and his love for America, then segue into the threats against the country and his hawkish solutions for them. War, war and more war.

That son of a bitch Henderson had sent her here to listen to a speech he already had. She only half listened to Menlo and Wes chitchat, still seething. Henderson wasn't cooperating; he was just pretending to, putting her the last place on earth she wanted to be, with the last person she wanted to encounter, to learn nothing.

Melissa slid through the crowd like a silver knife cutting through a multilayered cake.

"Governor," she said in a low voice one might use with a lover. "We're ready for you over there now. You get more handsome all the time."

"You can't flatter an old man, Melissa. Just quote me correctly this time. In case you need some help—" He plucked another set of papers out of his bag. "It's all here."

"Aren't you going to improvise?" she asked.

"I'll leave that to you lovely ladies." He took them both in with his smile, as if they were interchangeable. That he might not be the only one in this cozy group who thought so made Corina want to scream.

"Sure you don't want a drink?" Wes asked.

"No, thanks." A bottle of tequila and a hypodermic, but not right now.

"I would," Melissa said. "I'm burning up. But we have to tend to business first. You ready, Governor?" Only Corina could have felt the insult beneath her lilting tone. Wes looked uncomfortable as Melissa led Menlo to where the television cameras waited.

Wes turned at her. "I don't know what to say."

"I'm working, remember? By the time I'm finished looking around here, maybe you'll think of something."

"That damned pride of yours."

How dare he speak of pride, he who had smashed hers, smashed her whole damn life? She stared straight back at him. "What did you say?"

"Not a thing."

"Good. Now, I need to move around, talk to people, and I'm sure you do, too."

"As a matter of fact, I do. I'll catch up with you later."

With that, he drifted off into a sea of slapped backs, shaking hands and television cameras. That Wes could be part of this world was something Corina couldn't understand. It must be another gear, like the one she went into at weddings and *quinceaneras*. And Melissa? When the hell had she happened?

She stood there alone, watching the mingling and the by-rote banter, knowing that she'd never learn a damned thing about Skin Burke from these people tonight. The real Skin was truly dead, one of their own replaced by the fantasy Menlo's talk would cement in their collective mind. A hero felled too young.

Looking toward the entry, Corina spotted Eugene Belmont and his senator daughter, Nan. Just in time, too. They were making their way out of the tent. Danny, Nan's nondescript, muscular husband, trailed behind them like a bodyguard. What self-respecting Dan let himself be called "Danny" after age ten, Corina wondered. That would be a story in itself.

Eugene, more stooped than she remembered, held on to his daughter's arm. Nan, several inches taller than he, wore a pale pink suit of raw silk.

Her handbag was composed of overlapping petals of pink leather, one of them embossed with the word *Chanel*. Hanging from a bronze-linked strap, it looked like a very expensive rose, and on a smaller woman it would be excessive. Nan pulled it off, though, as she did the severe blond hair pulled straight back, nothing but face between her and the rest of the world. On her lapel, a bejeweled pin of the American flag sparkled in the light. Real jewels, Corina guessed.

She was one of the best-financed and worst-performing state senators in the history of California. Anti-everything except money for those who already had it. Pro-everything that hurt the poor, the elderly and people of color. Absent from meetings, uncooperative to the press; Nan was all this and more. It wasn't surprising, considering that she was the daughter of Eugene Belmont, "the son Eugene never had," Wes used to say of her.

Eugene stood just outside the tent, still clinging to Nan. Corina bolted toward them.

"Mr. Belmont," she began. "Do you have a minute?"

He paused, leaned on his cane and looked up at her. Always crude and outspoken, he'd gotten worse with age. "Not for you."

Nan darted between them, maneuvering expertly in her pale suit.

"I'll handle it, Eugene."

"Do you always call your father by his first name?" Corina asked.

"Only in public. It sounds more professional than 'Daddy,' don't you think? Honey, help him to the car, please."

Eugene went along with his son-in-law, muttering under his breath a word that sounded distinctly like "bitch."

"Did you say something?" Corina called after him, as he climbed into the limo.

"He said he prefers that you fax your interview questions to him," Nan said sweetly.

"I'd really like to talk to him now."

Nan gave her a tight smile. "I understand, of course, but those are his rules."

The limousine pulled away, and Corina knew her chance at Eugene was lost.

"I'm not looking for a formal interview. I just had a couple of questions about Skin Burke."

"No exceptions. I'm sorry. He's been misquoted too many times by you people." She underscored the *you people* with disdain.

"What about you, Senator? Did you know Skin?"

Nan's angular face paled. "We were acquainted, of course. He was a major supporter in my campaign, a fine man. His death is a tragic loss for this community."

"How long was Belmont Construction involved with Vineyard Estates?"

"I'm sorry." She continued smiling, but her eyes glittered bright as the pin on her lapel. "You'd need to talk to Eugene about that."

"As you just observed, he won't talk to me. I just wondered if he was a founding partner of Vineyard Estates, or if he joined more recently."

Nan glanced back toward the tent, still smiling, as if looking for someone to rescue her. Then she directed her gaze to Corina and lowered her voice. "Look. I think I've tried to cooperate with you, but this event tonight is about something a lot more serious than a housing development. I'd appreciate your practicing your interviewing skills on someone else."

Corina fumed. To think this woman had a damned

good chance of being the next governor of California once Menlo moved into the national arena, as he surely would. "You think Skin Burke's death isn't important?"

"That's not what I said, and you know it. Just fax your questions as Eugene requested, and we'll do our best, as we always have for the press."

She walked away, into the tent, sleek head held high.

Corina started to follow her, then realized it would do no good. She'd receive only rehearsed answers about the great tragedy of Skin's death.

She stood inside the doorway watching her fellow media members chasing down interviews. Another hour of this, and the speech would begin, the speech Craig Menlo had already sent to Matthew Henderson.

Wes appeared beside her carrying two glasses of wine. "Would you like that drink now?"

"No, thanks. And you need to get back to your date."

"Melissa has friends here. She's agreed to find her own way home."

"There's no need for that."

"I'm hoping there might be. And why don't you take one of these? I must look pretty silly holding them both."

She nodded toward a table cluttered with empty glasses. "I told you I was on assignment."

"What happened? You strike out with the Belmonts?"

"I didn't expect them to exactly open up to me."

"What are you trying to find out?"

"Vineyard Estates," she said. "Do you know who owns it?"

"Skin and his silent partners," he said, and placed the extra glass on the table. "He never went into any venture alone. They call Vineyard Estates turnkey mansions, and they go over well in wealthier areas. The home comes complete with everything right down to the silverware."

"Do you know who his partners are?"

He frowned, looking out to where the limousine had been. "You were just talking to him."

"Eugene? Are you sure?"

He sipped his wine and nodded. "My dad told me. He thought Skin was nuts to get involved with Eugene again, but Skin was like that. He was a big supporter of Nan Belmont, and he and Eugene got along, as much as anyone can get along with that one."

"Why do you think he kept the partnership quiet?"

"I don't know. Eugene's a secretive man, always has been."

The chairman of the Building Industry Association moved up to the makeshift stage, preparing to talk. "You've got a copy of Craig's speech," Wes said, grinning down at the papers she held. "And you know what this guy is going to say. Why don't we get out of here, maybe grab some dinner?"

She forced out every feeling she had, staring into the blue eyes she once would have trusted with her life. "Absolutely not."

"We need to talk. You know we do."

"We talked last July. You said it all then. There's nothing to say now."

"My dad was sick. I was under a lot of pressure."
Wes reached for her arm. His touch shot through her.
"I made a mistake, Corina. I've had time to think
about it."

He'd also had time to date Melissa Henson, alive
at five. "I've had time to think, too," she said.
"Now, I need to go. Belmont wants a fax. He'll get
a fax. I'm not going to learn anything else here tonight."

"You might learn something from me, over dinner."

His voice softened with promise. His eyes didn't
change.

"I'm not going to play games with you," she
said.

"It's not a game."

"Of course it is. If you know something you think
is important, I'd appreciate your telling me, but I'm
not going to waltz off to dinner with you, not for
anything. Good night."

She marched toward the door, shaking inside. This
was worse than she'd thought it was going to be.

"Corina, wait." He caught up with her in the
parking lot. The air felt heavy with leftover heat and
the scent of overripe fruit.

"Let me go, Wes."

"I don't want to. Have dinner with me, please."

He hadn't changed, waiting with that expectant
smile, as he asked the impossible.

"I can't," she said. "I'm sorry."

"And I respect your wishes." She got into the
car, and he stood before the open door. "Call me if
you change your mind. If you insist, we'll keep it
business, talk only about the Belmonts."

"Good night," she said and closed the door.

She sat in her car as he walked back to the tent. At the entrance, he turned and waved, as if he knew she'd been sitting there. Corina watched him until he disappeared inside. His scent remained with her long after he was gone.

Rojito greeted her impatiently at the door to her condo.

"¿Como te vas, Rojito?" she said. *"¿Quieres comida? ¿Un poquito, un pedacito?"* They spoke only Spanish at home.

She'd always been a dog person, probably because she was raised with them. However, when Rojito appeared unnamed, unfed and without anything but hope in his yellow eyes one day on her patio, she knew, just like that, if she turned away from those eyes, everything that mattered would be lost forever.

It didn't save Wes for her, which was probably the deal she was trying to make with the universe.

"But I showed him tonight," she said to Rojito. "I may be dumped, but I'm proud."

The red tabby stared at her, without moving, his amber eyes glazed. Corina reached down, stroked his coat and repeated what she'd just said, this time in Spanish.

Twelve

Thursday, June 7, 8:00 a.m.

On Corina's way into the office that morning, J.T. caught up with her in the hall. "You okay?" he asked, his somber expression reflecting a concern that appeared genuine. It was the first time she'd seen him since she'd discovered Skin's body.

"I guess."

"I've seen my share of that shit. I know how it feels."

"Yes," she said. "I'm sure you do."

"You don't just brush it away, you know. It keeps coming back. We're reporters, not cops."

Corina tried to move away from him. Too much had happened too soon. "I really can't talk about it right now."

"It will be a long time before you can. You know we have benefits that cover—" He paused while he pondered it. "We have medical benefits here."

"Mental health benefits, you mean?"

"I've used them. You might consider it."

"I'll let you know if I need to."

"No need to tell anyone. Just call the number and

book an appointment. I have all the information in my office. I'll e-mail it to you, if you like.''

"It's not a shrink I need. It's cooperation.''

"Oh?''

She couldn't seem to turn down the rising volume of her voice. "I found a dead man, a man I knew, okay? My job is to write about it, but Henderson isn't letting me write about it. He made me tell him about it and grabbed the byline. Then he sent me to cover the governor's talk last night when he already had a copy of the speech.''

J.T.'s brows rose. "Matthew wouldn't do that. We're all overreacting right now with what's going on, all this rotten stuff in Mexico. And on top of that, you find your first dead man.''

First, she thought, as though there would be a succession of them. She glared at him and tried to hammer the point home. "I'm not overreacting, J.T. Henderson stole my story.''

"I'll check into it.'' He moved closer to her. "Look, if you need time off, anything, just ask, and I'll see that you get it.''

Her throat tightened, and she tried to swallow. "Thanks, but I really need to work. There's nothing wrong with me.''

"I understand.'' He fell into step beside her. "You did a good job on the Tina Kellogg story, by the way.''

"Thanks.''

"As good as any of us could have done.''

Meaning Henderson, of course. "I appreciate that.''

He turned and began walking with her in the direction of their offices. "I may not approve of new management, but it's my job to support it, and to support the people they promote.''

"Like me?" she asked.

He nodded. "What's happening in the Middle East brought down the economy, and lots of papers didn't make it. I don't blame management for the budget cuts, and I don't support the acts of vandalism around this place.''

"I never suspected you would," she said.

"There was another one Monday morning. Did you hear?''

"What now? Another broken window?''

"Worse. Someone wrecked Brandon Chenault's office. Poured chocolate syrup over everything. They announced it at the managers' meeting. Chenault's furious.''

"Oh, no." She stopped. The ache in her stomach turned into a burn. "Do they think it's connected to the smashed front window and the flat tires on Ivy's car?''

"That's what security's saying." J.T.'s expression grew thoughtful. "I understand their frustration, believe me, but I don't like thinking that people in this building, walking down this hall, working next to us, are doing this stuff.''

"Security will catch them," she said. "In the meantime, it's going to take more than chocolate syrup to scare me away." She intended it to sound light, but she couldn't quite pull it off.

J.T. didn't smile. "Are you sure you're okay?''

"I will be. I just know there's a connection between Vineyard Estates and those two murders.''

"You need to work with Henderson." She couldn't

miss the judgmental tone in his voice. "And if you feel you need any time off—"

"I'll let you know," she said before he could finish.

Nan Belmont hated bowling alleys and bowling in general. Leave it to Craig Menlo to try to make her feel like the lone woman in a man's world. Blackstone Lanes hadn't changed much over the years and had long been a quiet, almost secretive watering hole for numerous politicians when they didn't want to be noticed. Craig was supposed to travel with bodyguards at all times, but, always a loner, he preferred to leave his outside.

"My father built this place," she said, guessing that he didn't know.

"Thought it was part of a franchise back in the sixties."

"It was. Some singer planned a bunch of them. Daddy built the two or three that actually happened."

"I forget how well you know local history." He smiled up at the waitress. "Two of the mango iced teas." As an afterthought, he asked Nan, "Mango all right?"

"Bourbon, for me," she told the waitress.

Menlo scowled. "Didn't know you drank before five."

"I drink whenever I like, and I prefer to order for myself."

Menlo glanced from her to the waitress. "Make it two bourbons and water."

"Short glass, for me, no ice," She wasn't fond of the stuff, but she wanted to make it clear that he was not in charge. As the waitress returned to the bar, Nan asked, "Why did you decide on this place, anyway?"

"Because it's not suspicious," Menlo said. "It looks social, two old cronies out for a visit, running into some friends, exchanging pleasantries."

As if she'd socialize with him of her own volition. But she sure didn't want The Trio at Daddy's. "Where are the others?"

"They'll be here. Is Eugene coming?"

"The heat's got him down today. I told him I'd handle it."

"Did you mean what you said about my speech last night, or were you just being polite?"

This man was so hungry for strokes he'd actually beg her for compliments. "It did exactly what it was supposed to do. The builders are behind you, the rest of the Valley, too."

"So we're in great shape except for that one little problem," he said. "It's not the end of the world."

"It could be if we don't watch it." She folded her hands on the table, looked directly into his eyes. "We need to be absolutely honest with each other if this is going to work."

"I have been honest, Nan, with you and your dad."

"Then why the hell did you kill Tina Kellogg?" The crash of bowling pins buried her words, but she knew he'd heard.

His skin grew even lighter than its ghostly white. "I didn't. I swear. You think I'd jeopardize my political career, not to mention our cause?"

He'd do whatever it took to be president. That was the only cause he wouldn't jeopardize. The job, the power, meant more than Mexico. She took another sip of the whiskey. Nasty stuff, but it worked, in moderation, as Daddy always said. That was something these clowns had never learned.

"I don't mean that you actually did it yourself," she said.

"I wouldn't hire it to be done, either, if that's what you're implying. Besides, I wouldn't betray your family. You and your dad have done too much for me."

"If not you, who?"

He raised an eyebrow, so shiny she'd bet he waxed it, the way men once did their moustaches. "There's always our silent partner."

"No balls," she said. "It has to be somebody else, maybe somebody trying to bring us down."

"Skin told our silent partner he thought it was your dad." He sipped his drink and glanced up at her as if the thought had just occurred to him.

"That's ridiculous. Tina's murder is the worst thing that could have happened to us."

"Unless she told the press what Skin told her."

"Unless." She laughed. "As Daddy says, everybody has a price, and if somebody hadn't gone off half-cocked, we might have found hers. We could have done something, bought her off, tried to reason with her."

He shook his head. "Wouldn't have worked, not with her."

"At the least we could have made her think it was smaller than it is," she said. "Instead we've got the newspaper poking into Vineyard Estates. That reporter, Wes Shaw's ex-squeeze, is a defiant bitch."

"A looker, though. If I were Matt Henderson, I'd

worry. This Corina is a bimbo who got her job because of her last name and her sweet little ass, I'll bet you.''

Nan wished she could believe that. ''She doesn't act like a bimbo. You should have seen how she treated Daddy.''

''She doesn't know anything. She's a novice.''

''I still think Skin was out of his mind to trust her.''

''Maybe he didn't,'' Menlo said, leaning across the table, his fingers laced around the glass. ''Maybe he just said he was giving her the stuff to scare us, so that we'd let him out.''

She knew better. Skin never made idle threats, never traveled without insurance. ''My guess is he didn't tell her anything, or it would be all over the paper.''

''What, then?''

''Maybe he did give something to her but didn't tell her what it was.''

He nodded. ''Sounds like the bastard.''

''If something happens to her, someone else could get to it before we do,'' she said, ''so no more bright ideas, okay?''

''I told you I had nothing to do with what happened to Tina.'' Liquor made his eyes mean or maybe just revealed the meanness that had been there all along. ''And you might be right about the reporter. She may not know what she has.''

''Another reason we need to find it immediately,'' she said, ''before she shows it to someone else.''

''Whiplash?'' he asked.

She nodded. ''Let me give him the instructions.''

"I thought you said you wanted as little direct contact with him as possible."

"I do, but I want to make sure he understands that no one is to be hurt. Somehow I don't think you were clear with him previously."

"I was clear, I told you that. Whiplash is an old military man, like me. He knows how to take orders."

She'd give him that one. The thought of dealing with Whiplash turned her stomach, anyway. And if anything happened, and he were traced back to their group, she'd be better off letting the others handle him. "Okay," she said. "Just do it right this time."

He sucked air through the ice, frowned at his glass. "I think I'll have another. You?"

"Not in the afternoon," she said. "Bad for your public image, not to mention mine. Once you're president, you can swill the stuff day and night, for all I care."

"A delightful conjecture," he said. "By then we'll be on the way to accomplishing what we've planned all these years." He toyed with the remaining ice in his glass, a smile playing on his face.

She was amazed he'd gotten this far, and he wouldn't have without her. "It takes a strong organization," she said, "to create change."

"We can thank your dad for that."

"Don't you forget it. Once this Mexico thing is settled, I want something nice for him, something with some honor attached to it."

"Count on it," he said.

"And this Corina Vasquez? Can I trust you to handle getting back whatever Skin gave her?"

"If you can't trust the governor of California, whom can you trust?"

It was a chilling question. Fortunately Nan didn't have to answer it. Just then, their silent partner walked through the front door, and feigning surprise, smiled and headed toward their table, hand outstretched.

And not a moment too soon. Nan was still disconcerted, unable to decide whether or not Menlo were telling the truth about Tina's murder. Besides, this whole bowling alley was just too strange. Those crashing pins hadn't changed since she'd come here with Daddy as a little girl. The waitress looked the same, just older, more lined and bleached.

Nan looked across the room as she adjusted herself in the booth for the addition to their group. An odd-looking girl with shocking purple hair sat at a table by herself, watching. Nan glared, and the girl seemed to stare right through her.

When Nan thought to look back once more, the girl was gone, but her root beer mug remained on the table. She'd barely touched her drink; its foamy top was still visible over the rim of the mug.

Thirteen

Thursday, June 7, 8:10 p.m.

That's all she needed—J.T. trying to send her to the company shrink. Probably hoping she'd go on disability and disappear as others had. She was too busy to worry about him. Henderson was out of the office all day, which left Corina to cope with their daily deadlines by herself. J.T. had looked in on her twice, frowning his approval when she told him everything was under control. Ivy Dieser also came by.

"Flying solo?" she asked.

"Just for today."

"Commendable." Corina pictured her sticking a gold star next to "Vasquez" in that mental ledger she so clearly kept.

Now, after about twelve hours here, she was exhausted, hungry and ready to go home. The meeting with Wes had reminded her of what she had lost. What it was like to be loved and cared for, to have someone to listen to her. But to think about it now would be to remind herself that she had believed in a lie.

She wondered if she should take Wes up on his offer to talk about Eugene. He was the best source she had, and if she could put her emotions on hold, she might learn from him.

She signed out at the security guard station and started down the ramp. The usually crowded parking lot held only delivery trucks and the vehicles of the night shift now. More than eight hundred people worked in this building. By day, it was like a tiny city, a microcosm. At night, though, it consisted of little pockets of activity within a large, abandoned structure.

When she had first started, Sam, the printer who supervised the night shift, had told her that the newspaper business was habit forming. "Printer's ink gets into your blood," he'd said. He was right. She loved this place, even on the bad days. She was, she thought, one of those rare and lucky people who'd discovered what she wanted to do with her life. She wasn't going to let Matthew Henderson or J. T. Malone stand in the way of that.

If talking to Wes again would help her, she would do it and pay whatever emotional price it extracted. Given a chance, she could be a good reporter, but nobody was going to hand her this story. She'd have to track it down on her own.

As she cut across the parking lot toward her car, she heard a movement behind her. Before she could turn, a sharp blow knocked the wind from her, and an arm grabbed her from behind. Corina's scream was muffled as a hand clamped over her mouth.

"Settle down, now. You got something I want. From Burke. Just keep quiet, and you won't get hurt."

Corina froze as the meaning of his words sank in. Then, just as suddenly, adrenaline pumped through her, and all she wanted was to break away, even if she had to kill him to do it. She tried to scream again, to kick from behind, but he was strong.

"Bitch," he muttered. "Come on. I'm getting you out of here."

He began dragging her across the asphalt, and she tried desperately to dig her heels into the ground, forcing sputtered screams through the hand over her mouth, trying to attract the attention of the security guards.

At that moment, she heard the blaring of a horn, felt herself being pushed out of his grasp, falling. Fabric tore as she rolled across searing asphalt. She stopped her fall with her hand, felt the slow burn, shook her head to stay conscious.

"Vasquez? Damn, are you okay?"

There before her, chalk white, looking on the brink of tears, stood Geri LaRue, the computer geek.

Corina heard a faraway screech of tires and looked around, fearing for a moment that he might be returning. "Somebody grabbed me."

"He's already gotten away," Geri said. "Come on. You've cut yourself. Let me help you up."

Geri's car stood just a few feet from them, the driver's door still open. She reached down, and Corina pulled herself to her feet.

"I tried to run him down, but he jumped out of the way. Damned mugger. I have pepper spray in my purse, was going to use that, too. Wish I'd gotten the license number of his van."

Corina sagged against her, no longer able to hold up her own weight. "What did he look like?"

"Terrible. He was wearing dark glasses. I couldn't

see his face. There was something wrong with his neck, though.''

"Wrong like how?" Corina asked, her mouth so dry she couldn't swallow.

"Like this." Geri tilted her head to the left. "It was slumped over to one side, like he'd broken it or had his throat cut, maybe. The creep had a scar from ear to ear."

Corina remembered the words of the janitor that night of Skin's murder.

"Did he have straggly hair, really pale?"

"Good guess," Geri said.

"Not a guess. I know that man. He was with Skin Burke, the developer, the night Skin was killed. He said he wanted something Skin gave me."

Geri's expression froze. "He gave you something?"

"Nothing. I can't imagine what he thinks I have." She turned to Geri. "I owe you."

"No big. I saw the guy dragging you across the lot and just figured I'd run him down if I had to."

A security guard pedaled up to where they stood. "Any problems, ladies?"

"I'd say so," Geri told him. To Corina, she added, "Come on. I have a feeling this is going to be a long night."

"I'm really lucky you came by when you did," she said.

"Yeah," Geri said. "Lucky."

"Did you actually see the guy grab me?"

"I was already in my car, had been there for a while. Don't know where he was." She shuddered. "He just stepped out of the shadows. I saw what was happening, and I gunned it."

Corina's head rang with questions. She had to piece this together, figure out what fit and what didn't.

A few more steps into the parking lot, moon hanging low, and her fear pushed back to make way for pain in every part of Corina's body. How could the night be so clear and her mind be so foggy? How, with that horrible man's arms locked around her, could she still be conscious, not to mention alive?

"What do you think this is all about?" Geri asked.

"I don't know," she said, looking up at the sky and the hazy moon that lit it. "And that's the scariest part of all."

Sleep that night was impossible, exhausted as she was from the questions of the police. Geri insisted she take her pepper spray, and when Corina finally did doze off at dawn, it was with the tiny can under her pillow.

She was terrified that someone could grab her just a few hundred yards from where she worked every day. Henderson would have no choice but to cooperate with her now. It wasn't just the story that was at stake. It was her safety. There was only one way to protect herself, and that was to find out what happened to Skin and Tina.

Friday's above-the-fold story focused on the trouble in Mexico. Baja was practically part of California. Americans had kept extravagant homes there long before O.J. Simpson had alerted the rest of the country to the lavish retreats of Cabo San Lucas. Now, local police had exercised their power to get rid of Americans. This, coupled with the drug prob-

lems and the missing DEA agents, would only stir
up the politicians trying to push the president toward
military action. The thought of loose canon Craig
Menlo in the White House, or of Nan Belmont as
governor, was alarming.

Henderson showed up as late as always, gave her
a weary nod and went into his cluttered office. Corina followed.

He looked up, as if he could force her to disappear
by sheer willpower. "You're looking a little weary,"
he said. "How goes Operation Elephant Hunt?"

She sat on the chair across his desk. "There's no
easy way to tell you this."

Henderson gulped more coffee as she explained
what happened the night before.

"You've got to go home, get out of here, take
some time off," he said. "Your life could be in danger."

"It may be, anyway. What I've got to do is work.
We have to figure out what happened to Skin and
Tina." She was too weary to fight him anymore.
They'd have to work as a team.

"I don't know," he said. "Tina's son was no help
at all."

Corina sat straight up in her chair. "When did you
talk to Tina Kellogg's son?"

"Yesterday. I tracked him down."

"I thought you said he wasn't important, that we
couldn't go around interrogating people as if we
were cops."

"I changed my mind." He bit his lip as if craving
a cigarette. "He's a loser. Lives over in Pismo,
works in a surf shop."

He was still doing it to her, still trying to sneak behind her back. "I want to talk to him, too," she said.

"Fine. I'll give you the contact information."

"I would have liked to go with you."

"One of us had to be here." He glanced down at his watch then back at her. "So, did the movie-star mayor give you anything useful?"

"Just that he thinks Eugene may have been one of Skin's silent partners in Vineyard Estates. If that's true, why would Skin accuse Eugene of killing Tina?"

"I don't know, unless she were involved in Vineyard Estates, too."

"Not while she was mayor. She was too honest."

"Trusting, aren't you?" he said, placing the cup on his desk.

"Until I have a reason not to be."

"You talk to the Belmonts?"

"I tried, but they demanded that I send the questions by fax."

"Did you do that?"

"Of course. I haven't heard back."

"It's a long, drawn-out process. They run everything by their attorneys."

Still angry, she stood and reached for the door. Then, she stopped and turned back to him. "By the way, Craig Menlo said you already had a copy of his speech."

She caught the flash of surprise in his eyes the instant before his expression hardened into an unreadable glare.

"As a matter of fact, he did send something over. He does that now and then."

"So I gather."

"I wanted you at that event for a number of reasons, not just to hear his speech."

"Is there anything else?" She couldn't stand there another moment without bursting into a barrage of accusations.

"Nothing for now. Just take it easy, and if you need time off—" He paused. "One thing about this company is that we do have good health benefits."

"So I heard. Maybe you should look into them."

"Only trying to help," he said. It was all she could do to keep from slamming the door behind her.

She wrote a second request to Belmont, sent it and tried to return to work. No way, she thought, as she stared at the screen of her computer. She'd been jumped in a parking lot by someone who thought Skin had given her something, someone who knew who killed Skin and maybe Tina. She couldn't trust Henderson, and Eugene Belmont was doing his best to avoid her.

She stared at her telephone, trying to ignore it, then lifted it almost playfully and punched in the number.

"Mayor's office," a friendly female voice answered.

"Wes Shaw, please."

The voice hesitated. "Mr. Shaw is in conference. May I ask who's calling?"

She ought to hang up, without a word. "Corina Casares Vasquez," she answered, then sat back and waited. It was too late now.

"I don't believe it." The hope in his voice was

enough to make her believe in him all over again. Almost.

She wanted to tell him about Henderson's lack of cooperation, about the man in the parking lot, but she couldn't, no matter how terrified she was, no matter how safe he had once been able to make her feel. But he did know more about Eugene Belmont than anyone in Pleasant View.

"Okay, Wes," she said. "Lunch."

"I thought we discussed dinner," he replied, in a voice that failed to hide his pleasure.

"I'm discussing lunch," she said. "Are you still interested?"

He made a noise that sounded like a chuckle. "As you wish. Today? I have an appointment, but I can change it."

"No, not today. I look a mess." Another chuckle. She realized how foolish she must sound.

"So this is an impulse call? What about dinner tomorrow night?"

"I told you lunch, Wes. Don't make fun of me."

"I'm not." His voice softened. "I want to see you. You name the day."

"Tuesday," she said. Yes, that was far enough away to give her time to think. "Let's do it Tuesday."

"It's going to be a very long weekend," he said. A long weekend with Melissa, no doubt. She needed to get off this phone.

"I'll see you Tuesday," she said.

"Not so fast. I have something for you. Don't know if it will be of any help."

"What's that?"

"The unlisted phone number for Betsy Webster, Skin Burke's fiancée."

Corina reached for her pen. "Can't hurt to try. You think she'll talk to me?"

"I told her she ought to."

She took down the number, stared at the black numerals, her little gift for being a good girl. "Would you have given me this if I hadn't called you?"

"Of course," he answered, a little too quickly.

When she hung up the phone moments later, she couldn't shake the uneasy suspicion that he had lied. Betsy Webster was her reward for getting in touch with him. Feeling like a pawn in a game she didn't want to play, Corina dialed the number, anyway.

Fourteen

Don't think about anything, Wes told himself. *Just taste, just touch. She's a beautiful woman. She wants you, only you, damn it.*

What the hell had he started? It was his own fault, his own needs that had driven him into a too-soon relationship with Melissa. Now, he was disappointing her, unable to capture the magic they had together.

"Having problems?" She gave a husky laugh and propped herself up against her padded headboard, her small, pink nipples still knotted in anticipation.

"Don't give up on me yet. We have all night."

"Do we?"

"Of course." He bent over, kissed her slim ankle, massaged her foot, the shiny, slick red-painted toes. "Let's do something different tonight. You be the queen and let the servant boy service you." He began trailing his lips up her leg.

"Two glasses of Cakebread Cellars chardonnay didn't do it. My legendary oral sex skills didn't do it. So now you're relying on the old fantasy trick?"

"I'm sorry," he said. Lying to her would only make it worse.

She pulled up her legs, then leaned down and touched his cheek. "Ah, the paragon," she said. "She's back in your life."

He could pretend ignorance, but that would be worse than the truth. "No, she isn't. She doesn't even want to see me."

"But she is lovely."

"She's a lot more than that."

"And you're still in love with her."

"I don't know."

"That means yes. You know that, don't you?"

"It means I don't fucking know."

He got out of bed and began searching for his clothes in the soft light.

"Wes," she said.

He turned. She'd spread herself on the bed like butter, the reading light aimed at the silky, fragrant patch between her legs. She reached down, parted the hairs. Finally arousal. Finally some blood through his veins.

"You can have me," she said, "right now, anyway you like. Just pretend I'm her. What's her favorite position?"

"Mel, I can't."

"Sure you can. It'll be fun. I'll bet she likes it like this, doesn't she?" She got on her hands and knees, then shoved her ass up, taunting him. This was not sexual arousal. It was punishment. "That's what it takes for you to get it up, isn't it? Pretending the woman you're with is Corina."

"I'm leaving," he said. "I shouldn't have come here in the first place."

"You're right about that. How do you think it feels to be the third person in this tragic little triangle? Or don't you think I have feelings?"

"I know you do. I'm sorry." He sat down on the bed, put his arm around her shoulder. "You're one of the most wonderful women I've ever known."

"Just not wonderful enough." Her eyes glittered like the eyes of a bird seeking the most sensitive place to peck. "Thought you were Mr. Commitment, Mr. One At A Time."

"Don't hate me, Mel. I'm not a jerk. I didn't lie to you about anything."

"Except how you feel about her." She got up and wrapped the robe around her. "Tell me one thing, and then leave, do whatever you want, and I'll just chalk it up to bad judgment on my part."

"What do you want to know?" he asked.

"If Corina is so perfect and you're still so hung up on her after all this time, why did you leave her in the first place?"

The question pierced him as he was sure she intended it to. "I didn't leave her. I needed some space. That's all."

She bore down on him, a partially clothed parody of the television reporter. "Were you cheating?"

"Christ, no."

"Did you want to? One last fling before you settled down, maybe?"

"You wouldn't understand," he said, buttoning his shirt, wanting to be anyplace but there with her pain, her accusations and his own memories.

"No, Wes," she flung at him, as he walked from the room. "You're the one who doesn't understand."

Monday, May 28, 2:23 p.m.
Skin

Security, safety. That's what it's all about. Memorial Day traffic stretches out this time on the freeway, eating into the third hour. If I get stuck behind one more lame-ass trailer, I'm going to drive right over the top of it.

I've been to Sacramento dozens of times, but today's different, and I know Nan could hear it when I called.

"Stick around, and we'll have dinner," she'd said, but her voice was hushed the way it gets when she can feel trouble coming.

She meets me in her office. The building is empty and unnerving without the bustle and the bodies that usually charge through it. She puts out her hand, and I'm glad she doesn't try to hug me.

"I know this must be important," she says, sitting on the sofa beside her desk.

I pull up a chair, feeling the cool stain of sweat on the fabric of my polo shirt. Sweating like a hog. Betsy's right. I've got to lose some weight.

Nan looks like she never heard of sweat. Not a pore on her face, blond hair pulled straight back into a knot. She's dressed down but not too down. Some kind of pantsuit thing in a soft greenish blue. The word seafoam comes to me, probably something I absorbed from all those shopping trips with Betsy. Osmosis or whatever you call it.

"Don't look so uncomfortable," she says. *"Just tell me why you're here."*

"I came to you because you're the only sane one." I don't mean to say it that way, but it's the truth.

"I'm not part of The Trio. You know that. If you have a concern with them—"

"You do whatever your dad tells you to."

She sits up straighter. *"I'm proud of the relationship I have with my father."*

"The group is losing it." Might as well just come out and say it. *"They're out of control."*

"My father would remind you that this is a war."

Polished. That's what she is. So polished you could almost see yourself in her reflection. But I'm not backing down. I have security. *"And I'd remind your father that people are getting killed."*

She gives me that too-good stare, shaking her head as if I'm a kid who's misbehaved. *"Oh, Skin. You know you believe the way we do. You helped raise the money to put our people in office."*

"I believe in the concept," I say.

"It doesn't come without a price."

I stand, look down at her, trying to keep my voice steady. *"Does that price include Tina Kellogg?"*

For a moment she can't answer. She just sits there like a photo on a campaign brochure. The only way I can tell she's heard me at all are the two red blotches on her cheeks. Then, she stands, too. I've never seen her this angry. For a minute, I think she's going to strike me. Or worse.

Fifteen

Betsy Webster returned her call early that Monday.

"I'm so sorry about Skin," Corina said. "Although we were business acquaintances, I considered him a friend."

"Skin didn't trust just anyone, that's for sure." Her husky voice carried the traces of a drawl.

Corina flashed on her final image of his body, splayed in the pool he never used. "I know that."

"Neither do I." She cleared her throat. "Wes Shaw speaks highly of you, too. Tell you the truth, he's the only reason I decided to return your call."

"I'm glad you did. I hope—" Corina couldn't finish the sentence. What could she possibly say that would change the horror this woman must be living? "I'd like to stop by and see you," she said.

"Wes told me. Said you'd have to ask some tough questions, though." She inhaled heavily, as if the thought of it were too much for her.

"I'll make it fast, just a few minutes."

"Got nowhere to go, anyway." Betsy took a deep breath, and Corina recognized the sound, the same one she heard every time Matthew Henderson drew on a cigarette. "I promised Wes I'd talk to you, so that's what I'll do. He's a good guy, isn't he?" Before Corina could concoct a response, Betsy continued, "Sweet as his daddy. You ever meet Big Wes?"

"He was a charming man." Finally one question she could answer. "I interviewed him when he won the Chamber of Commerce award."

"Sure, that's right. You know Melissa Henson?"

The words dug into Corina. "I've known her for years," she said, stretching the truth.

"I think Wes has finally met his match, and they sure make a beautiful couple, don't they? Skin just adored that girl."

Traitor, Corina thought, then chided herself. Skin was allowed to find Melissa Henson adorable. Wes was. Anyone was. The whole damn world could adore Melissa for all she cared.

Clenching her teeth against the image of the beautiful couple Melissa and Wes made, she agreed to drive up to Betsy's house at Vineyard Estates after work.

In the meantime, she helped Henderson with the updates on Tina and Skin. The autopsy revealed that Tina's skull had been crushed. Skin's body bore signs of trauma. Murder. It was real to her now, in a way it hadn't been before. Tina Kellogg and Skin Burke were murdered.

During the afternoon, Corina made several fruitless trips to the fax machine.

"You're wasting your time," Henderson said, as she passed his office. "I told you they'd run it past their attorneys."

"You think I should phone and kind of nudge them?" she asked.

"You'd just piss them off." He glanced at his watch. "By the way, I've got to leave early today. I have an appointment."

"Fine with me," she said. "Nothing's happening, anyway. See you tomorrow."

He left at three, then returned ten minutes later.

"Forgot my jacket," he said, dashing into his office. "Running late." He looked almost sheepish. Why would he, who dressed like a relic from the sixties, care whether or not he wore a jacket to an appointment? And in the middle of a heat wave at that? For a moment, she wondered if Henderson had a date, but nothing about him indicated any great affection for women. Probably working on his own again, trying to hide whatever he learned from her.

Not long after he left, the phone rang.

"Matthew Henderson, please." A strained female voice.

"You have the wrong number. I can take a message or connect you to his extension."

"His line's not answering. The front desk connected me with you."

The brusque tone clearly belonged to some old-school clerical person who thought professional interaction had to border on rudeness.

Corina started to say he was out of the office, then stopped herself. Investigative reporters investigate, she thought.

"Mr. Henderson is away from his desk right now," she said, mimicking the clerk's tone. "I'm his assistant. How may I help you?"

The caller hesitated briefly. "Did he— Do you

know if he has any appointments scheduled for this afternoon?''

"Let me check for you." She shuffled papers on her desk. She was getting good at this, she thought, picking up the phone again. "Hello? Yes, he has several appointments scheduled. Who's calling, please?''

"This is Senator Belmont's office.''

A secretary, she realized, who thought she was speaking to one of her own kind. She forced the excitement from her voice. "Let me see here. Yes, he does have an appointment with Nan Belmont this afternoon. He's running a little late.''

"Thanks for your help,'' the caller said, friendlier now that she had the information. "I'll let Senator Belmont know. She was just concerned.''

"I understand.''

Corina hung up feeling victorious. No wonder Henderson had acted so nervous. Any guilt she had felt about talking to Skin's fiancée behind his back evaporated on the spot.

She left through the front door that night, down the front steps and into the first row of cars, where she'd been lucky enough to snag a place that morning. Two large pine trees provided the only color in the dry flower bed in front of the building. A flag, one American and one Californian, draped from tall, gold-knobbed poles on either side of the trees. The American one hung at half-mast.

It was tradition. If an employee died, the flag was lowered. *Who?* Corina wondered. Then just as rapidly she remembered that Sam the printer had told her that Tim Boatright, a retired printer, had suffered a fatal heart attack that weekend. She slowed down, watched the flag, so still against the translucent blue of the sky and felt herself choke up. She'd met Boatright only once, at his retirement party, the month she'd started working as an intern at the *Voice*.

He'd seemed happy but subdued that day, as if working off a script someone had written for him, carefully following the etiquette of being, for one moment in his career, the center of attention. A man of few words and a shy smile, he'd introduced Corina to his wife, offered her a piece of cake, and talked about the trips they'd planned in their motor home.

Eight years without a thought of him, and now this.

How many companies of eight hundred, she wondered, would lower their flag because a retiree had died? Regardless of the cost-cutting measures, regardless of so much that was unfair at the *Voice*, there was also a deep current of goodness. More than that, there was a connection that linked all of them who worked in this tall, sprawling building to each other and to the building, the very newspaper itself. She looked at the flag again, felt the connection and liked the feeling.

She was part of something bigger than just a factory that printed newspapers. She belonged here in this noisy, deadline-driven world more than she'd ever belonged anywhere, even with Wes. The thought both saddened and frightened her. As much as she wanted to prove herself as a journalist and earn her place in this world, she didn't want to end up like Skin Burke. She didn't want that flag at half-mast for her.

Sixteen

Monday, June 11, 5:30 p.m.

Summer had already burned the foothills a brittle brown, yet Betsy Webster's home sat in a sea of winding kelly-green fairways. Located in Vineyard Estates, not far from Skin's home, the house looked deceptively simple at first glance. As Corina drove up the curving driveway, she took in the high beams and expanses of tinted glass. Even this late in the day, clumps of golfers stood around with their clubs and their beer cans, as if placed there to attract passersby to the good life that waited beyond these gates.

Corina refused to judge those who had time and money for such pursuits any more than she would want to be judged by them. Still, all that grass, those silly carts, those overweight bodies, primarily male, striding with purpose. Okay, so she was judging. She parked her car and walked, as Betsy had instructed her to, into the back.

Wearing a white T-shirt and khaki shorts, a wiry woman took a practiced swing that sent her ball flying across the lawn. She stood back, satisfied with herself, then turned and saw Corina.

"There you are. I timed it just right." She tossed her club at a giant bag sprawled nearby.

There are faces that, regardless of how attractive they are, inspire pity, and Betsy's was one of them. Sun did it to some; alcohol to others. And often that leathery, deeply lined skin just underscored years of exposure to elements, human or otherwise, stronger than they. Betsy had probably been pretty once, maybe even traded on the shapely legs and top-heavy form that was now borderline dumpy. A lifeless coral tint bled from thin lips that looked as if they'd spent years drawing on a steady stream of cigarettes.

"Betsy?" Corina asked, not knowing how else to begin.

"God, you're young."

The raw voice matched the one on the phone. Corina glanced down at her black capri-length pants.

"Older than I look, actually. We dress casually at the newspaper."

Betsy smiled, erasing some of the sadness from her dark eyes. The white visor with its green insignia on front made the artificial blond of her hair more glaring against her coarse-textured complexion.

"Can I get you something to drink, some iced tea?"

"No thanks. I appreciate your talking to me, and I'm so sorry about Skin."

Tears filled Betsy's eyes. "Silly, him living in his big house by himself, me over here in mine. It's like that song, 'The Morning Side of The Mountain.' Ever hear it?"

"I don't think so."

"No, you're too young. So close, so far apart, and never, ever together, don't you see?"

"I could come back," Corina said, "if this is a bad time for you."

"It's all bad now. We were going to get married, sell one of the houses. And now, here I am knocking around this place." The tear ran down her cheek. She led the way to a mosaic table with canvas-covered chairs.

As if suddenly weary, she took off her visor, fingered her brittle hair. "Skin wasn't much of a golfer," she said with a sad smile. "I shouldn't have always thrown him into our mixed scrambles. It embarrassed him having to play with scratch golfers like Wes Shaw."

In the distance, carts crawled like bugs as dusk crept up. Did golfers play at night? Corina wondered. Were turnkey mansions such as this strung with special lights for the restless and obsessed? Obviously not. Betsy chewed her bottom lip and surveyed the coming darkness with something less than anticipation.

"Does it worry you," Corina asked, "staying here by yourself?"

Betsy reached for a pack of cigarettes on the table and shook one into her hand. "Yeah, it does. I've got a sister down in San Diego. Might go there for a while. I just don't want to leave town until they know what happened. Do you have any idea?"

"Only that it might be connected with Vineyard Estates."

"Damn, that's what he thought." Her hand shook as she lit the cigarette with a black-enamel lighter. "That's why he called you."

"He called me Sunday, because he'd heard that we'd found Tina's body."

She shook her head vigorously. "No. Before that, Friday, I think, he said he was getting in touch with you. Said Vineyard Estates was going to blow sky-high, and he wanted to get out before he woke up dead."

"That's how he put it?"

"Yeah," she said, her voice shaky. "'Before I wake up dead one morning.' Those were his words, exactly."

Corina's pen stopped on the notebook. Skin had known, and he'd tried to get help, from her.

"He didn't say anything about Tina Kellogg?"

"Not a thing. It was Vineyard Estates he was worried about. Said you were his only chance, that he was going to give it to you."

"Give what to me?"

Betsy drew on her cigarette and exhaled like a sigh. "You don't have to lie. I know he had something on the Vineyard Estates group, and now you have it." Irritation cut into her voice.

"Please believe me," Corina said. "Skin didn't give me anything. There wasn't time."

"If you say so." She squinted as if to see the truth more clearly. "I don't know who to believe anymore."

"He didn't tell you what was going on?"

"Thought it would be too dangerous for me to know."

"Did he talk about his partners?"

"Not by name."

"Eugene Belmont?"

Betsy's lips tightened. She looked over her shoulder, out past her lawn toward the country club, as if someone might be out there overhearing their conversation. "Skin went to Sacramento Memorial Day to see Nan, the week before he—" She toyed with the visor, studying her crimson nails.

"Why wouldn't he have just waited until Nan was in town?"

"That's what I wondered. She keeps that office here, and is always checking in with her father, but Skin said he couldn't wait. It kind of made me jealous at the time, even though Nan's not exactly cheating material."

Corina looked at Betsy's time-beaten face and nodded. "Senator Belmont and I met briefly the other night."

"She's her father's stooge, senator or not. The old man still runs the show. He hates you media types."

"We're not exactly fond of him."

"In some ways, you can't blame him. Eugene did a lot for this city, but you never read that in the *Voice*."

"He did a lot *to* this city, too. Don't forget that."

The outlines of other golfers blurred in the last fading light of day. Corina sensed Betsy was running down, as well. Something in her face had changed. Her gaze darted from any attempt at eye contact. Her smoker's voice echoed a distrust Corina didn't know how to alleviate.

Corina stood up. "I'd better go now."

"Me, too. I've got an appointment later on." Finally eye contact, an equal amount of relief and fear. "You'll tell me if you hear anything, won't you? I'm going to stick it out as long as I can."

"I'll keep you posted," Corina said. "Call me if you think of anything else."

"I will." Beneath her heavy floral scent, she smelled like an ashtray.

They rose, and Betsy hesitated before she spoke. "I know you're doing your best, but honey, you don't have any idea the kind of monsters in this business. You can't."

"Oh, I know," Corina said.

"Not the way someone my age does."

Corina thought of the monster she'd seen at close range recently and tried to think of the least horrifying way to phrase the next question. "There's someone else involved in this," she said, "a man with stringy blond hair and a heavily scarred neck."

Betsy closed her eyes briefly as if trying to picture him. "I've never seen anyone like that around here."

"He's dangerous."

"Do you think he had something to do with what happened to Skin?"

Corina decided she'd said enough. "If you see him, call the police at once, and let me know, too."

"Oh, great." She smashed out her cigarette in the ashtray, the large house looming before them, empty and dark. "Now I've got one more thing to worry about. Maybe I should go to my sister's for the week, after all. You don't know what it's like to lie awake every night and wonder if someone's standing outside the window. You just don't know."

But of course she did. "Do you have a key to Skin's house?"

"Of course. I lived there half the time." She

paused. "Do you think there might be something there that would explain why this happened?"

"I don't know," Corina said. "It's worth a try."

"I can't do it tonight. Is tomorrow soon enough?" By the quiver in her voice, Corina guessed she was buying time to gather the courage to face the house and her memories.

"That will be fine," she said.

They talked a few minutes more until the darkness softened the harsh lines from Betsy's face and, they both agreed it was safer to be inside than out.

Geri followed the curve of the road, a few cars behind Corina's black Corolla. She cranked up Peter Case at top volume, loud enough to blow anyone else from there to the coast. Her after-hours tailing, combined with her habitual sleepwalking was short-changing her big-time in the rest department. Had it not been for massive amounts of caffeine, she would have nodded off at her desk today.

She was starting to get a feel for Corina's patterns now, and this after-work jaunt to Vineyard Estates wasn't part of the plan. After what happened in the parking lot at work, she felt differently about Corina. She'd seen the fear in her eyes and felt sorry as hell for her. She was doing this as much out of curiosity as for the group. After what happened to Corina, all of the rat fucking seemed kind of petty, anyway.

Corina drove fast, as if eager to get away from whatever she'd just experienced. Not a social visit, her little meeting with the lady on San Joaquin Drive. Geri glanced over at the laptop beside her in the bucket seat. It had provided the details while she waited, parked down the street from the house. Betsy

Lorraine Webster, born August 12, 1950, occupation, real estate broker. Those were the answers. Now all Geri had to do was come up with the right questions.

Case began belting out "Crooked Mile," appropriate, Geri thought, because she was going to drive that crooked mile to the top of the hill right now. Feeling the song vibrate through her, she turned the car around, and, as she drove, began spinning the fantasy she would lay on the woman after she rang her front doorbell.

She'd say she and her folks had just moved in to the house at the end of the cul-de-sac, maybe, and that she had gotten locked out. Yeah, cool. Weird kids were common in ritzy neighborhoods like Vineyard Estates. Couples too busy with what it took to land in a place like that didn't pay attention to what was going on at home, then one day, bang. Purple hair. Geri patted her gelled spikes. Since she'd come this far, she might as well check out Betsy Lorraine at close range.

Parental guilt call 649

"*Mija,* are you all right?"

"Great, Mama. I've been meaning to call."

"That's okay. Don't spend your money on the phone. We missed you at the birthday dinner, last weekend. We had some wonderful news. Lydia's engaged."

"She called me. That's great. Pete's a nice guy."

"And so successful. We need to get started on the fittings right away. Lydia's so organized. She's got the whole wedding planned down to the last detail.

Wait till you see your dress. Pale turquoise tulle, tank top. They're in all the magazines."

So much for taupe. So much for blending in.

"*Mija*, are you there?"

"Right here, Mama."

"Well, why aren't you saying anything? Aren't you excited for your sister?"

"Really happy. I'm just tired, that's all. It's been a long day."

Seventeen

Tuesday, June 12, 9:53 a.m.

Corina knew she should have expected Betsy's distrust, but it still bothered her, not that she could blame the woman. She had no reason to believe Corina, let alone believe in her abilities.

She reminded herself that Betsy had talked to her only because Wes had insisted. No, Wes never insisted. He didn't have to. He simply asked. Refusing him was no easy task. Better to be drugged into the logic of his argument, his warm, rational voice. Besides, as Wes was fond of pointing out, he almost never asked for favors to benefit himself. Again Corina wondered if he would have helped her contact Betsy if she hadn't agreed to have lunch with him today.

She couldn't worry about that now. She couldn't even allow herself the luxury of sorting out her feelings for him. Instead she needed to think about what Betsy had said. Skin had planned to give her something and was killed before he could. Now, the man with the twisted neck was after her.

Maybe she could have done something. Maybe her inexperience had gotten Skin killed. No, that was crazy. She had no way of knowing how much danger he was in. Nevertheless, Betsy Webster's distrustful face still haunted her.

The local headlines reminded her how the once-serene San Joaquin Valley had changed, even in the last decade. Car Kills Turlock Man. Prostitution Sting Nets 18. Chase Ends In Fatal Accident. Drug Raid Yields Arrest. 246 Drivers Cited For Running Red Lights. It was a free-verse poem, attesting to the constancy of violence and desperation, both escalated it seemed now as the heat continued to rise.

Geri LaRue appeared at her desk around ten that morning. She carried a folder and wore either the same Doc Martens she'd had on earlier in the week or a pair that looked just like them. As she sat down and crossed her leg, her olive-drab pants slid up over her ankle. She wore the tags out, sticking straight up the back of her leg, the way the kids did. Black laces, too. Corina knew from her younger sister, Lupita, that Doc Martens were a favorite of certain gangs, also that the color of lace was related to the gang to which one belonged. She looked up to see Geri staring at her through the narrow rectangles of her glasses.

"Just admiring your Docs."

"Thanks. Bought them in Haight-Ashbury at a head shop."

"They sell boots in head shops now?"

"In San Francisco, they do." She looked down at them as if weighing what she was going to say next. "Got 'em used for twenty-five bucks. You'd never know it, though. They were barely worn."

That was the most Geri had spoken to her the entire time they had worked together. She'd changed since Thursday night in the parking lot, and she wasn't really weird, Corina thought. There was something else not quite right about her, maybe just extreme shyness. "I got this stuff from the archives," she said.

"The stories about Belmont prior to 1986 are on microfiche, and the really old stuff is here." She opened the file of dated clips.

"Thanks," Corina said. "You work fast."

She colored slightly, then looked down at her violet boots. "Good luck with it. I went through some of the articles. The old man's a tough one. Did you know he did time when he was in his early twenties?"

"I think I read it somewhere," Corina said. "Paid his debt to society and became a community leader, something like that."

"But it was some mean debut. Belmont killed a guy, knifed him in a bar." She pulled out a photocopy of an early article and handed it to Corina.

"This is all I had time to dig up. There might be something in the file. This particular story came out right after some politician accused him of an attempted bribe."

"Big surprise."

"Was at the time, I guess. It got a little weird. Belmont made some threats—alleged threats, that is. That story there is about the politician's claim, but it goes into Eugene's background. Served time on Alcatraz. Hard to believe that cool island was ever a prison."

"Well, it was," Corina said. "Al Capone and Machine Gun Kelly were there, too. They didn't close it down until the sixties." She could feel her anxious itch to learn more. Maybe it was only morbid curiosity, but Eugene had killed once. Skin had believed he killed Tina. "I'll go through the file," she told Geri. "Would you mind checking out what you have on microfiche?"

"This a priority?" Geri clicked gears and switched to her computer voice again.

"Depends on what you find."

"What's your pub date?"

It was the question she'd been dreading. She looked into Geri's intelligent dark eyes and knew that to lie would be to insult both of them.

"To be honest, I don't have one," she said. "I'm just checking out background right now for those two murders we're covering. If something about Eugene Belmont ties in, then it will be top priority. I'll appreciate whatever you can do, within the constraints of your schedule, of course."

Geri studied her through her glasses. "You'd appreciate, or you and Henderson? You're working as a team, aren't you?"

"We're supposed to be." Corina paused, trying to think of what to say next. "It's not the way it looks. I'm not after his job the way some of the old-timers think. But this isn't just a story to me. You saw what happened in the parking lot. I have to find out why that man was after me before something like that happens again."

Sympathy seemed to shimmer in Geri's eyes. "I'll get back to you," she said.

Eighteen

Tuesday, June 12, 6:12 p.m.

Skin's house looked like a testament to wealth gone wrong. It had no style, a fusion of Tutor and Grecian, for starters. Maybe that's what had been wrong with Vineyard Estates, Corina thought. Even with the regulation golf course, it suffered from an identity crisis. Unlike other developments of Skin's and Eugene's, it lacked something, something that had to do with soul.

Corina was almost relieved that she'd had to postpone her lunch with Wes, but it was the only way she could be sure of leaving work early enough to meet Betsy. She tried to forget the last time she'd been here, the night she'd left her car in this circular drive and followed the path out to the back to the pool.

Betsy's Lexus was parked in front of the entry. Its odd color, a cross between gold and silver, reminded her of nail polish her sister Lupita might wear. On the back window was the decal of a small American flag, and beneath that a second decal that read, "I'd rather be driving a Titleist." Enough daylight remained for Corina to make out Betsy's sharp profile and the glow of her cigarette.

The glow disappeared, and the Lexus door opened. Betsy stepped out. Again she wore a sleeveless top and shorts that moved easily over her muscular legs. This time the shorts were white, and the top was khaki. Only the lifeless coral lipstick remained the same.

"How are you doing?" Corina asked. Betsy's ravaged face was the only answer she needed.

"Same as yesterday. Not sleeping. Not eating. Sitting up all night with the gun Skin gave me pointed at the bedroom door. But I'm hitting those golf balls. That's what's keeping me sane. You find out anything yet?"

"I'm working on it." When she saw the doubt clouding Betsy's eyes, she added, "The research librarian at the *Voice* is helping me."

"How old is she?"

"I don't know, but she's excellent at her job." Corina looked at the house before them, a turnkey mansion, as the Vineyard Estates's brochures read. At close range, it looked like any other house, only bigger. Large, faux-Mediterranean columns flanked the entry. "What will happen to this now?" she asked.

"It will go to Skin's mom in Alabama. She's in her eighties. I was the one who had to tell her. It was horrible." She shuddered and opened her shoulder bag, pulled out the brown leather box that held her cigarettes. "I don't think I can do this."

"Wait here, then."

Betsy's gaze darted from the house to her, as if

trying to determine if she were capable of this simple act. "You don't mind?"

"No." The last thing she needed was Betsy getting inside and then freaking out. "You stay here. It's better to have one of us out here, anyway, just in case." She didn't elaborate. Betsy was shaky enough as it was.

She reached back into the bag and handed Corina a single key. "You'll find all of his business stuff in the upstairs office. I wish I could go up there with you, but I just can't."

"Wait in your car. It will be fine."

She'd felt like an intruder the night she'd come here in search of Skin. This was worse. She was going through a dead man's files in search of something that might not even exist.

She kept the mask of bravado in place for Betsy's sake, until she stepped inside. Although she'd been in this house before, it felt different without Skin's presence. The enormous living room could have held a crowd, and had on many occasions. The black-leather wraparound sofa and entertainment center in the step-down living room looked abandoned, as if the audience had left at intermission.

At least the electricity was still on, and the room was well lit, probably as part of the elaborate security system Skin had designed for all his homes.

The staircase curved above her into the upper level. Skin would want her to do this, she reminded herself. He'd relied on her as he did few people outside his own conservative, white-male clique. She could hear his voice as she climbed the stairs. "You're the only one down there I trust."

She would do what she had to, and Betsy could wait while she did it.

The office was the first room to her left at the top of the stairs. It was lined with file cases. She began opening drawers, figuring out which were tax-related and which had to do with Skin's various properties. He'd made his first serious money in the manufacturing and sales of security systems, and his records went back that far, progressing toward his segue into land development.

She found copies of his will. Betsy was right. His mother, Gladys A. Burke in Montgomery, Alabama, inherited everything.

The Vineyard Estates information was in the third cabinet. Corina sat on the hardwood floor, paging through receipts and agreements that made little sense to her. Another file was labeled Contracts, Vineyard Estates. Corina reached for it. Empty, except for a file labeled, in Skin's block printing, Mexico. Corina picked it up, opened it. Articles fell out in her lap, all of them about the problems in Baja, the large influx of drugs, the growing difficulties at the border. Some of the paragraphs were highlighted in yellow, as Skin often did with text he sent her. Quotes from Governor Menlo and Nan Belmont jumped out at her. She tried to make sense of what she held, of what it all meant. Attached to one page was a penciled note in Skin's squared-off letters. "Waite and Flannigan. July 4. San Quintin. $50,000, American."

Waite and Flannigan, the kidnapped DEA agents. What did they have to do with the Bay-area prison? What did Skin know about them, and what was worth fifty thousand dollars?

Corina stared at the note a long time, trying to
make sense of it, wondering how much Skin had
known about the kidnapping that occurred the night
before his murder. She shoved it in her pocket, then
picked up another file labeled, Personal. She hesitated instinctively, then realized that anything that
had been personal to Skin could not hurt him now.

Inside was a photograph of a younger Skin than
she had ever known, a Skin with hair, lots of it, and
a military uniform. He had his arm around a woman
who already looked old beyond her years. A pink
Hawaiian-print dress barely covered her chunky
frame. She grinned at the photographer, pulling
Skin's face close to hers with a grasp so tight Corina
was sure it would leave marks. Her smile was all
pride. She had to be his mother, Gladys. Poor
woman. In her eighties, Betsy had said.

Another photo showed Skin and Gladys again. In
this one, his mother's hair was darker, her skin older,
and she held a little boy. A younger brother, perhaps,
a cousin, similar features. Other photos showed Skin
at various ages with others who looked like relatives.
The room grew warmer. That was the problem with
an upstairs office. How did Skin stand it up here?
Maybe people this rich didn't care about energy
costs and PG&E bills.

She tried to take a breath and realized it was an
effort. The sting in her nostrils blossomed into
smoke. *Smoke.* Something was burning somewhere.
No, something was burning here, just outside the
door.

Corina jumped up and threw it open. A wall of
fire crackled on the other side, pushing her back into
the office with an explosion of heat. She shoved the

door closed, choking on the stinging fumes. Only one window. Could she survive if she jumped from it? She grabbed the files. It was the only way.

Smoke crowded the air from her lungs, strangling her with heat. "I can't," Corina said to no one, but it was Wes's face she saw in her mind as she slid to the floor. She had to breathe somehow, had to find the window. It was the only way; the window, the only way she could live, but first she had to walk. She reached up, grabbed the desk and pulled herself to her feet. Smoke-blind, barely able to navigate, she lifted the glass and heaved her weight against the screen.

As it fell from the window, an alarm went off in piercing cycles. Leave it to Skin. She poked her head through it, gasping air into her burning lungs.

God, she could breathe, finally breathe, but now she had to jump. How the hell was she going to do it without breaking every bone in her body?

She looked down and saw them. Heard them. Firefighters, calling to her, holding a net. For a moment, poised there, the flames and smoke bursting into the room behind her, she focused on the shrieking burglar alarm she'd set off when she broke the screen. Skin was a security freak, she reasoned, her brain dull with fear. Why hadn't his fire alarm gone off, as well?

And then, she jumped.

The EMTs didn't waste any time. She was asked her name, what day it was, where she worked. The questions were easy. Her smoke-stung eyes and lungs were the problem. She could barely see, speak. She knew the answers to the questions, but that wasn't the point. "Where's Betsy?" she finally croaked out.

"Right here, honey."

She turned her head. Betsy sat upright beside her in the ambulance, a large bandage on her forehead.

"How'd you get that?" Corina asked.

"That guy you told me about, the one with the neck."

Corina gasped and tried to jump up. Practiced hands pressed her down.

"He hit me," Betsy said, "tried to drag me upstairs."

"Please," Corina said. "You've got to get me out of here."

"I will, honey, but they have to check you out. You breathed in a lot of smoke."

Corina pulled herself to her feet, glaring at Betsy, at the tubes still attached to her, to the men who'd attached them.

"I'm going back in there," she said, "right now."

"I'm sorry," a disconnected voice said. She turned to see who was speaking and then felt the sting of a needle in her arm.

Corina woke up confused. Someone, a man, was asking her name, her date of birth, the day of the week. "Let me up," Corina said. "I'm okay."

His smile was a manic grimace that blurred in her face. "You're in the emergency room. You can't leave until we check you out."

Although Corina still wasn't focusing too well, she could make out the watch on his wrist. The face of Mickey Mouse grinned back at her like a surreal dream. *M-I-C-K-E-Y...*

"The hell I can't," she said. And she did.

By the time she returned to the house, firefighters had the blaze under control, and Skin's once-lavish home had been reduced to smoldering planks and ash. God, Corina thought. She could have been killed in there. Betsy, too. And it wasn't an accident.

She felt someone move up behind her, take her arm.

"You doing okay?"

It was Henderson, his grim expression broken with something that actually looked like concern.

"How'd you find out I was here?" she asked.

"Source with the fire department. They suspect arson."

A smoky cloud settled in the night air. Corina couldn't get the smell of soot out of her nostrils.

"At least no one was hurt." A stocky man wearing a suit came puffing over to them as they stood outside. "You from the *Voice*?"

Henderson nodded.

"Heard one of your reporters almost got killed in there."

Henderson started to speak. Corina interrupted him. "How'd you hear that?"

"I called it in, live right next door." The man was breathing hard as if the excitement had over-exerted him. "Firefighters got here in no time, but it was too late."

Corina reached into her bag for her notebook. "About what time did you notice the fire?"

"Oh, let's see. Had to be around seven or so." He glanced at his watch, then back at the crowd gathered around the destruction. "Lookie-loos," he said. "They don't have enough excitement in their lives so they have to feed on someone else's tragedy."

Henderson took down the man's name and contact information. "Did you know Skin Burke?" he asked.

"Yeah, poor guy. His girlfriend, Betsy, sold us our house. Still can't get over what happened to him, right next door like that."

"Were you home the night Skin died?" Corina asked.

"Yeah, but the lots are so big we wouldn't have noticed anything going on next door. Since what happened to him, we're being a lot more careful. Just had our security system checked out. I've been keeping my eye on Skin's house, too." He shook his head. "I sure missed this one, though."

"You didn't observe anything unusual tonight?" Corina asked.

"No, and I made a point of checking before we went to bed. There's been a van hanging around lately, and I was afraid it might be someone who knew the house was empty, maybe casing it for a robbery. They do that kind of thing."

Corina's skin went clammy. "What kind of van?"

"Green, almost black. What we used to call British Racing Green back in the old days. I'm not saying the guy was responsible for the fire, you understand. He's just been hanging around the place a lot."

"The guy," she asked. "You saw the driver?"

"Couldn't make him out very well." The man grew thoughtful. "I think he was just watching the place."

"Could you describe him?" Corina asked, trying to swallow the dread.

The man made a face. "His neck," he said. "There's something wrong with his neck."

When Corina returned to the hospital, Betsy was still in the emergency room, a plastic drape pulled partially around the gurney on which she lay.

"Hey," said the doctor on duty, recognizing her. Corina walked past him to Betsy. Her eyes were wide, her thin lips swollen.

"Are you feeling any better?" she asked.

"I would if I had a cigarette." Her voice was a strangled rasp. "It was that guy you told me about. I saw him."

"I know." Corina moved closer to the gurney. "This is important, really important. Did you tell anyone you were going to meet me at Skin's house?"

Betsy nodded, choked. Corina offered her the water. She waved it away. "Just two people," she said, sputtering out the words.

"Who?"

"Wes Shaw, and your boss, that Matthew Henderson."

Parental guilt call 767

"Finally I get a real person. A mother shouldn't have to talk to a machine."

"Sorry, Mama. I went to bed early last night."

"Is something wrong? You don't sound good."

Having a murderer after you will do that, Mama.
"I'm fine, just tired."

"You work too hard."

"No harder than you at the restaurant."

"That's different. It's family. I have been busy, though, with Lydia's wedding and all. Lupita has been *imposible*. Do you know she has a tattoo?"

Yes, Mama, and you've known it, too. You just pretended not to. "Oh really? Where?"

"Let me just say that the bridesmaids' dresses will have higher necklines than I had planned. When can you get home for a fitting?"

"What's the rush? The wedding's almost a year away."

"And it will take that long to make it happen."

"I'm working on a big story right now. Let me check with my boss."

"I want to see you, *Mija*. It's the only way I can tell if you're okay."

"I'm okay."

"It's been a year almost since that trouble, and you ought to be over it by now. Time heals all wounds."

"That's what I hear. I'll call you back when I know when I can come."

"All right, but make it soon. I miss my daughter."

"I miss you, too, Mama."

Corina lay on her back, Rojito humming beside her. How had she gotten herself into this mess? How was she going to get out?

The telephone rang again. She picked it up without waiting for the answering machine. Mama, probably, with some forgotten last bit of advice.

"I wasn't trying to kill you, Corina." The voice came out in a grating whisper, and she knew at once who it was. She scrambled out of bed, hanging on to the phone.

"What do you want?"

"I'm calling on my own, not acting on orders. You're ballsy for a chick. I've seen guys wouldn't dive out of a window like you did."

"You set that fire."

"But not to hurt you. Acting on orders, that's all. I didn't know you and the old broad would be at the house."

Corina clutched the phone. "Whatever it is you're looking for, I don't have it. Please believe me."

A rasping laugh. "Don't matter what I believe, little girl. I'm just doing what I'm told."

"Who do you work for?"

Mirthless laughter. Corina knew she'd never forget the sound. "You know I can't tell you that."

She thought of Skin's desperate voice, of Betsy's haunted face. "Murderer."

"I'm a person, not a thing. Some women like me."

Corina shuddered. "Why are you calling me?"

"Like I said. You got guts, not like other chicks I know. I didn't want you to think I was trying to kill you in that fire."

"What difference could that possibly make?"

"Because I'm good at what I do, Corina, and you should know that. If I'd wanted to kill you, I would have."

Before she could reply, the phone went dead.

Nineteen

Wednesday, June 13, 8:03 a.m.

Ivy Dieser learned of the fire by way of Melissa Henson on the television news the night before. Once she knew that Corina and the Webster woman were safe, she allowed herself to imagine the kind of story Corina would write about the experience, once she felt better, of course. She'd left a message at her home, telling her not to come to work, but she bet Corina would be there.

Ivy's headache was on its fourth day. The pressure around here was getting too much for her. She had what she wanted, everything she wanted. Why was she so miserable? She felt like an advertisement for an estrogen commercial. Weepy, tense. And so damned alone.

Her ex-husband would love that. He'd always said that *she* was the real problem. Ben, the bastard, never took responsibility for anything, whatever the issue. He'd be thrilled to know she was thinking about dumping it all, just getting out of this place. "I'm the one who carried you," he'd say, the way he had the day she'd left him. "Without me, you're nothing but a good piece of ass."

She *was* a good piece of ass. She knew that. She was a good editor, too, a damned good one. Ivy passed through features on the way to her office, smiling in at J. T. Malone through the glass partition that separated them. He was part of the problem. Instead of supporting her appointment, he let the pressures build, didn't even pretend to respect her. She had no idea Janie Penny, the editor she'd replaced, had such a fan club, or that **Matthew** Henderson did.

That had to be the reason the employees hated her, why they barely spoke to her and why they moved away from the cafeteria table the moment she sat down. They resented her promoting Corina Vasquez as Henderson's assistant. As Brandon said, management wasn't a popularity contest. She'd be even less popular when she got rid of Henderson, but it was the only way.

Taking over his job would be a stretch for Corina, but she could do it. Contrary to what Henderson and the others thought of her, Corina had more than looks going for her. Not that she was that good-looking, anyway. Exotic maybe, with the cheekbones and those almond eyes. With the right makeup, she could be stunning, but not a true beauty. Her lips were a little too tight, her stance a bit too arrogant.

Ivy's office was backed against a glass window with a view of the parking lot with its palm trees and glimpses of the Sierra Nevada mountain range beyond. Given a choice of facing the view or facing her staff, she'd placed her desk to overlook the metro department. Something was wrong with it today, though. Ivy stood inside the door, trying to figure out what. It was clean, absolutely clean, not a paper in sight.

Stupid janitors. They'd tried to tidy her sundry piles in the past, and she'd told them repeatedly to leave the desk contents as they were.

A feeling of dread gripped her. The janitors left everything in a single pile. There was no file on this desk, not even a pen.

In an instant, she knelt before the file cabinet, pulling out her key. No, they couldn't have gotten in here, not where she kept her private records, her journals? She yanked open the door. Empty. Even her hanging folders. Gone. Everything gone. The keys dangled from the lock, useless and mocking. Ivy ran down the hall, tears blurring her vision. By the time she reached Brandon Chenault's office, she could barely see. She brushed past his secretary and went inside without knocking. He looked from his desk, the question in his eyes.

"What is it?" he asked. "You heard about Corina, the fire? She's okay. I just talked to her. She's coming in today."

"It's not that." She hesitated. "Are you busy?"

"Never too busy for you."

He took one final glance at the papers before him and stood up. "Tell me," he said.

She ran to him, and to her horror, began to sob. "I can't take it anymore. I just can't. Please help me get out of here."

"What is it? What's happened?" He put his arms around her then quickly stepped back, as if trying to read her eyes. More than that, he needed the distance, she knew. It was the only way Brandon could operate, and it made him much more interesting.

"They stole my files. All the information I've collected on J.T. and the rest of them. Even my journals."

"I'll have their jobs for that."

"But we don't know who they are."

"We can guess, can't we?"

Her tears stopped. "Henderson?"

"And?"

"J.T., maybe?"

"And?"

"Maybe a couple of people in advertising."

"And?" His rough voice nudged her on.

"The printers' union?"

"And?"

She shook her head, unable to fathom what he was saying. "Why are you asking me all this? How can it help anything?"

"Simple," he said. "I was brought in here to cut costs, and that's what I'm going to do. A group of employees is trying to keep that from happening. What we're going to do is terminate their employment, starting today, one by one."

Twenty

The rumor spread fast. Brandon Chenault had fired a veteran photographer early that morning. The photographer's wife was on dialysis. They needed the insurance.

The official reason was cutbacks in all departments. The unofficial reason was that the photographer, Wally Lorenzo, was involved in the vandalism that had occurred in the last couple of months.

Corina couldn't believe it. Although she knew Wally only through their grisly visit to Tina Kellogg's burial site, his crusty edge was just that. A family man, he would use any conversation for an excuse to pull out photos of his kids and grandkids.

Someone—one of the RF-ers—had lowered the flag in front of the building to half-mast, something that was done only in the case of an employee's death. The building was unusually quiet that morning, out of respect for Wally, perhaps. Or maybe it was the silence of realization, that if this man could be fired without reason, so could any of them.

Corina considered begging out of lunch again, but when she phoned Wes, and listened to his barrage of questions regarding her safety, she knew it would be easier to see him now and get it over with. They met at Lizabeth's, an upstairs restaurant in the renovated building that had once been Pleasant View Ice House. She was desperate, scared, and he was her only possibility. If it took this, she'd do it, anything to find out what he knew.

The restaurant was close to her office. A group of artists had taken it over, painting the high beams the blue-green of aging copper and putting in a bar of glass bricks. Paintings hung from every exposed surface, including the black walls of the enclosed staircase.

As she came up the stairs, she saw only a few couples at the tables scattered about a black-and-white checkerboard floor.

A woman finishing lunch at the bar turned when she saw Corina and looked as if she were going to speak. Corina recognized her from somewhere in the past, college maybe. No, she was too old to be a former classmate, with black hair pulled straight back from her face, and a long, lemon-yellow dress. As Corina walked past her, the woman turned away and reached for a cell phone on the counter. Phones in restaurants ought to be outlawed, she thought, like cigarettes.

Wes sat in an alcove above the parking lot of the Basque bakery, looking, in his navy sport coat, as if he could play himself in the movie of his life. He looked up and spotted her. When he did, he rose, putting out both hands.

She had no choice but to take them. Immediately she felt awkward, the way she had when she saw him at Craig Menlo's talk. They'd been apart almost a year, yet seeing him that night had brought back all of the pain.

He stretched out his arms. His fingers dug into her palms, refusing to let go. "Tell me what happened. It was arson, wasn't it? Why didn't you call me? I didn't even know until—" He stopped dead in his guilty tracks.

"I'm sure Melissa filled you in." She pulled away. "That's not why I'm here. We can talk about it later, if you like, but not now."

"If that's the way it has to be." His kept his gaze focused on her, trying to make her remember, she knew, trying to make her feel helpless again, the way she used to be. "I've missed you, Corina."

For how long? she wanted to ask. *Since you dumped me last July?* "Let's just have lunch," she said, hearing the hollow echo of her words. "I'm not sure I can deal with more than that right now."

"You don't have to. I ordered herb tea. Raspberry. Do you still like it?"

"Raspberry's fine." She sat across from him at the table.

"Iced. You still drink it with ice?"

"Wes, please."

"Sorry." He looked down at his hands then back at her. "I thought an attempt at civility might make it easier on both of us. It's not doing much good, is it?"

She shook her head. "I wouldn't have come, especially after what happened last night, if I didn't need your help."

"I know. You made that clear." She tried to read his eyes and failed. True-blue eyes, they had proven to be anything but. Right now, they were intense with concentration, directed at her.

"I know you never talked about Eugene Belmont before, not even—" She couldn't finish the sentence.

"My dad's wishes. He never gossiped about anyone, not even his enemies."

"And Eugene was an enemy?"

Wes picked up his menu, glanced down at it then up at her. "Let's just say he wasn't the most trustworthy partner Dad ever had."

"They made a lot of money together."

The server, a white-aproned woman with pulled-back auburn hair, high cheekbones and eyes squinting with humor, arrived with their tea. Wes introduced her as the chef and owner, and Corina wondered how many times he'd been here, and with whom. Seemingly oblivious, Lizabeth described the lunch specials.

"Pasta or salad?" Wes asked. "Want to split a couple of orders?"

"Sure." That was how they'd always done it. Yet this didn't feel the way they'd always done anything. They seemed wrong, mismatched—the movie-star mayor, the somber reporter, a table of distrust spread between them. Once Lizabeth left, Corina took out her notepad and placed it, unobtrusively, she hoped, to one side.

"Was your dad involved in Vineyard Estates?"

"No, he got sick before that thing was off the ground."

"Did he know who was involved in it?"

"Not exactly."

"How?"

He looked directly at her. "I don't want to lie to you, but this is confidential."

"It's also important. Can't you trust me with it?"

He sighed. "They say that, in your business, nothing's off the record."

"Who says? Eugene Belmont?"

He grinned, that old Wes smile filled with spirit and self-deprecating humor. "As a matter of fact."

"Are you going to let Eugene dictate how you treat information that might affect my safety?"

He put up both hands. "Okay," he said. "You've convinced me. Dad was asked to be part of it."

"By whom?"

He looked down at the table, then back up at her. "Will this really help you?"

"More than you know."

"By Craig Menlo."

The information hit her, almost like a physical blow. "Why would the governor of California try to get your dad involved in a housing development in the San Joaquin Valley?"

"I don't know, but he did. Dad told me about it, said he didn't want any part of that operation."

"Why?"

"Maybe because he'd had it with Eugene. That's what I thought."

"Because of something Eugene did to him? There must be a reason."

"A culmination. Sometimes it's not just one incident that ends a relationship."

"Sometimes."

"I wasn't talking about us." His gaze sought hers, held it.

"Neither was I." She looked away. Wes was a

human lie detector, damn it. "I have reason to believe Vineyard Estates is involved in the motive for both killings, Tina's and Skin's."

"You can't be serious. Tina was a player. Skin did business with the wrong people. Vineyard Estates couldn't have had anything to do with it. It's not worth enough money."

"Not with all those million-dollar homes?"

"Turnkey homes, they called them. Did you know you could buy them complete with furniture and silverware? That's what Betsy did."

"I'm not surprised."

"But an investor can't make any money if no one buys a house, and they're too far out of town right now. Ultimately, once the freeway's widened, it will be a different story."

"Could Menlo have been one of the silent partners?" she asked.

"A middleman, at least that's what he told Dad. Belmont's a given. Skin and Eugene were involved in deals before."

The food arrived, and he served her from the plate of curry parpadelle, chilled and lightened with snow peas. She picked at it, as they talked, unable to concentrate on the food.

"How's the pasta?" he asked.

"Excellent."

"Then why don't you try to enjoy it?"

"Guess I don't have much of an appetite." The smell of smoke seemed to have lodged in the back of her throat. "I'm not sure getting together today was such a good idea."

She needed to get out of here. As if sensing her anxiety, he leaned back in his chair. "Did you know

Eugene Belmont and my dad were best friends since grade school?''

Feeding her just enough to keep her there. Always feeding her just enough. Corina sat without moving. ''They made some amazing deals together,'' she said. ''What happened?''

''My dad changed. Eugene didn't. He wanted to rape the vineyards, places like the one my grandparents slaved in. He forgot his roots. My dad never forgot his, and I haven't, either.''

''And Vineyard Estates?''

''That was a strange deal,'' he said. ''The development's been sitting there for almost three years. At first they lobbied to widen the highway, Skin did, that is. But no one applied any real pressure.''

''Why not?''

''I don't know. Maybe they were earning enough off their other investments to ignore it.''

''Who did the actual building?'' she asked.

''Subs. The same ones my dad and Belmont used. Vineyard Estates was built by subcontractors, then sold through Betsy's company, because of Skin, of course.''

''So Eugene is involved. Why would he want to keep it quiet?''

''That's the part I don't understand, unless it's just typical Belmont paranoia.''

''Do you know anything about his serving time?''

''He supposedly killed a man, but Dad thought somebody paid him off. Said Eugene had nothing when he went to prison, and when he got out, he had enough capital to start their first business.''

She sat back trying to make sense of it. Eugene Belmont serving time for a murder he might not have committed. Governor Craig Menlo trying to involve Wes Senior in Vineyard Estates, a development of silent partners who didn't seem to care about the success of their development.

"What about the man he was supposed to have killed?" she asked. "The newspaper said Eugene knifed him in a bar fight."

"That's all it was. A bunch of guys drunk and arguing. One gets knifed, and Belmont takes the blame."

That didn't sound like the crusty old man she knew. "I wonder," she began, but she couldn't complete the thought. She glanced down at the plate before her. Nor could she take another bite. She looked up, realizing Wes was watching. "I'm sorry."

"You need to go home, get some rest. Do they have any idea who started the fire?"

She shook her head, unable to tell him about the call she'd already shared with the police when she turned over the scribbled note about the DEA agents she'd taken from Skin's.

"I'm worried about you," he said. "Why don't you go back to the business department? You didn't start out wanting to write about murder, did you?"

No, she hadn't. She'd wanted normal hours, a normal life, a normal man. Him. "I couldn't stop now if I wanted to. And I don't think I'd be any safer if I did stop." She thought of the stringy-haired man and shuddered.

"Then all I can do is be here for you."

His words surprised her, but they shouldn't have. His unconditional support was one of the reasons she'd fallen in love with him. "Thank you," she said. "Your help means more than you can imagine."

"Corina." He took a swallow of water, his face a mixture of expressions. "What happened with us was a terrible mistake on my part."

She thought she hated him. She didn't. She thought she'd lost all hope for them. She was wrong. The tiny voice of *maybe* whispered nonsensical phrases in her brain.

He reached across the table. She kept her hands in her lap and stared out the window, wondering what she really needed to hear. That he loved her? And if he said that, what then? Could she ever trust him?

"I've never stopped wanting you, Corina."

There, it was said, real and solid, almost as palpable as the table with its white, starched cloth. She sat very still, glancing out the window at the bread trucks poised like toys below.

I've never stopped wanting you, either. The words ached to be spoken, but she couldn't take that chance, couldn't risk her heart again, not now, especially not with Melissa Henson in the picture. She looked back at him. He waited expectantly, his hand poised on his water glass.

"My life is crazy right now," she said. "Do what you have to do, and I'll do what I have to do. Then we'll see."

"You don't give me much choice." He looked as miserable as she felt. "If you need more information, you know I'll do my best to help. Try to keep what I said about Menlo to yourself. I don't want anything to hurt my dad's reputation."

"I understand." She pushed back her chair, stood. "And I do need to go now."

"Are you sure? You've barely touched the food."

"I'm sorry." She was out of words, out of explanations, empty.

He rose from the table. "Let me walk downstairs with you."

"Please."

He hesitated. "Are you sure?"

"Yes." Being with him like this had wrenched too many conflicting emotions from her. She needed to be alone, to plan her next move.

She couldn't avoid talking to Henderson. His fifteen years at the paper gave him an edge she didn't have. Something she knew might trigger a memory in him. They'd have to agree to work together on this, that's all.

She stepped into the parking lot and was greeted by two cameramen and the woman she'd seen upstairs. A Channel 5 van sat parked at the curb.

"Could you tell us what Skin Burke gave to you?" the woman asked.

Corina remembered then that she had, indeed, known the woman in the yellow dress in college, and she remembered where the woman had gone after graduation. She'd become a reporter for a television station. Channel 5, where Melissa Henson just happened to be an anchor.

Twenty-One

Wednesday, June 13, 2:35 p.m.

Corina remembered hearing somewhere that, "No comment," was the most damning phrase to use in response to a reporter. She answered the woman's questions quickly. No, Mr. Burke hadn't given her anything. Yes, she'd been in the fire at his home. She'd accompanied his fiancée there to retrieve some of her possessions. A *thanks very much for your time.* A *have a good day.* And she was back on the road, wondering how to tell Henderson her face would be plastered all over the news that night.

Thank goodness Wes hadn't walked to the car with her. It would have only made the speculation worse.

Wes. Corina drove toward the freeway, her emotions at odds. Wes Shaw had betrayed her, broken her heart. Now, he said he still cared for her. As she turned onto the freeway that would lead her back to her office, she pondered a new question. What did she want?

Her e-mail included a curt message from Henderson. "Going to check out something at Vineyard Estates." Check out what? Another story? The Vineyard Estates clubhouse bar? Hating his lack of co-operation, she decided to do some checking out of her own. She picked up the phone and called Geri LaRue. She knew it wasn't Geri's preferred form of communication, but she didn't want any e-mail evidence of her request.

"LaRue." Geri's voice sounded hollow as if coming from far away.

"I need you to check into Eugene Belmont's early arrest," she said, "anything you can find."

Geri paused. "Your pub date?"

"I'm not sure, but it's important. I need to know anything you can find out about the man he knifed in that bar."

"Name's in the story I showed you."

"I want anything else, what they were fighting about, who else was there, as much as you can dig up. And I need it ASAP."

"I'll do my best, but it was a long time ago," Geri said. "Besides, I'm still working on Henderson's project. Which one you guys need first?"

Corina sat up with a start. "Go ahead and finish his. How are you coming on it?"

"Not so hot at all. Nothing I can find to indicate that Wes Shaw Senior was anything other than a nice old, very rich man with an eye for the ladies."

"Oh?" She tried to think fast, to say anything to elicit the truth out of Geri. "Henderson's hunches are usually right."

"Not this one, leastways not that I can tell. Even the stuff Shaw was in with Belmont looks clean, clean as developers get, at any rate. Are you guys sure he was a silent partner in Vineyard Estates, or is it just a guess?"

''Everything's a guess right now.'' Corina could barely get the words out. That bastard Henderson was going behind her back again, this time trying to smear Wes's dad. ''Do the best you can with it. Monday morning's early enough for my job.''

''Cool beans. Talk to you then.'' And Geri's voice snapped into silence.

Monday, Corina thought. Monday, and no later, she'd deal with Henderson. In the meantime, she'd try to piece together the information she had about Vineyard Estates. But not on an empty stomach. Rojito needed food, and he wasn't the only one. She returned home after eight that night, carrying two bags of groceries.

The complex was built in a U-shape, around the pool, two condos on either side, with Mama and Papa, the old Chinese couple, on her right. To the left, lived a young couple with an invisible but very audible dog named Zorro.

In the end unit, the manager, a real estate saleswoman in her fifties, lived with her elderly mother. She was the only tenant who owned her unit. The condo to the left of Zorro's couldn't stay rented. Two gay men who drank margaritas beside the pool had occupied it for six months, followed by a woman in a Carrow's uniform who'd stayed about six weeks. Currently it was empty again. The air still carried a faint odor of exotic food and peanut oil.

Corina put the bags on the sidewalk outside her condo and fumbled for her key. The neighbors' door opened, and Papa, the old Chinese man, ventured out. Close to eighty, he still performed his tai-chi exercises each morning. When Corina bought melons or squash from the roadside stands, she purchased extra for Mama and him, and they always reciprocated. Just yesterday, he'd presented her with a six-pack of Chinese beer.

As he crossed the narrow flower bed that separated their units, she noticed his agitation and wondered if she'd thanked him properly for the beer. The last thing she wanted to do was offend such a good neighbor.

"Hello," she said with a smile. Although they didn't speak the same language, they understood each other. Not tonight, though.

Papa gestured wildly, speaking in Chinese and pointing at her condo door.

"What is it?" she asked. "Are you all right? Do you want to come in?"

She reached for the door. It swung forward. She looked from the key in her hand to Papa's silent stare.

"Wait here."

She stepped inside and flicked on the light by the side of the door. Her sofa balanced on its side, slashed open, spilling white, fluffy fiber. The contents of her buffet drawers lay scattered on the carpet. The photographs of her family had been torn from their frames. The room felt as if its soul had been ripped from it.

Rojito! The reality of what had happened began to break through her numb shock. "Rojito? Where are you?"

She ran through the debris of her possessions, calling her cat, again and again. The bed. He always hid beneath the headboard when she vacuumed. *Please be there,* she thought, getting on her hands and knees before the shredded ruin that had been her mattress.

Through the darkness under the bed, she spotted the tight knot of red fur at the far corner beneath the headboard.

"Rojito," she called softly, her breathing labored. *"Mi gatito."*

He began to move slowly from his hiding place.

"Sí, Rojito. Ven, ven aquí, por favor."

He crept closer, terrified but not hurt. She heard a loud click behind her. In the silence of her bedroom, it sounded like a gunshot. Still on the floor, she whirled around to face the intruder.

Sunglasses wrapping his narrow skull hid the rest of his face. The man who had grabbed her in the parking lot. His colorless hair fell in strings to his shoulders, and his head lay at an angle, roped by thick, ugly scars. He took one step toward her.

"Finally," he said. The same scratchy voice from the phone. Corina couldn't move. "You know what I'm here for. Acting on orders. You can make it easy or rough."

"I don't have anything." She barely gasped out the words.

"Don't lie to me." His fingers closed around her arm. He brought his face close to hers. "And don't piss me off."

"Please believe me." She was trying to reason with a crazy man, a killer. There was no hope. Corina began to sob.

"I told you not to piss me off." His grip tightened on her arm, far too powerful for her to be able to escape. "Just tell me where it is, and I'll let you go. If you don't—"

Corina heard the heavy slap of footsteps. The man heard them, too. He jerked toward the noise.

A male voice shouted, "Police."

A uniformed officer sprang into the room, his gun drawn. She felt the movement, didn't see it, felt herself smash to the floor. Heard the blast, the moan, the thud. She tried to scramble to her feet. Still holding the gun, the intruder dashed out the back. The officer, a young Asian man, grabbed his bleeding shoulder.

"I'm okay," he gasped. "My partner's outside." As he spoke, the second officer appeared. He rushed to his fallen partner, who struggled to stand.

"Out there," he said, pointing. His partner headed in the direction the intruder had taken.

"How'd you know to come here?" Corina asked.

"Him." The officer pointed at the figure in the doorway. Papa stood just inside the bedroom, carrying a clublike object. He bellowed in Chinese, loud enough to summon every neighbor in the complex. The Asian officer answered in the same language.

"My neighbor called you?" she asked.

"Yeah. Said there was an intruder next door, someone carrying a weapon." He reached for his shoulder, moaned.

Papa muttered concern. The club hung from his wrist.

"Are you sure you're all right?"

He nodded, and spoke to Papa again in Chinese.

She went into the living room. Rojito crouched in the front window, his pupils large and dark. She stroked him, speaking calming phrases in Spanish.

Papa's shout summoned the neighbors. Corina as-

sured them the police had been notified, and they
returned to their condos. Papa didn't leave her side.

"It's okay," she told him, trying to reassure herself, as well. "Everything will be okay now."

If only she could believe it, as well.

Twenty-Two

Wednesday, June 13, 9:55 p.m.

While they waited for the police to finish their business, Corina walked aimlessly through the condo. Violated, she thought. The man with the lopsided head had violated her life, handled her personal possessions with his filthy fingers. He'd even ripped the ice cube trays from her refrigerator, slashed open packages in her freezer.

"Why the refrigerator?" she asked Papa, feeling the tears slide down her cheeks.

Somehow understanding, the old man just frowned and shook his bald, freckled head.

"You're a good friend, Papa," she said slowly, trying to make him hear the feelings beneath her words. "A really good friend."

He responded with a solemn nod and slowly reached out to stroke Rojito.

Just then, an angry voice exploded into the room. "What the hell?"

Matthew Henderson stood in the open doorway. He wore a pair of jeans and a black T-shirt. His florid face registered shock. Papa moved between them, surprisingly agile for his age.

"It's all right," she assured Papa. Then she turned to Henderson. "What are you doing here?"

"That's beside the point now." He moved slowly inside, taking in the damage. "Cops are all over the place. What happened?"

"Someone broke in." She shuddered again, and he took over, stalking into the kitchen and over to its jimmied sliding glass door.

"Must have come over the back wall and gotten in there. You see anyone?"

She nodded slowly, not wanting to remember, but unable to forget. "He grabbed me, that man. The same one who jumped me in the parking lot."

His frown turned suspicious. "What was he looking for?"

She sank down into a kitchen chair. The man hadn't come with the intent of vandalizing or even frightening her.

"The same thing. He thinks Skin gave me something. He even destroyed my ice cube trays."

"The first place they go," Henderson said, as if thinking to himself. "Is anything missing?"

His questions hammered at her. "It just happened," she said. "I sure as hell haven't taken an inventory."

He went to her refrigerator, took out a green bottle of beer and opened it as if he drank Tsingtao every day.

"Want one?" he asked.

She glanced down at her hand on Rojito's back. How long had it been trembling? At least Henderson planned on sticking around for a while. She didn't want to be alone, not yet.

"Sure," she said.

The investigator seemed to be working from a script he'd long before committed to memory. He confirmed Henderson's suspicions about the intruder entering from the back patio.

They'd be back, he told Corina. Did she have another place to stay? She phoned the manager and explained her problem. She could move into the vacant condominium, the manager said. Would that work for her? Would it work? Did she dare occupy the unit so close to where she had been violated?

Henderson sat across from her at the kitchen table with his second bottle of beer. "You sure Skin didn't give you anything?" He seemed to measure her with his eyes.

"I told you he didn't." Her head ached from questions. "I do know I can't stay here tonight. I don't know if I'll ever feel safe here again."

"You have a gun?"

"I don't believe in them."

He regarded her in silence. "Is there anyone I can call for you?"

For one crazy moment, she thought of Wes. Then, just as rapidly, she dismissed the thought. She didn't need complications. She needed a friend.

"Geri LaRue," she said to her surprise.

"Why her?"

"I don't' know." It had been a silly idea. What could Geri possibly do? "Ignore me," she said. "I don't know what I'm saying."

Henderson placed the green bottle on the table. "I'll stay here with you for a bit."

"That's not necessary. My neighbor's right next door. If he hadn't been here tonight, I don't know what would have happened to me." She shuddered.

He took a swallow of beer, then spoke as if measuring his words. "Come on, Corina. What did Skin give you?"

Her head spun. He didn't believe her. Something had convinced him that she was lying. Someone.

"You talked to Betsy, didn't you?"

"You shouldn't have met with her behind my back like that."

"The way you met with Nan Belmont?"

"That was different."

"To you perhaps. How did you get to Betsy?"

"She called."

He hesitated, and she could read the thoughts behind the flicker of his pale eyes. "She called *me*, didn't she? You took the call."

"Last I heard I'm still the supervisor. Yeah, I talked to her. Went out to Vineyard Estates. She said she remembered something she hadn't told you. The group that owns Vineyard Estates calls themselves The Trio. Betsy thought that might help."

"The Trio? That man who was here today is involved with them in some way."

"And he's looking for whatever Skin gave you."

"Which was nothing."

Somebody thought she knew more than she did. A second fact revealed itself to her as she studied his face. Henderson thought so, too. He still didn't believe her.

"So is that why you came over?" she asked. "To tell me what Betsy said?"

"Not exactly. We can talk about it later. I want you to take tomorrow off."

She set her bottle firmly on the table. "Let's talk

about it now, Matthew. Why did you come here to-night?''

He sighed and looked down at his hands. ''I don't think you're ready to hear it.''

''Don't play games with me. What could be worse than what's already happened?''

''You really want to know?''

''What does it take?'' she asked. ''Another beer?''

She'd crossed the line. She could see it in the reddening of his face, the narrowing of his eyes. ''You want the truth, lady? After I talked to Betsy, I realized you've been doing a lot more work on this story than you pretended.''

''I'm not the only one,'' she retorted. ''What about your meeting with Nan Belmont? What about your trying to dig up dirt on Wes Shaw Senior?''

His cheeks flushed a deeper shade, making his eyes, by contrast, paler, more dangerously angry than ever. ''I have to cover every possibility, and I thought your emotional involvement might get in the way. I don't want to see you end up like Skin, okay?''

She felt an involuntary shudder. ''What makes you think I might?''

''This mess here, for one,'' Henderson said, gesturing at the room. ''And for another—''

''What?''

''After work, I got home and started thinking about all this. When I realized that you'd used your contact with Wes Shaw to get to Betsy and that Skin claimed he'd given you something connected to the murder, I got concerned.''

''Concerned, Matthew?''

''I got pissed, okay?''

She looked down at Rojito and stroked his head. "At least the man's honest." Rojito gave her a unilingual glance.

"You asked a question, and I'm trying to answer it," Henderson said. "I went back to the paper, okay? Took a lot of shit from Geri LaRue. There's something weird about her and not just her hair. She asked me what I was doing hanging around that late, then actually followed me down to the first floor."

"What did you do that attracted her attention?"

"You're good. You know that?" He stared into her eyes as he drained the rest of the beer.

"Please answer my question."

"I know how you document every interview, how you file each notebook," he began. "Got another beer in there?"

She felt her stomach turn to water. "You didn't break into my files at work? Tell me you didn't." If he as much as touched her notes, she'd go straight to Chenault, screaming harassment, threatening a lawsuit with the newest lawyer in her mother's family.

"Didn't have a chance." Henderson lowered his voice. "Somebody beat me to it. Your files were scattered all over the office."

"No," she said. "What about my notebooks?"

Henderson leaned forward in his chair and lifted his empty bottle. "I'm afraid they're gone. And I *am* sorry."

The sense of violation that had knotted itself in the back of her brain became a full-blown, splitting headache.

"Sorry for what?" He had the nerve to take the self-righteous stance of the victim instead of the accused. "Sorry that somebody trashed my condo, my office and everything else in my life? Or sorry that you had to admit you'd stoop so low as to try to break into my files? Which is it, Matthew?"

"You'd better watch it," he said. "I know what you're feeling right now, but—"

"No," she said, rising from the kitchen chair. "The truth is that you'd better watch it, Matthew Henderson. And you'd damn well better get out of here right now."

"That's the first thing you've said that's made any sense." He flung open the door, then stopped, started to say something, and without a word, shut the door behind him.

After he left, she sat in the shambles of her kitchen and thought that, as much as she hated facing this violation by herself, there were some fates far more frightening than being alone.

Rojito pressed his red face against her palm. She held him close to her and wept.

Twenty-Three

Wednesday, June 13, 11:05 p.m.

Corina's landlord, the real estate woman from the end condo, came to survey the damage and assure herself that the property was safe. Her questions were careful but decent. She insisted that Corina stay in the furnished condo where the waitress had lived the month before. Corina agreed and numbly took a key, signed papers and wondered how she could sleep in a strange bed just a few feet away from her own wrecked home.

She had told everything to the police. How Skin had called her the night of his death, saying Eugene Belmont had murdered Tina Kellogg. How the janitor had said Skin had left with a man with a scarred neck. How that same man, the man who had just torn apart her condo, had jumped her in the newspaper parking lot, demanding she turn over something he thought Skin had given her. How he'd telephoned her later, boasting that he could kill her if he wanted to.

They had Skin's scribbled notes about the DEA agents. They had the couple of files she'd been able to rescue from the fire. And now they had her account of everything she could remember since that day she'd stood not far from Tina Kellogg's remains. After they left, she realized how much better she felt.

Just talking through the story again gave her more ideas. The intruder must work for Eugene Belmont. Certainly the police would check on that. And Belmont was after her because he thought Skin had told her something about his involvement in Tina's death. The key was Vineyard Estates, a development no one cared about. But somebody cared a great deal. Corina tried to straighten her kitchen, then stopped out of frustration. She couldn't tackle this tonight.

She went into her bedroom and looked through a bureau drawer tossed on top of the bed. She'd never been able to throw away any of the cards Wes had given her. Now they were scattered along with her jewelry and underwear. Carefully Corina gathered the cards into a small packet and found a rubber band to hold them together. That was the best she could do for now, and it wasn't enough. She pressed the cards to her chest like a bouquet of flowers. Her life had collapsed around her. She had no one, nothing.

She couldn't call her parents. They wouldn't understand. Her father would demand that she quit her job on the spot. And her mother—Lord, she didn't even want to think about her reaction.

Corina felt weak, drained of courage, but she knew she couldn't take any immediate action yet. She had to regain what the intruder had taken from her; she had to get herself back.

She reached for her cell phone, the way she might reach for a box of chocolates, not really admitting to herself what she was doing until the act was too far gone to stop.

He answered on the first ring.

"Wes?" She tried to say more. Couldn't.

"Corina, what is it? Are you all right?"

"Oh, God. I don't know how to start." More tears escaped. She couldn't stop shaking.

"It's okay," he said. "I'm on my way."

She was still holding the phone when he arrived. "What the hell happened?" he asked.

She choked out her story.

It was the first time she remembered seeing him look afraid.

"I should have been here. I should have done something."

"No, Wes. Don't blame yourself. It doesn't have anything to do with you."

Rojito entered the room and went straight to him. Wes bent down to pet him. "You remember me, don't you, boy? We're going to get you out of here, both of you."

"My landlord gave me the condo over there. It's furnished. At least I'll have a place to stay."

"You've got to get out of here. What if he comes back?"

She shuddered. He put his arms around her, and she buried her head in the soft folds of his loose-fitting linen shirt. "My fault," he whispered. "I never should have let you go. I knew it was wrong when I did it."

"It doesn't matter."

"It does. Everything that's happening to you is my fault."

"No." She stepped away from him, looking into

his eyes to make him understand. "You're not responsible for my safety. My job is what caused this, not you."

"I'm just so damned worried about you." He looked down at her hand, touched the packet she still clutched. "What's that?"

"Just some things I picked up from the bed. They were scattered everywhere."

She tried to pull them away, but he held her hand firmly in his. "I know what they are." He drew her into his arms. His shirt felt safe. She kept her eyes closed, smelling his freshly pressed scent. God, she loved him. She'd never stopped loving him. She lifted her lips to his, no longer caring what a risk she was taking.

He tasted familiar and new, frightening and wonderful. She wrapped her arms around his neck. Finally she knew where she needed to be.

"Come with me now," he whispered.

"I can't. Not to your place." She couldn't do that, not yet.

He seemed to understand. "We can go anywhere you like. Anywhere you say."

"Next door." A place she'd never seen. A place without memories or history. A place where she could be safe and alone with him.

He kissed her again. "Are you sure?"

"About going next door?"

"About that and about me. About us."

They kissed through her answer. Kissed through the grabbing of personal possessions, through the transporting of Rojito. Kissed against the locked door of the strange but familiar condo, its bed without sheets, its clean-smelling shower. They kissed in

the spray of water that washed away Corina's pain
and tears. Kissed her well. Kissed her back to life.

They lay next to each other on the strange bed,
only a large bath towel thrown across its mattress.
Wes had spread his shirt over Corina. It lay, gossa-
mer-like, cooling her sweat-drenched body.

He propped himself up over her, leaned down and
kissed her throat through the linen. "Talk to me."

"Can't talk."

"I know. Me, neither."

He sank down beside her, his heat and his scent
part of her heat, her scent now.

"Clock," he whispered into her ear.

He was right. In the rush of leaving her condo,
she'd grabbed up her clock along with her other possessions.

"Remember the game we used to play?" he
asked.

"Every night."

"It's not the same when you play it alone, is it?"

"No."

After making love, lying in the dark, barely able
to speak, they would count the sounds of the night.
She thought for a moment, listening into the silence.

"Purring," she said. "Rojito's."

"Train."

"Dog."

"Drums."

"I don't hear any drums," she said. Wes had been
known to make up sounds when he was drowsy and
drifting toward sleep.

"Thunder then."

"No, a vacuum, next door maybe."

"Radio, too, from somewhere."

Yes, she could hear that. An oldies station. She could hear the beat. And another beat, closer. "Water dripping in the bathroom," she said.

He rolled over, placed his cheek against her chest. "Your heart."

She turned into his arms. "*Your* heart."

"You win," he said, and kissed her again.

"Wes," she said much later, softly, in case he were sleeping.

"What is it?"

"That man."

"I won't let him harm you. He'll never have a chance to get close to you again."

She didn't say anything else. The thought of her ruined possessions, almost everything she owned, humiliated her, as if she were the one who had done something wrong. But she hadn't. She who abhorred violence had been violated. Her life had been attacked, but she would be okay. She had herself back. And now she had Wes back.

Twenty-Four

Thursday, June 14, 5:30 a.m.

She awoke in the tangle of his arms, then slowly remembered what happened—the terrible part first, the rest later. He roused beside her, mumbled love words to her.

"Of all the places I've dreamed of taking you, this is the last place I would have imagined our getting back together," he said.

She pulled the soft linen to her breasts. "I've never had more elegant bedclothes." Awakened by their voices, Rojito stretched on the window sill and headed in their direction.

She had to get to work, to protect her story, and it was her story now. She had paid too much to hand it over to Henderson. Whatever the man with the twisted neck wanted had to be important if he'd risk breaking into her condo and the newspaper office.

That was it! Of course. Adrenaline pounded through her. Every visitor to the newspaper had to sign in, regardless of the hour. She needed to get down there and talk to security.

Wes read her mind, touched a finger to her lips. "You're not going anywhere today."

"I have to."

"You could have been killed."

"But I wasn't."

"Not this time. You need protection, a body-guard."

"Wes, please."

"I mean it. You can't keep risking your life for a stupid story."

"It's not about the story. It's about something Skin was supposed to give me."

"What was it?"

"I don't know. I never got it."

"I'm giving you a gun," he said.

"Isn't that illegal?"

"It might keep you alive."

"I don't believe in guns," she said. "I don't even know how to use one."

"Then, I'll teach you."

She snuggled next to him. She would keep him warm, close and quiet for a few minutes more, although she knew she'd never be able to hold, let alone fire a gun. It had something to do with the violence she had witnessed since Tina's body had been found, and her feeling that a weapon would be her admission of more violence to come.

With the help of the landlord and a locksmith, she would secure her condo against attack. The intruder would be able to find her, anyway, if he wanted to. He must have started to figure out that she didn't have what he was after. If she couldn't feel safe in the condo again, she'd move. All that mattered right now was to find out who was after her before he had a chance to do more damage.

Against Wes's wishes, she dressed and went to

work. Shaky as she was, she felt wrapped in his love, strong and less alone. Maybe it wasn't wise to rush back into his arms like this at a time when she was fragile and frightened, but she didn't care. She needed him, and she knew now that she'd never, in the eleven months they'd been apart, stopped loving him.

When she arrived that morning, she found her office clean. Someone, probably Henderson, had arranged the photos and books on her desk in some semblance of order. She approached the file cabinet. The door slid out easily, free of contents. Nothing but empty folders. She closed the door.

"This is terrible."

She whirled around to see Ivy Dieser standing on the other side of her desk. She wore a black linen suit cinched at her small waist. "When will this vandalism stop?" she said. "They did the same thing to my office."

"I'm not sure this was vandalism," Corina said. "Someone's been after my notes. They think Skin Burke gave me information about Tina Kellogg's murder."

Dieser's face went white beneath the blush. "Are you certain? Do you really think anyone could get in here?"

"Somebody did. They also broke into my condo."

"Then what are you doing at work? You should be home."

"Doing what? My condo's as secure as it can be. The police are investigating."

Dieser swallowed and stepped inside the office. "You talked to the police?"

"Of course."

"That explains it."

"Explains what?"

"Brandon Chenault received a phone call from Nan Belmont this morning saying her father's threatening to sue."

"Oh, no."

"It's not the first time Eugene Belmont's threatened us, but Chenault wanted me to let you know what she said. Her father is ill apparently. The interview you gave Channel 5 and the police showing up to question him about Tina Kellogg's murder further upset him. I guess Nan was pretty hot."

"Well, she can be hot," Corina said. "Vineyard Estates is connected to those murders somehow. Eugene is involved in it. I think he hired the man who's after me."

"That's quite an accusation. I'm sure you have facts to back it up."

"I'm getting more all the time."

"Commendable." It must be her favorite word. "I have great expectations for you, Corina, and so does Brandon Chenault. You've been in this department such a short while, and you've uncovered what could be a major story."

"I'm trying," she said.

"I've made J.T. aware of our feelings. I think now he's beginning to see how right I was about your abilities."

"J.T. and I are okay with each other," Corina said.

Dieser ignored her comment. "He was in diversity training last week, but I'll bring him up to date when I see him today."

Diversity training for J.T. That was a laugh, but Dieser said it with complete sincerity reflected in her wide brown eyes. "What about the lawsuit?"

"Legal will handle it, if it really happens. Nan Belmont made it sound as if you accused her father of murder. From what you say, you repeated only what Skin told you."

"That's correct. And he said that Eugene was responsible for Tina's death."

"I'll pass that along to Chenault. Depending on what happens, he may want to talk to you himself."

"Of course." From behind Dieser's pile of hair, Corina could see Henderson making his way to the office. "I'd better get to work now," she said.

Dieser turned, strictly business. "Good morning," she said, glancing at Henderson and then at the clock on the wall above his office.

"Everything okay?" he asked.

"As okay as it can be, considering." Dieser smoothed her skirt. "I'm going to call maintenance right now. We need stronger cabinets with better locks." She said it as if the old ones were Henderson's fault.

He grunted a response.

"We'll talk later," she said to Corina, and left.

Henderson didn't move until she was out of earshot. Then, to Corina, he said, "What the hell was that all about?"

Worried that she'd snitched about his going through her files, she thought. "Eugene Belmont," she said. "Nan called Chenault, threatening to sue."

"It's not the first time."

"So I hear."

"Listen." He glared at her, his cheeks aflame.

"I'm going to say this once and only once. I didn't have any right to go through your files without telling you, supervisor or not. I was pissed about your talking to Betsy, and I acted without thinking it through."

"Am I to take that as an apology?"

"Take it any way you want. I told you I was saying it once, and that was it. Now, let's get to work."

He cut in front of her and strode into the office. She could smell the faint, sour odor of the night before. He was still a bastard, but less a bastard than he had been, and his stammered, obviously rehearsed speech was at least a step toward communication. She needed to reciprocate, but she wasn't about to gush.

"I need a cup of coffee," she said. "Can I bring you one?"

He stopped before his desk, turned, his eyes narrowed.

"You buying?"

"Sure."

"I never turn down free coffee," he said.

She shrugged and headed for the hall. Not exactly sparkling repartee, she thought, but maybe it was a start.

Twenty-Five

Thursday, June 14, 8:36 p.m.

Finally the night crew arrived. Henderson had already gone home. Corina hadn't seen Ivy Dieser for the rest of the day and had no idea if she were still in the building. The Mexico story was leading again. The president of Mexico was meeting the president at an undisclosed location. Governor Menlo was putting pressure on the president to demand the return of the missing DEA agents, Roxene Waite and Norman Flannigan, implying that the Mexican government was behind the kidnapping.

J.T. stepped into her cubicle, his face set like a mask. "Working late?" he asked, clearly disinterested.

"Diversity training must not agree with you," she said.

"Punishment."

"For what?"

"You'll hear soon enough. I'm tired of being harassed by that woman."

"Dieser?"

"None other. She wants to get rid of Henderson, and I'm not going to play her game."

"Does that mean you and I can't be friends?"

He stared at her, taken aback. "Depends on how involved you are with what she's planning."

"I'm not. I'm just trying to do my job."

"Then why don't you try to work with Henderson instead of against him?"

"Because he won't work with me."

J.T. shook his head. "Would you want to work with someone you thought was after your job?"

"But I'm not—"

"*Would* you?"

"No, of course not."

"Henderson's a good guy and a hell of a reporter. Give him a chance, why don't you?"

She started to tell him that Henderson had gone through her files, but decided against it. Once when they had been on better terms, J.T. had told her that his family was from the South, that his father had moved to California because he said at least the racism was hidden there. He knew what it was like to be judged before having an opportunity to prove himself. On a lesser scale, so did she. His eyes looked weary and older than his years. She couldn't turn away from them.

"Okay," she said. "I will give him a chance."

"You will?"

"I'll talk to him. Maybe there's a way we can work together."

"I'd like that," he said. "Thanks." The smile he gave her was brief and genuine, but it did nothing to change his eyes.

A television set with four miniature screens flashed on four different locations inside and outside the building. The young security guard at the front desk went through the previous night's sign-in sheets. The black moustache he wore did little to hide his age.

"I already showed these to your boss last night," he said, looking up from the counter that separated them.

That didn't surprise her. The guard station would have been Henderson's first stop.

"Everyone who comes through that door after-hours has to sign in here?" she asked, gesturing toward the door that led to the ramp.

"Everyone, no exceptions."

"Yet, you didn't ask me to sign in just now."

He looked up with a frown, as if she'd tricked him. "That's different. I know you."

"Are there others you know who don't have to sign in, either?"

"Yeah, I guess so," he said, clearly irritated. "You guys are supposed to wear your ID badges."

"But not all of us do."

"So?" He regarded her with narrowed, suspicious eyes.

"So, this is important. Can you tell me how many passed through that door last night without signing in?"

"Just the usual." He glanced down at the papers before him then back up at her. "And your boss. He came in around eight, and no, I didn't ask him to sign in, either."

He wouldn't cooperate if she got him angry, she knew. She leaned against the counter and spoke in a low voice.

"Someone broke into my office last night. They could have only come through this door."

"Oh, man. I'm in for it now. Verna will have my butt for this."

"I'm not blaming you for anything," she said. "I just want to know if you saw anything or anyone unusual."

"Just the same old crew. I don't know their names, all of them, but I know their faces."

"This was probably a man, about forty, thin, blond hair, his head tilted to one side, thick scars on his neck." Even describing him gave her chills.

"I don't think so," he said. "I'd remember someone like that."

"And you were here all night?"

"Till midnight."

"And you didn't leave the station?"

Guilt clouded his eyes. "Except a couple of times when I went into the caf over there for coffee."

"Was one of those times before eight?" she asked.

He nodded warily. "Might have been."

The door swung open, and a few of the night-side printers entered and moved down the hall.

Sam, the former shift supervisor, lifted his hand in greeting. He'd lost the index and middle fingers in an accident years before, but no one pasted up pages with more speed or dexterity. Not that speed was that essential anymore. The newspaper had outgrown its need for printers. Editors composed pages on their PCs and sent them directly to prepress now. Only Sam and a few others who had yet to retire remained, counting the hours in what had once been an hectic, deadline-driven composing room.

She motioned him over.

"How you doing, kid?" She could tell from his voice and his solemn expression that he'd heard what happened.

"Got a minute?" she asked.

"For you, sure."

They stepped outside onto the ramp and leaned against the still-warm metal rail overlooking the back parking lot. She studied his thin, narrow face, his even narrower grizzled beard that shot down a good eight inches past his chin.

"You know that someone broke into my office?"

"Your stuff was all over the place. That tech chick, Geri LaRue, was down there when I came in."

"You don't think she had anything to do with it?"

"No, Geri's different, but she's good people. She was all over Henderson's ass. Claimed she caught him poking around in it."

"What did he say?"

"Denied it, of course. You sure he didn't do it?"

The question caught her off guard. "Henderson wouldn't have any reason to fake a break-in," she said. "And officially he is my boss. He can check out my files anytime he feels like it."

Sam lifted an eyebrow. "If it was your files he wanted."

"What do you mean?"

"He's an old union man like me," he said, stroking his beard. "Nothing personal, but none of us is exactly turning cartwheels over the changes around here. Maybe he's just trying to spook you."

"Scare me away, you mean?"

"Yeah, or just find out what you're up to, maybe.

A lot of guys are saying Chenault promoted his spies into good jobs. There's the kid in my old job, the hot little honey in classified, pardon my French. Then there's Ivy Dieser, you. A lot of new faces."

"You've known me since I started here," she said. "Do you really think I'd spy for management?"

"I know you wouldn't, but I'm not Henderson. He doesn't know you."

"And you think he'd try to scare me away?"

Sam stared straight ahead. "Don't know what anybody's bound to do around this place anymore. Sure isn't the way it used to be."

Would Henderson stoop so low? Corina couldn't imagine it. Yet he had practically stolen her byline. He'd gone to Nan and Betsy behind her back, had been willing to break into her files. Her head hurt from trying to figure out Matthew Henderson and his motives. "I have to go," she said.

"Let me walk you."

"There are guards out there."

He made a sound of disgust. "What kind of protection are they? Kids on bicycles. They spend all their time drinking coffee in the caf. They ride around on those bikes like this is a park."

They stepped into the floodlights as a guard pedaled by, a cigarette glowing in his hand.

"I see what you mean," she said.

"It never used to be like this. Damn punks will come right in, steal your hubcaps off your car. Weird types hang out here like it's the neighborhood watering hole, and cops don't do nothing."

"What kind of weird types?" she asked.

"You name it, I've seen it. Druggies mostly."

"Have you ever seen a man—" She touched her throat. "He has something wrong with his neck."

"Oh, that dude. Wears shades at night? Looks like maybe he was burned?" He tilted his head toward his shoulder. "You seen him, too?"

She nearly choked, trying to find her voice. "What color van?"

"Kind of olive, only darker."

"Did you see him last night?"

"No." A frown creased his narrow forehead. "I did see the van, though, parked out there." He turned and pointed toward the back parking lot. "You think he had something to do with the break-in?"

She clutched his arm. "You've got to promise me you'll phone me if you ever see him out there again."

"We'll make it a conference call."

She released his arm, her throat so tense she could barely speak. "What do you mean?"

"Your buddy Henderson made me promise the same thing. Said to call him first if I saw the guy again. He trying to steal a story from you or something?"

"It's bigger than that, trust me."

He stared her down, as if trying to decide on a response. Finally he said, "I *do* trust you. Henderson used to be a good friend. Changed when he split with his old lady, though. If I see that weirdo out here, I'll call you both, just like I promised." He grinned. "But I'll call you first."

"Thanks, Sam."

"Now, get in that car and lock the door, so I don't get busted for being late on a shift I used to run about three times as good as that snot-nose they put in my place.''

She stayed in her car, watching his wiry body find its way back through the parking lot. He was one of a disappearing breed, a man most new reporters considered a dinosaur. She couldn't count the times he'd rescued her as a novice reporter, pointing out her mistakes on a paste-up before her editor could spot it, cutting space from an overset headline until it fit.

He'd just done it again, giving her enough evidence to go back to the police, confirming the involvement of the man with the stringy hair. The security guards hadn't done that, and Geri LaRue certainly hadn't. She hadn't even bothered to mention her confrontation with Henderson.

Corina knew what she had to do next. She had to talk to the police again. And, like it or not, she had to have a long-overdue talk with Henderson.

She returned to the condo, committed to barring the door, sleeping with Geri's pepper spray under her pillow and doing whatever it took, including drink the remaining Chinese beer in her refrigerator, to get through the night. It wasn't the best time to receive a visit from her baby sister.

Twenty-Six

Thursday, June 14, 9:41 p.m.

Although she was named Guadeloupe, she'd always been Lupita, the baby, and she'd used that for all it was worth.

As Corina came down the walk from the back, she could see her stalking back and forth in front of the condo, unaware that Corina was no longer staying there. In the still, starlit night, her sister needed only to throw back her head and strike a pose to look like a dancer from *West Side Story*.

"Lupita," Corina called out.

"What'd you do, change the fucking locks?"

She'd pulled her long hair up, and clipped it with a dangerous-looking silver object that seemed designed for holding papers in a binder. A low-cut black T-shirt tucked into her jeans did little to hide the offending tattoo their mother claimed to have just discovered. Corina looked at her sister's fragile, lovely features, her demanding pout and tried to decide if she should go for truth or fantasyland. Maybe she ought to say she was moving, redecorating, or maybe she shouldn't go into her place at all, just usher Lupita into the other condo.

"Well?" Lupita put a hand to her hip and sighed at this latest inconvenience.

Truth it was. "There was a problem here," Corina said. "Don't freak out at what you see inside."

She opened the door, let Lupita go in ahead, heard a gasp.

"Oh, Cori."

"I can explain."

"An orange sofa? And what, velvet? Holy shit. It's worse than Mama's."

"Hold on," Corina said. "My landlord just put this in here as a favor. She usually rents it out."

"People pay for this? Why are you borrowing it? I don't understand. Jesse's supposed to meet me here in fifteen minutes. I'll have to have him pick me up outside."

"Would you stop thinking about yourself for one second? A man broke in last night and turned the place upside down. Sorry about the old sofa. It's slashed to pieces." Corina meant it to sound harsh, but she hadn't counted on the catch in her voice, the sudden tears.

Something new flickered in Lupita's eyes. It looked amazingly like intelligence. "What do you mean?" she said. "What's going on?"

"You knew our mayor was murdered?"

Lupita nodded and moved to the couch, her scent trailing behind. Patchouli and sandalwood. She smelled like a candle. "What does that have to do with you?"

"A builder I'd used as a source was also killed, and there are people—" She sank down on the arm of the sofa next to her sister. "The man who broke in here thinks that Skin, the builder, gave me something. He tried to burn down Skin's home Tuesday, with me in it.''

Lupita sat mute on the rust-colored sofa, her eyes wide. "I had no idea," she said.

"Of course not. You're not really used to thinking about anyone but yourself.''

"That's not true. You've forgotten what it's like trying to live with Mama. You can't imagine what I go through with that woman.''

Corina wiped her eyes. "Oh, I can't? Like I never lived in that house?''

"It's different for me." Her pout was more fear than attitude now. "Lydia, the perfect lady. Corina, the perfect student. All the good roles were taken before I came along.''

"Lupita, the perfect baby." Corina shrugged. "Sounds pretty good to me about now.''

Lupita dug in her purse and handed Corina a tissue. "So you got pulled into someone else's nightmare?''

"I guess I did. We'll talk more later. The manager let me take the condo next door. You can stay with me if you like.''

Lupita stared at her, barely comprehending or able to respond. "I still can't believe it. What are you going to do?''

"What can I do?" She waved her arm at what used to be her home. "I don't even know what he's after.''

"And that Skin guy didn't give you anything at all?''

"Nothing''

"Maybe he tried to tell you something, used some kind of code.''

"There wouldn't be any reason for Skin to use code with me. We were talking on the phone. He could just tell me."

"Unless there was someone with him."

"He was alone." She sat down next to Lupita. "He was killed because of something he knew about a housing development on the river bluffs."

"Was he an honest man?"

Good question. "I thought so at one time. In fact, my first freelance piece was a profile on him I wrote for a builders' magazine back when I was still living at home."

"California Living," she said. "It still comes to the house. Mama bitches that you have to pay so much for it, ten bucks a copy or something."

She laughed. "Journalists don't pay. Once they have you on their list, they send it forever. Tell Mama to stop forwarding the damn thing to me every month."

"So," Lupita said, her gaze intent. "I asked you whether or not he was an honest man. Could you trust him?"

Corina no longer knew. "If I could answer that, I might have the answer to what happened to him," she said. "You know, I'll bet you'd make a good reporter."

"Spare my sweet ass. That would do Mama in for good."

They sat side by side on the sofa, silent. Corina thought it might be the first serious conversation they'd ever had. She smiled at Lupita, brushed a stray hair from her face.

"Don't look so scared, baby. It's okay."

"Does Mama know anything about this?"

"No, and don't tell her a word."

"You think I'm crazy? She'll find out sooner or later, though. You know how she is."

"I'll tell her when I'm ready, and I'm not right now. You've got to promise to keep quiet."

"Promise." Then as if sensing the doubt Corina felt, she added, "I might be a little flaky, but I know how to keep a secret."

"Good, because I need you to. Now, why don't you go meet Jesse? Don't let me screw up your night."

She shook her head slowly. "I'm afraid to leave." Her eyes shone in the dim light. "You're my rock, Cori."

"And you're thinking of yourself again. I'll be here when you get back, right next door. You can stay with me over there. Go try to have a good time."

"Well." She looked from the cell phone to Corina as if weighing the advantages of each. "There's not really much I can do here, is there?"

"Not after you fix your eye makeup. It's all over your face."

Lupita stood up and surveyed herself in the hall mirror. "You know," she said, turning to face Corina, "you'd really like Jesse if you got to know him."

"I do like him," she said. "And next to my high-school boyfriend, he looks like a primo catch."

"Really?"

"Yeah, but don't tell Mama that one, either."

"She never met your high-school boyfriend?"

"Of course not. You know I wasn't allowed to date in high school."

* * *

As high-school boyfriends go, Jesse wasn't bad, except for the small matters of tattoo, earring and baggy pants. He'd been raised by decent people and might be able to return to some semblance of civility once he got his priorities straight. Or he might end up above the fold on page B-2, among the convenience store shootings and hit-and-runs. She hoped not, for his sake as well as her sister's.

Love, she thought. Was Lydia the only one of them who was doing it right? No. Neither she nor Lupita would be happy with Pete, whom Lupita described as "too Mexican." Corina knew what she meant. But Lydia's chances of happiness were better than both of theirs combined right now. Maybe not, though. She knew Lydia couldn't love Pete the way she loved Wes, regardless of what happened. Theirs had not been a match of convenience or culture. They'd defied the odds, lost, but now, maybe… Oh, God, maybe, if she could just get through this.

For now, she needed to get next door, where Rojito waited and anonymity prevailed. She had just started outside when the phone rang. Who'd call her here? Wes would use her cell phone, wouldn't he? Maybe not. She'd told Mama to use the cell number, too, but Mama always did things her way.

She hurried to the kitchen, and as she answered, another possibility flickered through her mind. She remembered what happened the last time she had an unexpected caller in this place. But by then, it was too late.

"Corina?"

Damn. The jagged voice. "Leave me alone."

"Acting on my own again. That was a close call

yesterday. You are some babe, you know that? How'd you get the cops out there so fast?''

Corina forced the tremor from her voice. He hadn't figured out that Papa had summoned the police. ''Why won't you leave me alone?''

''You know why, baby.''

''I meant what I said yesterday. I don't have what you're looking for.''

''I've stood in the closet with your clothes, Corina, babe. I've smelled you. You have the tape, or you know who does.''

She bit her lip. *The tape.* It was a tape Skin had planned to give her. She clutched the phone, trying to buy time. She needed to keep him talking, any way she could.

''You're pretty brave calling me at home.''

''Not brave, just smart. I know all about you, so don't try to pretend there's somebody there. There's never anybody with you at night, and that's too bad, a good-looking girl like you. Nobody to talk about how nice your clothes smell in the dark.''

She took a chance. If he'd slipped once, he might slip twice. ''Why does Eugene Belmont want the tape?'' she asked.

''Don't get smart with me, girl.'' The grating voice dropped to a whisper.

Corina visualized his stringy hair, the raised slashes of scar tissue on his neck. ''Don't you think I'd hand it over if I had it? Believe it or not, I'd rather keep living.''

''Don't worry about that. Everyone wants you alive. Almost everyone, that is.''

The dread within her froze into a solid knot of ice. ''Who wants to kill me?''

"Just one person, but that's not any of your business, either."

"Eugene? Is he behind this?"

He made a noise that sounded like laughter. "You're not as cagey as you think you are. A guy like me could teach you a lot. Maybe our next little talk ought to be in person."

The phone went dead, and Corina didn't know if she were angry or scared to death or relieved. She had more information, but at what personal cost? She needed to get out of here, but now she was afraid to make the short trip from this condo to the one next to it.

Twenty-Seven

Thursday, June 14, 10:12 p.m.

Corina walked to the front door. Her porch light illuminated the area from her entry to the pool; there was nothing to fear. She had neighbors on all sides of her, police officers patrolling the complex. Still, she couldn't help reaching out and lifting the blinds beside the door. The pool lay like a silent, dark rectangle behind the chain-link fence.

Something moved to the right, on the walkway beside Papa's condo, a shadow, that was all. No, not a shadow, a shape, the shape of a man. She watched him cross in front of Papa's and disappear on the walkway along the bougainvillea-covered walls. Maybe someone out walking, taking a shortcut, but no. It was too much of a coincidence. Breathing in short gasps, Corina forced her legs to carry her into the kitchen, the newly secured back door with vertical blinds closed now. She took one in her hand, slowly parted it. Looking back at her was a face, hands cupped around it. Eyes met her eyes, so close their faces would be touching if there weren't glass between them.

Corina screamed, and the shape disappeared. Her

mouth dry, she screamed again and again. She needed her neighbors, the police, someone to help her. She couldn't deal with this alone.

Her cell phone rang just as she heard someone at the front door.

"Corina? What's wrong? Are you okay?" Wes's voice, and behind it, the sounds of traffic.

"I just saw someone outside my window,"

"I'll be right there."

Before she could answer, the connection was broken.

Corina carried the phone with her to the door. The condo manager stood outside. She'd thrown a hooded terry-cloth jacket over her thin cotton night-gown.

"There was a man," Corina said. "He was looking through the kitchen window."

Papa and the couple to the right joined the group outside the condo.

"I heard someone running," the manager said. And to the group, "Everyone's going to have to be on the lookout for everyone else. This could be a series of robberies."

But Corina knew better.

Her neighbors milled around by the pool, unsure what to do next. Just then, Wes burst through the gate.

"Where were you?" she asked. "How'd you get here so quickly?"

"Across the street. It's okay. I just talked to the cop outside. He was watching the back area and saw movement in your condo. He knew it was supposed to be vacated, so he looked in the window."

"It was a policeman she saw?" the manager

asked, pulling her jacket closer at the sight of the immaculately attired mayor.

"That's right."

Corina moved close to him. "I feel like such a fool."

"Don't. You can't take chances."

The officer came through the gate and crossed the lawn to where they stood. "Sorry," he told her. "I thought the unit was unoccupied."

"It is. I just stopped by for a minute. I saw a man and just freaked."

"That's natural."

No, it wasn't natural. It was sick, hysterical behavior. That's what the man with the scarred neck had done to her. She hated it. She hated him.

"Could we talk privately?" she asked the officer. "Just the three of us?"

"Okay, folks," he said to her neighbors. "Why don't you all go back inside now. Everything's fine."

He walked with Wes and her over to the condo next to hers. "The man who broke into my place called me again just a few minutes ago," she said.

"No." Wes took her arm. "You need to get out of here."

"It won't do any good. He'll find me wherever I am."

The officer took out a notebook. "What exactly did he say?"

How did she repeat the vile conversation, the exaggerated intimacy? "He said he was acting on his own," she said. "And he complimented me on how fast I got you officers here last night."

"You didn't tell him your neighbor called us?"

"Of course not."

"What else did he say?"

"That was it. Just that he thought Skin had given me a tape."

"A tape?" Wes asked. "You never said that before."

"I never knew it before. The man obviously wasn't aware of that, because he's convinced I have the damned tape."

"Did he threaten you?" the officer asked.

"Not directly." She swallowed through the tightness in her throat. "He did say that everyone wants me alive, except one person. That's all I can remember. Now, I need a drink of water."

The officer nodded. "Thanks for your help. You sticking around, Mayor Shaw?"

Wes glanced at her. "For a while."

"I'll be out here if you need anything. Sorry I startled you, miss."

Startled. A euphemism if she'd ever heard one.

The officer left, and they walked to the next-door condo in silence. Once they were inside, Wes turned to her, his lips tight. "You're coming home with me tonight."

"I'm not ready to do that yet. Please understand."

"You don't know how happy it makes me to hear that word."

"What word?"

"*Yet.* It's the first time you've said *yet.* That means that you're starting to think in terms of a future for us."

She looked up into his eyes. "And you can read all of that into one word?"

"Yes. All of that." He put out his arms.

She stood, a sleepwalker, moving across the room into them. They closed around her, pulled her to him. He leaned down, pressed his lips against hers, hard, almost taking the kiss from her.

She drew away. "Lupita's coming back later," she said.

"I understand. You haven't told her about us."

"She just found out about my condo. I think that's enough shock for one night."

"How'd she handle it?"

"Amazingly well, considering she's never had a serious thought in her life."

"I'm not so sure about that."

"You always liked her."

"I like all your family." He reached down and petted Rojito. "Even this one. How are you, red tabby?"

Rojito arched his back and moved against Wes's khaki pants.

"You'll have hair all over you," Corina said.

"For him, it's worth it. He's grown into a fine, big cat, hasn't he?"

"A fat cat. He still doesn't speak English."

"He understands me, don't you, boy?"

While Wes continued his one-sided conversation with Rojito, Corina went into the kitchen and poured two glasses of Barbera. Somehow he'd managed to trespass into her life. She'd sworn she'd never see him again. Now, here he was, sitting in her new makeshift living room, petting her cat, as if he'd never left. She wished she had a piece of string she could follow to find her way back to where she could trust him again, believe him again when he said he'd never stop loving her.

He stood up from the sofa and reached out to her, as if to say he understood what she was thinking, and that he would make it okay. She went to him, wrapped her arms around his neck and pressed herself into the safe scent of him. His breathing quickened.

"What do you say we drink this wine in bed?"

Her thought exactly. She turned toward the master bedroom, one arm still around his neck. "We'll have to hurry."

"That's what you think."

They did finish the wine in bed, pillows propped against the headboard, after they'd made love. Somehow she'd worked it out in her head. If Lupita came back and found them together, she'd be surprised but not shocked. She'd probably be delighted. And it was a two-bedroom condo. It's not as if they'd be hanging from the metaphorical chandelier. Love did that to her, put her in a drowsy state where she could rationalize anything.

Wes slipped a naked arm across her shoulder.

"You have an amazing body," she said, "even in the dark."

"I was about to say the same of you." He gave her a wine-flavored kiss. "Are you feeling better?"

She nodded. "I can't believe I let my imagination do that to me."

"Don't be so hard on yourself. You have reason to jump at your own shadow, or a cop's, for that matter."

"But I hate it. I never realized how much fear can weaken a person."

"I wonder if that could be the purpose of all this."

She put her glass on the bedside table, remembering her conversation with Sam the printer.

"The man made it very clear that he wants a tape he's convinced I have. I don't think anyone's merely trying to scare me off."

"Still, you've been asking a lot of questions about Vineyard Estates. Maybe you should lay off."

"I can't. It's my job."

"So, let Henderson cover it. That's what he wants. You do the paperwork."

"It's not that simple. I'm a reporter, not Henderson's scribe."

He paused, and for a moment, she thought he might argue with her. "I just thought of something," he said. "Henderson's on this story, too, yet no one's bothering him."

"No. I'm the one who talked to Skin."

"Maybe Henderson hasn't been bothered because he's involved himself."

"He's an arrogant jerk, but I don't think he's a criminal."

"You never know." He lifted the glass to his lips. "This is really good. A Napa Valley wine?"

"It's a Barbera from the university vineyard, and it wasn't that expensive. It's a gold-medal winner, though."

"You always had a gift for that." In his voice, she heard a wistful yearning that echoed her own.

"For buying cheap wine?"

"For recognizing quality in any form."

Her cheeks burned. Finally, just the two of them, naked, facing each other in a stillness where trust was like breathing and lying was an impossibility. "Most of the time," she said. "But when I do make a mistake, it's a big one."

"I wasn't a mistake. We weren't." He tightened his grip around her. "Come here."

"Wes."

She pulled away, but he drew her to him, kissing her softly with only the surface of his lips. "I love you, Corina. That's what I've been trying to say tonight, what I tried to say to you at lunch, on the phone, at the governor's speech. I never stopped."

There it was. She wanted to fall into his arms and never let go, bury her lips against his and never come up for air. "Then why?"

"I got scared." His face was a soft blur through her tears. "I've regretted it every day since then. Please give me another chance."

She forced herself to pull back. "I want to. But there's just so much going on right now." *And you left me. You left me when I needed you.*

"I'm not going anywhere. You won't be able to get rid of me."

The way you got rid of me.

"I don't want to," she said. "Now, we'd better get dressed and get you out of here before my sister gets back."

He rose with a sigh and went to the foot of the bed where his shirt had landed. She leaned back against the pillows and watched him as she sipped the last of her wine. What was wrong? Why did she feel as if her heart were being ripped out? Was it because he was getting ready to leave?

No, she couldn't get over the fact that he'd left in the first place. And now, in a few days, he'd moved

back into her life with everything except a tooth-
brush. This cozy reunion was just a little too easy.
He'd shown up when she needed help, and she'd
lulled herself into dropping her guard.

"Wes," she asked, toying with her empty glass.
"Why were you across the street when you called
me tonight?"

He looked up over his partially buttoned shirt.
"It's a good thing I was, don't you agree?"

"But why?"

"Just a little worried. I told you I didn't think you
should go back to the office. I wanted to be sure you
got home in one piece."

"So you waited out there for me?"

He shifted slightly but didn't look away. "I drove
by a couple of times. Is that okay?"

"I don't know. I'll have to think about it."

Her questions had killed the spell they'd woven.
The evening slowly drained away, leaving the two
of them staring at each other across an expanse that
seemed to widen by the moment.

He lifted his jacket, a muted combination of
denim and spice tones. Still holding it, he sat by her
on the side of the bed. "I love you," he said. "I'm
worried about you. If I lost you again, I don't think
I could take it." He leaned down, kissed her still
lips. "So let me obsess a little, okay?"

"Okay," she said, and gave him a real kiss.

She lay there after he left, smelling the scent of
them. He'd barely closed the front door, and the
room already seemed empty without him. Thus was
the power of Wes Shaw. Being with him, even momentarily, only made being without him that much
worse.

Her cell phone rang. She grabbed it, heart pounding, and pulled the covers over her as if the caller could see her.

''This is just in case you're getting any second thoughts.'' She could hear the traffic. Wes. He must be only blocks away.

''You know me well,'' she said.

''Second thoughts and hardheaded pride, your only flaws. But I have the solution to both.''

''What's that, oh brilliant one?'' she asked, smiling into the darkness now.

''I love you. Just remember that when that pride kicks in and tries to talk you into having those second thoughts.''

''I love you, too, Wes.''

''Tell me again.''

''I love you.''

''And if you get nervous or you hear anything at all, call me.''

''I will.''

Police outside. Wes on the phone. The bed tangled and warm with the memory of their lovemaking. She might be all right, after all, for one night at least.

And tomorrow she'd take some steps to deal with what the murders and the man with the twisted neck was doing to her mind. Tomorrow, damn it, she was going to take advantage of the company's mental-health benefits.

Monday, May 28, 2:46 p.m.
Skin

Security, safety. That's what it's all about. That's why I'll be okay, no matter how crazy these fools go.

Nan surprised me, though, jumping out of her chair like that when I mentioned Tina, staring me down.

"How can you even think that?" she demands. "We don't know any more about what happened to Tina Kellogg than you do."

"Funny she disappeared right after she warned me about the group."

"A coincidence. We don't operate that way." She sits down again, stiff on the sofa, as if trying to force herself into calmness. "You have my word, and I don't give it lightly. We don't know where she is."

I want to believe her, want to think she's right, that Tina got scared and took off. That she's undercover, gathering evidence against them. Still, I've come here for a reason, and I'm going through with it.

I reach into my briefcase, pull out the tape. "This is for you," I say.

"What is it?"

"Security."

"Are you crazy?" She's on her feet again, glaring at me, her features distorted. "Where did you get this?"

"You forget how I made my money? I can record these things in my sleep."

"What have you done, Skin?"

"I didn't want to," I say, *"but you people are scaring the hell out of me. This isn't the only copy. The other's my insurance."*

"For what?" Her voice goes frigid on me, her features animated like a character in a cartoon.

I stand, as well. *"I want two things,"* I say. *"Tina Kellogg safe and me out of Vineyard Estates."*

"I told you I don't know where Tina is," she says. *"Whatever has happened to her has nothing to do with us. And as far as your leaving the partnership, I don't think that will be a problem."*

"Last time I asked, it was."

"It's been discussed since then."

"I won't say a word," I tell her. *"Maybe you people are on the right track, and this is the only way. I just don't want to be part of it."*

"Where's the other tape?"

Should I tell her? Really shake them up, or just leave it like this? No, I have to let her know how serious I am, not just some wimp chickening out at the last minute.

"Unless I get what I want," I say, *"it's going to the Valley Voice."*

Twenty-Eight

Friday, June 15, 9:30 a.m.

Corina told Henderson she had a dentist appointment. That's probably what they all said, all of the employees who took advantage of those medical benefits J.T. touted. She'd dialed the number he'd e-mailed her, made the appointment, and now here she was, walking into the office of Dr. Sylvia Lopez.

A large woman with auburn-streaked black hair sat on the sectional facing a wall-to-wall aquarium. She rose when Corina entered and introduced herself. Corina had requested a woman and a Latina, figuring that might at least save her some time. Now she questioned her decision. This could be Lupita with thirty pounds and forty years on her. There was probably a tattoo lurking under that reptile-print shirt and pants.

She settled in the chair to the right of the sectional. Dr. Sylvia Lopez seemed to take note of that.

"I like your fish," Corina said.

"Good *feng shui*."

"I've heard that. If it's true, with a tank that size you should be able to retire next year."

The big woman's laugh was startling in the tranquility of the room. "So retirement is the ultimate goal, is it?"

A trick question, but what more could she expect from a Latina who practiced *feng shui?* "I remember reading somewhere that an aquarium works like a crystal. It blocks the bad energy so prosperity can come in."

"Close enough. Not to mention that watching the fish relaxes me." She leaned forward on the couch. "Would you like to tell me why you're here?"

Corina turned from her gaze, toward the bright flashes of color in the glass tank. "Because I'm afraid, and I hate it."

"What frightens you?"

"Being killed, for starters." She looked at her. No change of expression. Good. She'd go for more. "I'm a reporter covering a high-profile murder case."

"I know. I read the *Voice*."

"I was assured that our visit will be confidential."

"There'll be no record that we spoke, not even on the billing. We see many people from the *Voice* here. You people down there have high-stress jobs."

"This is more than stress."

"I understand. Now, tell me about the fear."

"It makes me feel weak, powerless." Damn, why had she done this? She could barely get the words out, and her voice was a mere quaver.

"Tell me about it."

"A man grabbed me in the parking lot of my own building, my own newspaper. He ruined my condominium, destroyed everything I own. And I'm afraid he's going to kill me. I'm twenty-eight years old, and I don't want to die."

"Do you have a close friend, someone you can talk to?"

"All of my college friends are married. They're into their families. The only one who's single is Dolores. She runs the Hispanic Drug and Alcohol Council, and she doesn't even have time for her own life."

A grim smile. "Yes, our abuses are so rampant that we have our very own council."

"She's a good administrator and a wonderful role model." She didn't add that when they got together for coffee the last time, Dolores confessed that her love life made Corina's look downright sinful.

"And your parents?"

"They own a restaurant. My grandmother started it as a bakery selling *bolillos*."

It began like that, with a little roll as much of a staple as tortillas in her culture. When women had begun working outside the home, they no longer had time to bake, yet their families still expected fresh *bolillos* every day.

"And they graduated from that to a restaurant?"

"Thanks to my mother, who does all the work. My dad greets the customers and takes all the credit."

She nodded. "Sounds like my folks. Not the restaurant—the family dynamics."

"More than anything in the world, I don't want to be like my mother. I don't want some man taking credit for my work." Immediately Corina felt guilt, for both the emotion and the voicing of it. "I love my parents," she said. "They're wonderful people."

"Have you told them about your fears?"

"Of course not. They don't know anything about what's going on."

"Do you have a partner you can talk to?"

She'd known they'd get around to this. She looked at the fish again. "I've recently begun seeing a former lover."

"How did that happen?"

"We were thrown together again because of the story I'm working on. I still love him."

"What caused your problems before?"

Corina had made up her mind in advance that she'd discuss the murders, admit her own fears, but she'd keep Wes out of it. She didn't want to rehash the story of his leaving to this garish stranger with the bubbling tank of fish. "I'm not sure. It just didn't work out."

"Do you think it will work out this time?"

"I can't trust my own judgment right now, not with everything that's going on."

It went like that the rest of their time together. They talked about her friends, her family, the fear that had driven her to seek guidance from a stranger.

"So, tell me," Dr. Sylvia Lopez said. "You want help, or you want a bandage?"

Corina didn't know how to answer. "I'd like to learn how to control my fear so I don't burst into hysterics every time someone walks past my window."

She'd come here in search of answers, and now she was as anxious and uncertain, if not more so, than when she'd arrived.

Dr. Sylvia Lopez stood up with a rustle of fabric. "You get three visits," she said. "After that, there's a ten dollar co-pay."

It didn't matter. Corina didn't plan on coming back. She'd have to deal with this on her own.

Twenty-Nine

Sunday, June 17, 4:40 p.m.

The truck rattled down the dirt road, shooting vibrations of pain through Roxene's body. She dug the heel of her tennis shoe into the side of the truck's bed to keep from being slammed into the splintered surface. Beside her, his hands bound behind him, Norm moaned. Alive, at least. For now. How long had they been moved from place to place? Two weeks? Longer?

"You all right?" Only a raspy whisper after all the screaming she'd done. Their captors just laughed, asking her who she thought was going to hear her.

"Can't get a breath." Norm struggled under the plastic tarp, managing to work it down so that some light leaked in. Roxene breathed in dust and sea air, nearly gagging. This was the fifth or sixth time they'd been moved. "How long was I out?" he asked above the loud rattle of the truck. "Did I kill him?"

"Missed. The other guy grabbed you as soon as the gun went off."

"Shit."

Typical Norm Flannigan, the big daddy who'd put himself in charge of taking care of the world. "There's just two of them. We'll go for it again when they stop the truck."

"We might have a chance. They should have known better than to turn their backs on us. If we can get the small one—" The truck hit what felt like the boulder from hell. They both cried out. Roxene's head banged against the wooden truck bed, and for a blurry moment, she thought she might pass out.

"Are you okay?"

She could make out his features, his eyes large and vulnerable without his glasses, the mouth she'd always thought of as smug, a dark, black line of blood. "That one just about knocked me out. Those guys don't seem to care if we arrive in one piece." She forced the thought from her mind.

"We can take them. I won't miss next time."

She didn't mention that the next time he wouldn't have a gun, either. Another bump. She rolled again, into Norm, then back to the side of the truck. Concentrate. She had to concentrate on survival. Don't waste precious energy talking, crying or thinking how this might end. Just focus on her strength. Draw from it. Next to her, Norm grew silent, a pro, as was she. This was part of the job, the chance they took.

After what felt like thirty minutes, maybe more, they grated to a stop. The tarp was pulled off them, and the two men dragged them out. Roxene blinked at the bright light and leaned against the old truck for balance. Sand stretched in both directions. A few hundred yards from them, a dirt landing strip lay desolate as the landscape. Beyond it, a Quonset-shaped shed, missing a few tin sheets in the walls

and roof, stood with an open door. The tattered remains of a wind sock hung from the top of it, wilted
in the heat of late afternoon like everything else in
this forsaken desert. Roxene felt the tall man's knee
in her back and knew that's where they were going.

A loud droning buzzed over them, growing louder
by the moment. Roxene looked up at the plane,
squinting against the sunlight blazing off its shiny
wings. It circled lower, lower, as if the pilot were
having second thoughts about the odds on making a
successful landing here. Norm stopped, too, and
looked up at the plane.

The runty one approached Roxene, thumbing the
edge of a service-issued knife. He looked at the knife
and then her, showing bright teeth under a dingy
moustache. In Spanish, he directed her to turn
around. She stared steady hatred into his face.

"Puta."

His free hand shot out. He grabbed her arm and
whirled her around, shoving her against the truck.
Norm surged forward, but the other man held him.

"No." She fought, tried to run. He struggled with
her, propelling her against the truck, sawing at the
tape around her wrists. Tears filled her eyes. He
wasn't going to stab her; he was removing her
bonds. Exhaling, she rubbed her numb wrists and
watched as the man freed Norm, as well.

The twin-engine plane looked too large for the
airstrip. Sand burned Roxene's eyes as wind
whipped her hair across her face. The plane touched
down, throwing up clouds of dust in a screech of
brakes against the grinding sand. The smell of burning tires filled the air. Norm moved closer to her.
The men didn't seem to notice or care. His face

looked raw from his fight with the taller of the two, and he was favoring his right leg.

He put his arm around her, leaned down to her ear. "They left the keys in the truck," he said.

Before she could respond, the tall man who had attacked Norm yanked him away from her, threatening him in curse-filled Spanish and shoving his service revolver under Norm's chin.

The side door of the plane opened and folded downward. Two men climbed down on the built-in stairs. The taller wore tennis shoes and jeans, bouncing slightly as he walked. His shoulder-length colorless hair blew behind him, but it was his neck that drew her attention. Heavily scarred, it tilted his whole head to the left, a grotesque doll.

The other man wore all black, from T-shirt to pants. "Good afternoon," he said.

His gaze lingered on her. She stared right back, memorizing his features, his face. "You know they're looking for us."

"You're DEA," he replied in a pleasant voice, "nothing more than soldiers, puppets in the hands of the politicians. Your deaths would be little more than a tick mark on the wall of the new world, expendable casualties of war."

She knew he was right, but she wasn't about to concede that. "They'll be looking just the same."

"What do you want with us?" Norm demanded.

"For now, just to see that you're comfortable, and to be sure you don't try to leave until we're ready for you to."

"I can take care of that." The man with the scarred neck moistened his lips with his tongue, as if contemplating how he might accomplish that.

Roxene broke eye contact, looking off at the distant ocean, trying to protect her thoughts, not just from them, but from the vulnerable part of herself.

"I don't think that's necessary at this point." The man in black turned to one of their captors and began speaking in Spanish, asking how long they'd had them, if they had given them any trouble. All the time, the creature with the twisted neck watched Roxene.

She glanced over at Norm, with the quick, ESP look that rarely failed them.

He met her gaze with a silent question. Should they try to escape? Get out of here now? The truck wasn't far from them.

She moved her chin, a slight nod, trying to get the message across with her eyes. *Let's run for it.*

A quick nod of understanding. He pointed with his index finger. *One. Two. Three. Go.*

Norm shoved the man beside him to the ground, and sprinted toward the truck. She dashed ahead, jumped behind the wheel, got it started, as he landed beside her. She heard the shouts, a blanket of noise behind them. The truck ground into gear. She held tightly to the slippery steering wheel and slammed her foot into the accelerator. The wheels skidded in the dirt. She steered back onto the path.

A noise exploded behind her. The truck skidded, and for a moment, she thought she'd been shot. Then she lost control of the truck, feeling the weightless vehicle fly across the sand and finally shudder to a stop.

The leader in black shouted orders to the others. Fingers dug into her arms, her shoulders. Her screams ricocheted from the plane to the tin shed to her brain. She tried to fight, but the bastard was too big. Reduced to deadweight, a bag of pain, she felt him drag her across the sand, then throw her down next to Norm.

"Idiots," the one in charge yelled to the two kidnappers. They cowered, making excuses in Spanish. The blond-haired man loped up to where they lay, his head cocked even more. He lifted his gaze to the other man, as if asking a question. Then he returned his gaze to her with a look that made Roxene shudder.

"Okay, Whiplash," he said. "You take care of them."

Thirty

Ivy Dieser strode down the hall, careful to keep her expression fixed. She just hoped her professional mask didn't betray what was really on her mind.

She passed J.T.'s office. He looked up and glared at her. She should have known the bastard would threaten to file a grievance when she gave him the unsatisfactory performance review. Now, the troublemakers would have a new reason to harass management. She flashed him a professional smile as she walked by.

Don't walk too fast. Just take your time. She forced herself to move slowly, hoping she wasn't wrong about what had passed between Brandon and her last Wednesday. She'd thought of little else since, and she knew she'd never forgive herself if she didn't try.

She paused outside his office and smoothed her skirt. He wasn't the first powerful man she'd ever lusted after, and that's what she had to keep reminding herself. Brandon Chenault was still a man. He put on his pants—and took them off—the same way every other man did. Remember that, and she might have a chance.

Even confined in a conservative charcoal suit the same color as his eyes, he exuded sensuality. Behind him, a bank of windows reflected the sky and gave the room a feeling of being set apart from the rest of the building.

Sitting in his office, across from his desk, Ivy filled him in on what Corina had told her about what happened Friday, including the fact that the man who broke into her condominium believed Skin Burke had given Corina a tape of some kind. He listened carefully, as if silently counting off each point she made. That was a key to his attractiveness, his ability to focus on one person and listen.

"Intriguing," he said. "When this is over, I think we should have Corina write a first-person account of her experiences. Run it as a series."

"She could do it," Ivy said. "Based on what I've seen of her, I think she could be an excellent investigative reporter. She just hasn't been given a chance."

"She's getting one now." Brandon's eyes darkened. "Regardless of how this story turns out, she's proven that she can handle herself under pressure. And she doesn't have the personal problems Henderson does."

"And she's not antimanagement. I think you were right about her."

"I'm not wrong about people. I wasn't wrong about you, was I?"

His voice resonated with self-confidence. She felt herself blush. "If I succeed at this job, it will be because of you."

"Only because I recognized what others overlooked." For a moment, his expression seemed to change, grow more intimate. Or was she just imagining what she longed to see?

"You won't be sorry," she said. "I've done everything you asked."

"You've done it well. Let Malone file his grievance. We have a procedure. Henderson will probably do the same thing sooner or later. We didn't expect him to hand his job to Corina."

"No, we didn't. I guess I shouldn't let it bother me."

"Of course you're bothered. You're a good manager. But we'll win. I was brought in to save this paper. September Eleventh just about killed the economy, and advertising revenue with it. My cuts haven't hurt the *Voice*. They've actually helped it."

"Corporate thinks you're God," she said.

"And you." He gave her that smile. "What do you think?"

"You know what I think."

She looked down at her lap, as if embarrassed by her own boldness. A man. Under that expensive suit, he was really just a man.

"Ivy." His voice transformed her name.

She let her gaze travel to his eyes, breathing deeply so that he could see the outline of her breasts against her suit, the skirt inching up over her crossed legs. The understanding in their eyes linked them, man and woman. Ivy felt the pull, rejoiced in it, willing all other thoughts from her mind. Brandon got up and walked to where she sat. His suit could have been ironed on; it was that smooth.

Even his scent emitted power, conjuring rich

leather, snow-covered mountaintops, tapestries in European castles. Light-headed, her heart beating faster than she could think, Ivy stood, put her fingers against his cheek.

Sweat shone through the smooth skin on his forehead. He took her hand, lifted her fingers to his lips, bit down. Exquisite pain.

"Oh," she said. "This is going to be so good."

"Ivy, please." His voice, his eyes helpless now. This was what she'd gambled on.

"Please, what?"

"Lock the door."

She did as he asked, then walked back to where he stood, trembling inside, still unable to believe it was happening. He put out both hands. She took them.

"I think perhaps we should leave."

"Where can we go? Someone might see us."

"There's the corporate suite at the Piccadilly. I'll just let them know we're expecting some people in from corporate. I'll leave the door unlocked."

She stepped away, smiling at him. This was the right time to let him see what was in store for him. "Brandon," she said. "I feel there's something you should know."

Surprise replaced the desire in his eyes. He was wondering now if he'd made a mistake with her, if this was a setup of some kind. It was, of course, but not the type he feared. "What is it?"

She walked back to where he stood, and wrapped her arms around his neck. "This suit I have on?"

He sighed relief into her ear. "What about your suit?"

She snuggled against his shoulder. "It's all I'm wearing."

He slid his hands under her skirt, his hands cool against her bare flesh. He moaned softly, then pulled away, lifting her face to his. She loved the questions in his eyes, the confused mixture of terror and delight.

"You knew?" he asked.

She lifted her lips, aching now, ready to claim what she'd come for. "I hoped."

Thirty-One

Tuesday, June 19, 9:20 a.m.

As she showered that morning, Corina had decided this would be the day she talked to Henderson. They couldn't continue to work together as adversaries, spying on each other.

In the steamy logic of the shower, her plan made perfect sense. By the time she got to work, she felt her nerve begin to desert her. Part of the problem was in her head: almost every conversation she initiated with Henderson turned into a confrontation. The thought of another one, first thing in the morning, kicked in a conditioned reflex of avoidance. The rest of the problem had to do with Henderson himself.

Brusque and strictly business, he stopped by her cubicle and announced as his brand of greeting, "Publisher's meeting today at four."

Chenault's monthly meetings were not mandatory, but it was duly noted, she knew, who attended and who didn't. Someone from the HR police was always there with their sign-in sheets.

"You going?" she asked, knowing the answer.

"I work for a living."

"You want me to stick around?"

"Go schmooze with the Brandonites. I can handle everything here."

She rose from her desk, trying to ignore his contentious tone.

"I'll stay if you want me to."

"I don't. Besides, Chenault is the reason for your season. You'd better go if you want to stay in good graces."

"I'll need to take a long lunch hour."

"That's fine." His intense look burned through her.

"I have to meet with the police," she said, "about what happened at my condo. I'll make up the time."

"Take as long as you like." He ran his palm over the stubble on his cheek, as if he wanted to say more. This might be the time to try, to make a stab at peace. "What?" he asked, his eyes narrowing.

"Nothing. I'll see you later."

The police department must be designed to make people feel there was no escape, Corina thought, a windowless purgatory of old furniture and stale air. Like the *Voice*, the department must be on energy alert. The still, hot air felt a week old. Even breathing it was a chore.

Mel Wise, the older officer who had come to her house the night she had found Skin, showed her digital photographs she knew would etch themselves into her brain, waiting for the appropriate nightmare to reappear. Old men, young men, men without lips, missing an eye, and one with a nasty chunk gouged from his cheek. "Take your time," Wise had told her, as if she'd want to spend a moment more than necessary perusing these faces on the screen. She clicked the mouse button for a new page, and there he was, looking back at her.

"This is the man." She could barely bring herself to touch the photograph on the screen.

"Are you sure?"

He was younger, his hair shorter, but there was no mistaking those lifeless eyes, that neck. "Yes. His hair's longer now."

"Can you tell me anything else about him?"

She thought for a moment, studying his face. "His voice. It's like a rasp."

Wise nodded. "Very good."

"I'm right, aren't I?"

"We'll need to check it out."

"I'm a reporter, Mel. Tell me what you know about him."

"I can tell you he violated his parole."

"What was he in for?"

His eyes, hardened by years of tragedy Corina could only imagine, softened. "I'm not supposed to go off the record with you guys."

"I'm not a guy, Mel. I've got to know about this man."

"His name's Winston Branch, but he goes by Whiplash."

Corina shuddered, looking down at the scarred neck, still feeling the man's arms around her. "What else?"

"Let's just say you're right about the voice." Wise shook his head. "He was in Vietnam. Screwed him up real bad, inside and out. The man's a pyro, not all there."

A pyromaniac. He'd probably enjoyed burning

Skin's home. "He's been doing more than setting fires," she said. "If I'm right, he killed Tina Kellogg and Skin Burke."

"You have any idea why?"

"I think he was hired to do it. Skin told me Eugene Belmont had Tina murdered. I think this man works for Belmont."

Mel processed the information, his expression hiding his emotions. "Unfortunately we have to deal with facts. You say you can identify him as the individual who broke into your home and grabbed you in the parking lot?"

"Absolutely."

Mel nodded. "Then all we have to do is find him."

Few publishers bothered spending time with staff members. Brandon Chenault held his meetings in two shifts, morning and afternoon, and invited everyone who wanted to attend. Except for the diehard union fanatics, everybody did attend and not just for the free coffee and croissants.

Corina watched him interact with everyone from pressmen to printers, from advertising sales people to the two women who operated the company credit union. More handsome from a distance, his whole was more arresting than any single part. Watching him, she thought of Wes, who got what he wanted in part because he could make the smallest cog in the wheel of his world feel like the most important.

Chenault was a crowd-pleaser, a superb one, and a politician. No wonder corporate loved him. He talked about teamwork while he bought out older, high-paid employees with golden handshakes and minimum-wage replacements. He blatantly promoted employees he liked. And, as Henderson had pointed out, Corina thought with a twinge of guilt, he was the reason for her season.

He caught up with her at the refreshment table. "Croissant?" He hit the *kwah* harder than necessary, as if applauding himself for the French pronunciation.

"No thanks. Tea's fine," she said. No way did she want to talk to Brandon Chenault with a full mouth and greasy fingers.

He took one for himself from the glass platter. "I'm really pleased with what I see coming out of your department."

Your department. "Thanks," she said. "I'm still learning my way around."

"Indeed."

He was a tall man. She found herself almost squinting to make eye contact.

"It's very challenging," she said, keeping her tone noncommittal.

He broke off the crusty tip of the roll and held it in his fingers. "Remember, I have an open-door policy with staff."

"I know."

His eyes flickered with shadow, but they didn't leave her face. "If for any reason you want to talk, off the record, of course, just stop by."

The intensity of his gaze unnerved her. It was as if he were saying one thing and telling her another. She knew this was not a casual conversation.

"Off the record?" she repeated.

"Without fear of recrimination. If there's a problem with your supervisor, say, and you feel it needs my attention, you needn't worry that it will go further."

An expectant silence filled the space between them. Corina sipped her lemon tea. "I'll remember that," she said finally. "Although I hope I'll never have to bother you."

"No bother at all. We want to keep good people like you, Corina."

"And I appreciate everything you've done for me."

Ivy Dieser approached from nowhere. The long-sleeved, V-necked blouse beneath her navy suit looked like the one-piece numbers Victoria's Secret guaranteed not to pull, ride or slip. For sure, it snapped at the crotch.

"Hi," she said to Corina as she lifted the plate. "Have you tried the croissants?" She pronounced the word phonetically.

Corina glanced up at Chenault, wondering if she imagined the slight grimace. "They look great," she said, "but I really need to get back to my office. We're on deadline."

She left the two of them standing at the table, Chenault still holding the broken piece of bread, looking as elegant and unfathomable as a statue.

She hurried down the hall toward Henderson's office, knowing she could no longer put off this conversation. She turned the corner, then marched inside. Henderson was gone. Probably slipped out early again, she thought, and wondered if he had another secret meeting. On his desk lay a folder, marked in black with a single word. *Burke.*

Corina reached out, then paused. No, she couldn't. But Henderson would, for sure. He would have even gone through her notebooks if the man with the scars hadn't beaten him to it. Besides, they were supposed to be working together on this story, together, damn it. Henderson probably wouldn't even care if she glanced inside his folder. She reached out again, and this time, she flipped it open.

Like the rest of Henderson's life, it was a mess. Sticky yellow notepapers clung to pencil-scrawled binder paper, pages and pages of it. Henderson needed her assistance more than he knew, she thought. Once they were really a team, she'd show him how to organize his notes. She moved closer, trying to decipher the words on the first page. Pencil was impossible to read, absolutely impossible, especially with his horrible handwriting.

Corina felt rather than heard the door close behind her.

Henderson blocked her exit, standing with crossed arms between the desk and the door. "Looking for something?" he asked without smiling.

They stared at each other, glaring, eye-to-eye. His office was suffocating, small, especially with the drawn blinds. Corina stammered. Henderson's shadowed face didn't change expression.

"I asked if you were looking for something." He took a step toward her.

Her body tensed. "Don't."

"Don't what? Don't defend my own turf? Suppose you tell me what you're doing in here."

His snide tone erased what remained of her fright. "I'm the least of your worries."

"Is that so?"

"You'd better believe it. Chenault all but begged me to spill my guts about you just now."

"You're lying."

She continued as if she hadn't heard him. "He calls it an open-door policy, the same one that got all those managers fired. You can bet it's what he said to Ivy Dieser about Janie Penny."

"He's a bastard."

The fire had gone out of Henderson's voice. She walked past him, opened the door and stood between the office and the hall. "Don't worry. I'm not a snitch, but before you raise hell with me, just remember he's gunning for you." The announcement left her more drained than victorious. She rested her head against the cool wood of the doorway. "Damn it, Matthew. Don't you think it's time we worked together?"

"Pretty hard to work with someone you can't trust."

"Tell me about it. You haven't exactly been straight with me."

"True." He sat down heavily behind the desk and sighed. "Chenault really encouraged you to snitch?"

She nodded. "That's how it sounded to me."

"And you'd end up with my job, of course, the same way Dieser ended up with Janie's."

"I don't want your job," she said. "If I did, I wouldn't be here, would I?"

"Then what do you want?"

"For starters, a cup of coffee, away from here. I'll even buy."

Henderson stood, his voice still tenuous. "I think this calls for a beer."

Thirty-Two

Tuesday, June 19, 6:25 p.m.

He lived in one of those sterile apartment complexes people pass through between marriages or jobs. A sign in front said, "Sparkling pool, weight room," probably the only advertisement needed to attract a clientele looking for the right price and an innocuous concrete decor.

His apartment was located on the top floor. She followed him up the narrow stairs.

"This is the place," he said, waving at the tiny patio area across from his front door. "Let's sit outside. It's probably cooler than in there."

"That's fine."

"Have a seat, and I'll be right back with our beer."

So, he wasn't going to invite her inside. That didn't surprise her. Through the open blinds of his window, she caught a glimpse of woven Bauer chairs and a pedestal topped with a circle of smoke-colored glass. On the wall hung a framed child's drawing of a house, a woman, a man and a child. The child and the woman had bright yellow hair. The man's hair was scribbled red. There was something sad about the painting and its simplistic, hopeful world children tried to draw into reality.

She looked away quickly as he returned. He carried two bottles of ale by their necks.

"Hope you like Red Dog," he said, lifting one to her.

She followed him to the patio overlooking a swimming pool. A couple dawdled in the shallow end. The woman smoked a cigarette and drank from a martini glass on the deck. Corina caught the piquant scent of barbecuing meat.

"Does this mean I didn't convert you to Chinese beer?" she asked, sitting on the edge of a chaise beside the table.

"Afraid not." He pulled up a webbed chair beside her. "Too hot for you out here?"

"You forget I was raised in this Valley. I'd opt for fog and rain if I had a choice, though."

"Not I." He lowered his voice. "I'm glad you came. It's time we cut the crap."

"Well, since you put it so eloquently, let's do that."

She told him everything then, leaving nothing out, speaking so rapidly that, when she paused for breath, she felt light-headed and giddy. She'd shared her information in chronological order—from everything Betsy had said, to the relationship between Wes and Eugene Belmont. When she finished, she turned to him and said, "Now it's your turn."

He took a swallow of beer and wiped the sheen from his forehead. "Let's start with Eugene Belmont."

"He's behind this, isn't he?"

"I think so. I've been able to trace Vineyard Estates to a dummy company in San Quintin, Mexico. He's the principal.''

"San Quintin." She repeated the word, chills shooting through her. Hearing him pronounce it made her realize what she'd been overlooking. *San Keen TEEN*. Not San Quentin, the prison, not the prison at all.

"I found something at Skin's," she said. "Waite and Flannigan. July 4. San Quintin. Fifty thousand, American."

"Roxene Waite and Norman Flannigan," he said.

"The DEA agents."

"San Quintin," he said. "Jesus."

"We have to go after them."

"First we have to call DEA. I have a contact there. This is bigger than a development scheme. You know that?"

She sat her bottle on the patio table. "Those receipts I found at Skin's house. Can you make any sense out of them?"

His jaw tightened, and he took another swig of beer. "I haven't tried. I figured you wouldn't give me anything that was worth something."

Corina's eyes burned. "I never wanted your job, and I'm not an idiot, either, by the way."

"I know that. All of this—the changes at the paper, the murders—just kind of came at a bad time for me, I guess." He looked older in the harsh sunlight, his ruddy face coarse. "My personal life, I mean."

"I'm sorry."

"Hey, it happens. I'm not trying to cry on your shoulder. I just want you to know why I've been distracted, and why I'm not thrilled about working with a woman right now. It's my problem. I'm not usually such an asshole."

"I can relate," she said. "Can't say I'm exactly thrilled by male authority figures."

"So we understand each other." He stared at the swimming pool, and Corina could glimpse his scalp through the thin strands of hair. "I saw Nan Belmont at her local office that day I left the office early. Thought I might be able to get something out of her."

"And?"

"Nothing. She's smooth. I thought I could shake her loose by threatening to go to Eugene, but she very politely told me to leave them alone."

The beer started to work down her throat in a bitter path of dread. "What about Wes Shaw Senior?"

He squinted and stared straight ahead. "I thought he might be involved. Doesn't look as if he was."

She didn't mention that Menlo had tried to involve him. She owed Wes—and his father—that much.

He lifted his empty beer bottle as a question.

"Why not?" she said.

He returned dangling two fresh ones in one hand and what must be a backup in the other. Once seated, he took a long swallow then looked at her as if expecting a response.

She straightened out on the chaise. Her neck felt knotted and tight from tension, and the backs of her legs sweated against the hot aluminum frame. "Whatever it is they're after was enough to get Skin killed, and maybe me, too."

"No, they won't kill you," he said matter-offactly. "If they'd wanted to do that, they could have. They want you alive until they get their hands on this tape they think you have."

"Until?"

"We'll find them before then."

"That's easy for you to say."

"But I wouldn't say it if I didn't believe it. What we have to do now is go over everything we know."

She happened to glance down at the ashtray. It was a crudely shaped piece of pottery, painted black where it was painted at all. Where it wasn't, the glazed clay glinted through like a stark white skull. "Okay," she said. "Tina was murdered because she knew something about Vineyard Estates. And because she tried to get Skin out of it."

"Perhaps." He nodded, mulling the possibility. "And Skin?"

"Because he was going to go to the press. Me."

He leaned forward. "And why did Tina want him out? Why did she care what he did?"

"I don't know."

"Well, think. Just start supposing, the more outrageous, the better."

"She hated Eugene Belmont for some reason, wanted to hurt him. Or she and Skin were involved in some kind of side business. Or Tina was the third member of the Vineyard Estates trio. She found out something Skin didn't know about, and it scared her."

"Again, why would she care about Skin?"

"They were business partners. Or political allies."

"Or?" He raised a questioning eyebrow.

"Scotch and sofa?"

"She was a player."

"But Skin wasn't. He was committed to work. Look how he moved up from security systems to land development, from Eugene Belmont's flunky to his partner."

"That never made sense to me, either," Henderson said. "Belmont's as rotten as they come."

"You know he served time," she said.

"Did you also know the man he killed was black?"

"No. Why didn't you tell me?"

"Didn't occur to me."

"Why the hell not?"

"Don't get salty. It just didn't."

"Salty, my ass. You kept it from me, didn't you, Matthew?"

"Why would I do that?"

Good question. Her mind grabbed the easiest answer. "Because you're on to something, and you didn't want me to know."

"Close enough." His smile was the only apology she was going to get. "Here's what I think," Henderson said. "Eugene took the fall for someone else when he served that term for homicide. The man he killed was involved with civil rights."

"And Eugene gets out of prison and has enough money to start Belmont Construction."

Henderson stood up, stretching his legs as if they were cramped. "More important, his wife, Nan's mother, had tuberculosis. It was a killer back then. The week after the murder, she was sent to Springville, received the best care."

"Eugene's reward for taking the blame for a crime he didn't commit."

"My question now," he began, "is how long he stayed connected with that group, KKK, or whatever that bought him off. Is he still connected? Was Skin?"

"Skin wouldn't," she blurted, then thought about it. No. Skin would. "And California's supposed to be so damned liberal."

"Hate groups are everywhere. I'm just wondering if Belmont Construction and Vineyard Estates are connected to a larger group."

That's what he'd been working on secretly, what he'd hidden from her. It didn't matter right now, though. Nothing mattered but trying to figure out what they were up against. Corina tried to remember what had bothered her earlier, something she'd found that day in Skin's file. "Among Skin's files there were some receipts, big ones, from an electric company. The offices were somewhere in the South."

"Can you remember where?"

She tried to picture the pink piece of paper. "Geri LaRue has the folder. She's trying to run down the company for me."

"Then let's call Geri LaRue."

"She's probably left the office by now."

"You never know with her. Besides, I have the employee database on my home computer."

He started toward the apartment, then looked down at her. "I know this is a touchy subject, but are you absolutely sure Wes Shaw isn't involved in Vineyard Estates?"

She hesitated only a moment. Was she sure? Did she know Wes as well as she thought she did? "I'm certain," she said.

"His dad and Eugene Belmont were asshole buddies. You talk about scotch and sofa. Hell, those two old farts invented it."

"Wes Senior was a sweetheart."

"By the time you met him, yes. And Wes Junior's done a good job of cleaning up his old man's reputation after the fact."

"How bad do you think he was?" Even mouthing the words made her feel like a traitor.

He shrugged. "He was a developer. That about explains it. And like his son, he was a charmer." The sinking feeling in her stomach must have registered on her face. "Sorry," he said. "It just slipped out." He dropped his cigarette in his empty beer bottle and looked uncomfortable enough to be telling the truth.

"Don't be so quick to judge Wes Shaw," she said.

He gave her a sheepish look of apology. "I'm the last person who should judge anyone, believe me. I know you and Shaw are friends."

"More than friends."

"Right." Although he spoke in a soft voice, the words tore into her. "Sorry I brought it up."

"Me, too, but you're correct when you say I'm probably not all that objective where he's concerned."

He started to respond, then cleared his throat. "Let's call Geri LaRue."

Thirty-Three

Geri wasn't used to company. She thought about changing out of her sweats, but what would she change into? It wasn't as if these folks didn't see her every day. More important than what she was wearing was what she should say to them, how much she should tell them.

Well, Geri girl, it all depends on whose side you're on. That was a tough one. She'd been on Henderson's when she thought Corina was after his job. Then she'd been on Corina's when she'd caught Henderson going through her files. And now? She couldn't think. Too much racket in her head.

She turned down the CD player so that it wouldn't blow a normal person out of room, and tossed Nathan an Altoids. Swoosh, and the tiny white breath mint disappeared like an insect on the tongue of a praying mantis. Damned dog was a vacuum, not to mention an Altoids addict. Her mind played with the word for a minute. Plural form. *Two Altoids. One Altoid?* Who the hell knew?

The light above the door flashed, indicating the buzzer had sounded from below, and she hurried down the stairs to let them in. Henderson smelled like a microbrewery, but he and Corina were at least working together. Management might play hell starting a war between these two, after all.

"Root beer?" she asked when they were back in her apartment, lifting her bottle of Henry Weinhard.

Corina accepted; Henderson declined. His florid face reflected an overdose of sun and whatever made him smell like that.

"You ought to try it," she said. "It's been hotter than blazes today."

"Where do you get Henry Weinhard around here?" Corina asked.

"You can find it at COSTCO sometimes. I order it by the case from Washington." After she said it, she realized how strange it must sound to people who weren't as particular about their root beer as she was. "Glad I have the file here," she said, trying to redeem herself.

"Sorry we called so late," Corina said.

"Late doesn't matter. I work at home a lot. My 'puter here's better than the one I have at the office."

"And you don't have to put up with reporters all day," Corina said.

"That, too."

"This is a really nice apartment."

"A town house. I got it because of the garage. Never had one before."

"Never?" Henderson asked.

"Not that I remember."

Corina gave her a quizzical look. "The file," she began.

"Got it right here." Geri picked up the folder

from the counter, not sure which one of them to hand it to. Instead she placed it in the middle of her kitchen table. They took seats on opposite sides of it, while she stood at the counter and Nathan went from one to the other, sniffing them out.

Corina flipped it open and handed Henderson a stack of papers. As she watched them, Geri pondered the singular form of Weinhard.

"What exactly are we looking for?" Henderson asked.

"I'm not sure. Some kind of receipt. I think it's pink."

"Only pink ones are the electric and plumbing companies." Geri surprised herself with that one. Funny how she could pull facts out of the air like that. Photographic memory, sometimes, but there was nothing selective about it. Give her an anthropology exam, and she was dumb as a box of rocks.

"Perfect." Corina began dealing the colored papers out like cards. In seconds, she isolated a stack of pink receipts. "These are the ones we want," she said. Her finger trembled as she pointed at the paper. "Bertram Electric. Montgomery, Alabama. San Quintin, Mexico."

"This is important?" Geri asked.

"Very." Henderson handed her the paper. "You got a photocopier around this place?"

"How'd you know?"

"Just thought you might."

She switched into business gear. "How many copies?"

"Two, please."

"You need any help checking out these places?"

"We might."

"Awesome possum," she said. "Just tell me what to do."

That's all she'd better say right now. The rest could wait until she thought about it a little more.

Thirty-Four

They hadn't been able locate Bertram Electric, not even with Geri's help. There was no phone number listed. The address was a mail drop, and the company didn't show up on any Web searches.

Corina woke early Wednesday morning after a night of restless, intermittent sleep. They were getting close to something big, something that had to do with the missing DEA agents. They'd meet with Henderson's DEA contact, then go to Baja themselves. It was the only way.

Making even tenuous peace with Henderson had freed her of a great burden. Not that they agreed on everything. But they shared a common cause now, and the information he provided had helped her make better sense out of hers. So stupid to be at war with each other when together they might be able to find out who murdered Skin and Tina.

Already the air hung heavy with humidity. As Corina zipped up a denim sundress, the lights went out. She glanced at the clock, its digital numbers snapped into blackness.

Rojito looked up from the foot of the bed as if to

ask what was going on. ''Power's out,'' she told him in Spanish. ''And me with wet hair.''

She opened the drapes and pulled her hair into a damp twist in back. As she prepared to leave, the lights came back on.

Their attempts at peacemaking hadn't changed Henderson's arrival time. His old navy Honda was nowhere to be seen when she pulled into the parking lot.

Just ahead, Geri climbed out of her car. Catching Corina's eye, she waved and waited. An actual attempt at friendship. This was a first. Last night had changed something.

''Hi,'' Corina said, catching up with her. ''Did you get caught without power today?''

Geri patted her glistening purple spikes. ''Can't you tell? What about you?''

''Oh, yes.'' She mimicked the motion. ''Dress code or not, here I come.''

''It's all over town. PG&E says to expect more of the same.''

''That's all we need.''

Geri grinned. ''Boy howdy, can't you see us if the power goes off at press time?''

''At least we have a generator.''

''Oh, that's right, sure.'' She hesitated as they neared the building. ''So how does all this stuff set with you?''

''The heat wave? I was born in the Valley. My folks had nothing but swamp coolers for years.''

''I'm not talking about the heat,'' Geri said. ''I mean all this stuff with the Brandonites.''

Corina laughed. ''That's what they call us, isn't

it? Because we're young and we don't earn anything close to what the old-timers do.''

"Just cause they call you something doesn't mean you have to be that something,'' Geri said. "You ever hear any of Peter Case's songs?''

"No, I'm not into much alternative music.''

"You think alternative's all I listen to?'' Geri asked. "Think I listen with my hair, maybe?''

"Of course not. Sorry if that's how it sounded.''

"This guy is cool beans, and he's a folkie, believe it or not.'' Geri continued, as if she hadn't heard the implied apology. "He does a lot of John Prine stuff. You don't have to walk anyone's crooked mile. That's what he's saying in one of his songs. And you don't, honey chile. Nobody does. Not me. Not you.''

"Meaning?'' They reached the steps leading to the entrance. Corina maneuvered ahead of Geri and opened the door.

"Meaning, we don't have to be Brandonites. Meaning we don't have to kiss ass just because we're perceived as ass-kissers. Meaning we can be young and still do a good job and not owe our collective soul to anyone. Meaning, we don't have to walk no crooked mile for no one.''

Geri stepped inside, and Corina followed, as the heavy glass door swished shut behind them. As they started down the hall, Corina said, "You're one of them, aren't you?'' She knew she didn't have to say more.

"What if I am?'' Geri's eyes glowed like onyx. "Like it or not, you and I and people like us got our positions for no good reason, except maybe our ages or something just as stupid.''

"Like our surnames?" Corina said.

"Maybe. In some cases, mine for sure, we replaced folks who were doing a good job."

"You didn't exactly replace Millie," Corina said. "She was going to retire, anyway."

Geri smiled at the door-side security guard, flashed her ID, then leaned over, whispering in Corina's ear. "Bullshit. That old lady could have cooked another eight, ten years easy, if Chenault hadn't wanted to slash the budget in our department."

"You think so?" Corina flashed her own ID at the guard.

"Hell's bells, yes. Henderson, too. He's still hot, in spite of what they tried to do to him."

"Henderson and I are working together now," she said. "No more games."

"I can see that. That's why I'm telling you this."

Corina stopped walking and turned to Geri. "Telling me what?"

Her face went blank. "Well, at first I thought you were the enemy. Now, I know you're not. If anything, you're in a heap of shit, lady, and don't even ask me how I know it."

Corina took her at her word. "Okay. So what the hell am I supposed to do?"

Geri's lips straightened out into her version of a smile. "Beats me. You need to work with Henderson, though. And you might start by telling him that Tina Kellogg's son was at Betsy Lorraine Webster's house the night you went to see her."

"There was no one there when I visited Betsy."

"There was when I did. He was driving a black pickup. I got the license number."

"What were you doing visiting Skin's fiancée?"

She shrugged. "Research. Kid lives at the coast. Pismo Beach. The name is derived from *pismu,* after the tar the Chumash Indians used to look for there."

Corina had learned to let Geri finish when she was in manic research mode. The news she'd just shared was worth enduring her recital.

They reached the main hall. Corina turned to Geri and said, "Thank you. I'll share this with Henderson."

"I'm glad." Geri paused. "I know you think we're nothing but a bunch of RF-ers."

"Chocolate syrup does strike me as less than mature," she said.

"It's more than that, what we're involved in. It's about people's jobs."

"I won't say anything," Corina told her, "but think about what you're doing."

"Whatever."

"And thanks again." But Geri, already walking ahead of her, did not turn around. Why would she be so helpful one moment and so rude the next? And had she really seen Tina Kellogg's son at Betsy's house?

Corina walked the rest of the way to her office alone. *A heap of shit,* she thought. *You're in a heap of shit, lady.*

Betsy Webster answered her phone as if she'd been expecting someone else.

"Oh, it's you," she said, when Corina announced herself.

"I wonder if I might be able to drop by this afternoon."

"Well—"

"It will take just a minute," she said.

A gnawing silence followed. Corina stared at her blank notepad.

"Betsy?"

"Look, I've been thinking. You might be Wes Shaw's friend, but you're still the press."

Something, someone, had changed Betsy's mind. "Don't you want to know what happened to Skin?" she asked.

"Listen, damn it. I can't talk to you."

"Betsy, I'm just—"

"I got to go." Before Corina could respond, she realized the connection had been broken, and all she was holding was a dial tone.

Thirty-Five

Wednesday, June 20, 3:30 p.m.

Two more brief power outages occurred that day, and reporters were already speaking the language of superlatives. They were right, though, calling it the hottest summer on record, the highest temperatures since 1936.

Stretching toward the eastern foothills, Eugene Belmont's ranchlike estate overlooked impeccable gardens set against a backdrop of Italian cypress trees. The house itself was unassuming, except for its size. Bigger no doubt equated with better in Eugene Belmont's vocabulary. Like Wes's father, he had started with nothing. Corina wondered for a moment about what all this had really cost.

The woman who opened the door was Corina's size and color. She wore a white uniform. The gold cross around her neck looked like the one Corina's parents had given her for eighth grade graduation. That, at her age, she still chose to wear it told Corina most of what she needed to know about the woman. The fact that she chose to serve, white uniform and all, a man like Eugene Belmont, told the rest.

In Spanish, Corina asked for him.

''Mr. Belmont is busy,'' she answered in heavily accented English. ''May I let him know who—''

Her eyes were large and shiny, the eyes of someone who didn't cry enough. When she realized Corina was staring at her, she looked down.

''Well, he needs to get this today. I'll just take it to him.'' Corina started to move past her into the house.

''No, no. He is in back. You must wait here.''

''Out there?'' Corina crossed in front of her and walked briskly toward the rear yard, the maid protesting as she followed.

''You can't go back there. You must wait, *por favor.*''

She heard the soft murmur of voices ahead about the same time she saw them. Eugene sat in a wooden chair, his skinny back to her, his thinning silver hair reflecting the sunlight. In the safety of her own territory, Nan looked softer and more feminine. She wore a long, gauzelike dress of black alternated with turquoise. A large silver-and-turquoise squash blossom hung from her neck. She stood beneath a columnar portico before a long granite table.

The table looked like a relic from a happier past. A deep groove filled with water ran down its length. Several wilting flowers floated there. It must have been purchased in the days when guests like Wes Senior gathered out there before the pool to drink, eat, dance and party.

Nan leaned down to say something to her father, then saw Corina approaching. The facade of femininity vanished. With clenched fists, she marched toward her before Corina could step into the yard.

"What is the meaning of this?" She turned to the maid. "Gloria, I told you—"

"It's not her fault," Corina said. "Your father never answered my fax, so I thought I'd deliver the questions in person."

"Please leave." Nan blocked the path, her face scarlet. "Your boss will hear about this. You're trespassing on private property, you're—"

"Leaving," Corina finished, backing up a few steps at a time.

"Nan," Eugene's voice rose above them, high-pitched and demanding. "What the hell is going on?"

"It's okay, Daddy. I'm coming." Perspiration dotted her upper lip. "You'd better not upset him. You think you've got trouble now? You sure don't need Eugene Belmont coming out here to see what the hell you're doing on his property."

"I'd be happy to explain," she said, trying to see where Eugene was. Nan wasn't having it.

"You'd better leave before he comes out here. He has an old-fashioned way of dealing with your kind."

Corina glared back at her. "My kind? Reporters, you mean? Women?"

"You know what I mean. Daddy's views aren't exactly politically correct, and on this property, he'll deal with you as he sees fit."

"As long as it's legal. In the meantime, I'd appreciate some answers to my questions about Vineyard Estates," Corina said. "And in case you're wondering, I've dealt with bigots before."

"What's it going to take?" Nan asked. "Another call to the paper? The police? What?"

"I told you I'm leaving."

"Then get moving. Don't you understand? We don't want you here." Nan followed her to the drive, counting off a litany of threats, including calling her editor, calling the publisher, and of course, filing a lawsuit.

"All I want are a few answers from your father," she said.

"Don't hold your breath, *Miss* Vasquez." She underscored the courtesy title in venom, her eyes as hard and cold as the granite table. "People like my father don't talk to people like you." Before Corina could respond, she added, "You're out of your league with Wes Shaw, don't you think?"

Corina tried to duck the anger. It was contagious, she knew. If she breathed it in, she'd spit it back, be contaminated by it. She took a deep breath, concentrating on the feel of the sun on her face. She forced herself to look past Nan at the trees, their leaves shimmering like shredded green cellophane. "He never talks about Eugene," she said, as if speaking to the trees.

"Well, Eugene has plenty to say about him *and* his father. Now, get out of here before I call the police."

Without another word, she turned and headed back the way they had come. Eugene was no longer visible, hidden behind the trees. Corina exhaled in a slow hiss. Her eyes burned, and she could almost smell the foul odor of hatred Nan had left behind. It had taken every ounce of self-control she possessed to stay calm. As Nan disappeared around the drive, she realized she was not alone. Gloria, the maid, stood a few feet from her, watching.

Corina whirled to face her. "You ought to be ashamed to work for these people," she said, waving her hand at the space Nan had occupied moments before.

"I need the job," Gloria said.

"Don't give me that." Corina stared her down, releasing all the contempt she'd been holding back. "You need the abuse."

She'd driven several miles down the road before she realized that she was still shaking, and that her anger had nothing to do with the maid.

Henderson sat at his desk, chewing on a red plastic straw in a paper cup of iced tea. He actually looked happy to see her.

"I traced the license number of that pickup Geri saw in front of Betsy Webster's," he said. "Had to go through the cops. That's why it took so long."

"Worth the wait?" she asked. "Who is it registered to?"

"Tina Kellogg."

"Which means Geri was right. That was her son at Betsy's."

"None other."

"Lawrence. That's his name." He bent the straw between his fingers. "Like I said, a loser."

"Wonder what he was doing there?"

"He didn't mention it to me when I talked to him. You think you can get Betsy to talk?"

"Not anymore. Something's changed her mind about me. She's scared."

He held the straw as if it were a cigarette, staring at it thoughtfully. "Well then, you think you can get the son to talk?"

"It's worth a try." She didn't bother to remind him that he'd tried to prevent her earlier from doing just that.

"Might be crucial to our story or just a post-script," he said. "That's the way it works sometime. Either way, you talk to Lawrence Kellogg. I'll try to reach Betsy, and we'll sit back and watch the shit hit the proverbial fan."

Something had changed about him, something subtle. He'd made some kind of decision, and he was no longer trying to hold her back.

"Want me to do it in person?" she asked.

"Absolutely. Drive over tomorrow. We need to deal with Belmont, too. He's never going to answer that fax of yours."

"I went by his place after lunch," she said. "Got attacked by Nan herself."

"You fight back?" he asked, trying to suppress a smile.

"It was a verbal attack. She threatened to call everyone from the cops to Chenault, and she literally ran me out of the yard."

"That had to be a sight." He fiddled with the straw, appearing to bite back laughter. "Did you get a chance to talk to Eugene?"

"Not this time."

He lay the straw on the desk next to an irregular-shaped container of paper clips. The dish, like the ashtray, was glazed in an uneven black. "You're planning a next time?"

She hadn't verbalized her plan, not even to herself, but now she saw it clearly. "Yes," she said. "I'm going back there."

Thirty-Six

The drive to Pismo Beach took less than three hours. After the gradual climb out of the Valley, the oppressive air grew less stifling. One day she'd have to leave this place. She didn't want to end up as bitter as Henderson. But then maybe his reasons were not entirely geographical.

The less guarded he grew with her, the more clearly she saw the firepower and energy he still possessed. Almost in spite of himself, he'd click into action and start processing information. Whatever the breakup of his marriage had done to him was temporary, she guessed. He'd bounce back or drift back sooner or later, at least she hoped he would. She was starting to trust him, and for the first time, she was beginning to realize how much easier it would be to have a partner she could trust working with her on this story. If Geri were right, she'd need a partner. If Geri were right, she was in a heap of shit.

Pismo had once been a blue-collar retirement community for those who were uncomfortable in less rustic coastal towns like Santa Barbara or Car-

mel. As prices rose along with the adobe-colored
waterfront condos, the innocence had remained. This
was no Laguna Beach of white shorts, blue eyes,
blond hair and pedigreed dogs. It was too-thick
chowder eaten from bread bowls with plastic spoons,
corny poster shops, RV-ing seniors and a heavy
sprinkling of Portuguese and Italian surnames
among the white-bread mix. Most of all, it was miles
of beach, where the tide heralded the time of day
and crashing waves accompanied the dramatic drop
of the sun each night.

She and Wes had walked this beach too many
times for her to face it alone. She entered the beach
from the Shell Beach side—past Kon Tiki, Sea
Crest, Whalers Inn, Shelter Cove, all of the oceanfront motels that used to promise magic to her. Even
the Shell Beach deli and Del's Pizza evoked memories she thought she had buried. She could remember what she'd ordered, what he'd worn, and the
sound of the ocean reminded her of all those times
she and Wes had lain in bed counting the sounds of
the night.

A few hundred feet from the ocean, sat the mall
that housed the surf shop where Lawrence Kellogg
worked. Even though he was the only person in the
store, she would have known he was Tina's son,
only on him the full lower lip looked more sullen
than sultry. But then he was only, what? Twenty-
five? And he'd just lost his only living parent.

Unlike his mother's dark hair, his was strawberry
blond, and he was already losing it. Pale brows made
his eyes appear even more narrow. He compensated
with oversize dark glasses that matched the ones on
the store display. Their heavy frames stretched all

the way to his ears. His self-consciously ratty cutoffs also matched the display. The kid was a walking advertisement for the lifestyle the store promoted.

When she introduced herself to him, he registered only mild surprise.

"I don't have anything to tell the press." He had the oxygen-starved breath of those who smoke a lot of marijuana, but he smelled clean, like starched fabric.

"I'm sorry about your mother. I'm trying to find out what happened."

He brushed his hand against the rack of sale shirts, hangers clattering. "You won't."

"Why do you say that?"

He gnawed on his full lower lip, so much like Tina's. "The people she was up against ain't going to confess. She'd take on anyone, my mom. It finally came back to get her." He swallowed hard and continued straightening clothes.

"Do you know who she was taking on this time?"

"Them Vineyard Estates people. That Eugene Belmont." He shook his head, started hanging up shirts. "You'd have to know my mom. She'd get something in her craw, and that was that. She uncovered something about Vineyard Estates. That's all I know, all I could find out. Now she's dead." He hit the rack of clothes. "Just when we were starting to know each other."

Corina wanted to turn away, leave him to whatever guilt and grief had hold of him, but she forced herself to continue. "You didn't get along with your mother?"

"I didn't *know* her." He said it in a whisper drained of hope, as if that should explain it all.

"First, she had to get through college, worked the whole time. Then there was politics. I lived with my Gram over in Morro Bay until she died."

"Did you go to school over here?" she asked.

He shrugged. "Dropped out over at Cuesta a few times. I can't handle school. Too much routine. Really pissed my mom off, but she didn't have any right to tell me how to live. No one does." The reality of his situation seemed to hit him again, like a wave. He ran a hand through his lanky hair, tucking it behind an ear. "She said it would take something big to wake me up, and by then it would be too late. As usual, she was right."

"I'm sorry," Corina said.

"No, you're not. You're just trying to get a story." He turned from her. "You probably just want to write some trash about what a bad mother she was, how she screwed around and deserted her kid."

"That's not my intent."

"Most chicks who started out the way she did would've ended up on welfare," he said. "Something had to fall through the cracks. You can't blame her for that."

Something *had* fallen through the cracks. Someone. "Lawrence," she said, "I'm not trying to blame your mother for anything. I'm just trying to find out what happened to her."

"She knew too much about that development group, that they were taking money or something. And they had her killed."

"Something bigger than taking money," she said.

"Whatever it is, you'll never be able to prove anything. Those people own the town, the city council, probably the mayor. My mom was the only honest politician in the bunch.''

She resisted the impulse to argue with him. Instead she looked into the khaki windows of his glasses at the faint shape of his eyes. ''What were you doing at Betsy Webster's?''

He stepped back, removed his sunglasses and squinted at her through watery eyes that looked as if they needed to cry. ''Trying to do the same thing you are right now. I heard what happened to Skin Burke, and I knew he and Mom were working together.''

''Working on what?''

He shrugged. ''That's why I went to Betsy Webster's.''

''Had you met her before?''

''No, but I'd met Skin Burke. I called Betsy's real estate office and told her I wanted to see her, but she didn't know anything about Skin's business dealings.''

''Did you believe her?'' Corina asked.

''She said it was a group called The Trio, and that she thought Eugene Belmont was behind it. Told me she was going to leave town, that she didn't want anyone coming after her. Tell you the truth, I felt sorry for her.''

''Did she say anything else?'' Corina asked.

He hesitated for a moment, and she wondered if he were weighing his response or just beaten down from her questioning. ''Not really.''

''Anything at all?''

He looked at her with eyes too old for the rest of his face. ''She said she was sorry for my loss, that she respected my mom. Big deal. If people hadn't respected my mom so much, maybe she'd still be alive. Maybe we—'' He stopped, looked around the empty store. ''I've got to get to work. This is killing me.''

''I'm sorry,'' she said again.

''How can you be? You don't know what it's like to be twenty-five years old with both your parents dead. You don't have any idea.''

She thought of her folks and dispensed with any platitudes she might have mouthed. ''You're right,'' she said. ''I don't, but I am sorry.''

He turned away without a word, heading to the back of the store, and she let him go. Outside, couples walked the beach, their arms around each other. A few kids surfed the waves. A black dog ran ahead of his master. She stopped for a moment, watching them, realizing how far outside this picture of life she was. It would be a long drive back.

Tuesday, May 29, 10:45 a.m.
Skin

*No way out of this deal. Not this time. I walk to
the balcony past Betsy's big bed with its blue-and-
white comforter, a room to relax in, but who can
relax? I see her below, a small, tan figure with her
golf clubs, not playing, just standing there, holding
a club and looking into the distance.*

*She knows something's wrong, has been pretend-
ing for my sake. I should have told her a long time
ago, before it got out of hand. But how do you begin
to tell something like this?*

*"A hothead," Nan said. "You've always been a
hothead."*

*And I replied with some lame-ass blather about
how I didn't know they were going to kill people.
Trying to kid myself, even then.*

*Betsy looks up, blows me a kiss. I wave and watch
her stride toward the house.*

*I pick up my briefcase from Betsy's overstuffed
chair. The tape sits solid and safe, my life insurance
policy, maybe Tina's, too, if Nan's telling the truth
and the others in The Trio aren't behind Tina's disappearance. I try to convince myself that she's safe,
maybe having problems with the boy again. But I'm
too scared to reason anymore, I know that.*

*Betsy comes into the room, her face lined with
concern. Too many lines, but shit, she's as old as I
am, and she's spent her life in the sun. She seems*

to have aged in the last year, and I know I'm the reason. She moves close to me, smelling of that perfumed sunblock she uses. Puts her hand on my shoulder.

"What is it, baby?"

"Vineyard Estates," I say. "The Trio."

"Eugene Belmont?"

"No names. I told you that."

"What are they doing?"

I shake my head. "I can't, Betz. I just have to get out, and they don't want me to. I know more than I should about what's going on."

With a sigh, she sits on the side of the bed, and I get the feeling she's almost relieved to know what's bothering me. Guess I haven't exactly been a barrel of laughs lately, not to mention dishonest as hell. "You can tell me, Skin. I wouldn't say a thing to anyone."

"Wouldn't do any good." I look over at the brief-case, then back at her. "I'm thinking of talking to Corina Vasquez at the Voice."

"A reporter? Are you crazy?"

"She's always been straight with me."

"But she's a reporter, honey."

"I've told her stuff before, and she kept it to herself."

Betsy stands up. "Are you sure you don't want to talk to me about it? I'm a good listener."

"Don't want to jeopardize you," I say.

"Jeopardize me? Come on, baby. We're engaged. You're really afraid to tell me?"

"Yeah."

"That serious?"

"Afraid so."

"Then I wouldn't call that girl at the newspaper."

"No?"

"Definitely not." Her voice is firm, and she gives me a look that suggests I must be losing it. *"You know better than to trust anyone in the media, Skin."*

"Yeah," I say. *"I guess you're right."*

Thirty-Seven

Thursday, June 21, 5:30 p.m.

"**I**f you can't bite, don't bark," Wes had often told her. Corina had barked to Henderson that they were going to get to Eugene Belmont, and now she had to do more than talk. As she drove home from the coast she realized how much she missed her parents. In spite of the way they could exasperate her, they were two decent people who did the best they could for their children. Monday was their day off. She'd phone them, suck it up and agree to be in Lydia's wedding. Hell, she might even curl her hair.

Her parental struggles seemed pretty minor when she looked at someone like Lawrence Kellogg, or Nan Belmont, for that matter.

When she reached Pleasant Valley, she didn't go directly home. Instead, she drove east toward Belmont's. The same maid waited at the front door before Corina could touch the bell. Although her manner was polite, her dark eyes registered panic.

"Please," she whispered.

"I need to see Eugene," Corina said, "without Nan around. Do you understand?"

"Go, please. She will take it out on me."

Any pity she might have felt melted as she watched the maid cower. She remembered something Tina Kellogg said in her talk that day Corina had heard her speak at the luncheon. *We're as evolved as our lowest common denominator.*

"This isn't the only job in the world," she said. "Where is your self-respect?"

A car drove by with a steady swoosh. The woman stiffened, her white uniform like a starched sheet on a scarecrow. Corina reached out for her wrist. It felt like cold steel in her fingers.

"I can't leave. I have two children. Please. She will be back any minute."

When she let go of her, the woman gasped as if she'd just been released from a trap.

"Listen to me," Corina said. "I'll help you find another job, a better job, but you must help me, too. It's important that I see Eugene without his daughter around."

She nodded, but the fear didn't leave her eyes. "If she finds out—"

"It won't matter. You'll be out of here. I have a friend who has an important job with the city. I know he'll be able to find a position for you."

"I am a good worker."

Finally, Corina thought, a spark of pride behind the fear. "Then go where you can be appreciated. When will Eugene be alone?"

She looked down, muttered, as if talking to herself. "She has a dinner with Governor Menlo tomorrow night."

"And Eugene's not going with her?"

She looked up, a strange light behind the dark veil

of pain in her eyes. "He never does. Now, will you leave?"

Corina dug into her purse and handed her a business card. "Call me to confirm," she said. "If she should cancel the dinner at the last minute or something."

"And the job with your friend?"

"I'll take care of it," she said. "I promise."

When Corina got home, she left a message with Wes's answering service.

Late that afternoon, the power at the complex went out again. Without air-conditioning, the air within her condo was sweltering. Her neighbors gathered by the pool. The manager brought out a portable radio and a large ice chest full of beer and soda. Compared to the rest of her day, it seemed a remarkably sane activity. Her neighbors were starting to relax, convincing themselves that the trouble at her condo was just one of the unlucky coincidences in a city that was growing faster than it was maturing.

She took a jar of still-cold sun tea from the refrigerator and knocked on Papa's door. When he hesitated, she motioned toward the pool. He and Mama joined her soon after. Although they passed on the sun tea, they mingled, listening to the news reports as if they could understand. The sense of camaraderie and the smell of chlorine actually made Corina feel cooler. The phone sounded far away, and it took her a moment to realize the ringing came from her new condo. Her cell phone. She'd forgotten to bring it outside with her.

She jumped up and ran across the yard, dashed into the living room and grabbed the phone from the table by the door. It was Wes. She felt the smile spread across her face when she heard his voice.

"I knew it would be you."

"I was concerned. Is the power out over there, too?"

"All over town, I think."

"What about you? You sound winded."

"I'm fine, but I need a favor, Wes, a big one."

"It's about time. Just tell me what I can do."

"You can help me change somebody's life," she said.

Parental guilt call 892

"*Mija*, I caught you."

"Just leaving, Mama."

"Going somewhere special?"

"Not really, kind of an assignment with my editor."

"Is he single?"

"Divorced, I think."

"That's no good. There are lots of nice single men out there."

"It's not a date, Mama, honest. And he's a smart guy. I can learn a lot from him."

"I've been worried about you."

"Don't be. I'm fine."

"The last time we talked, you sounded so—"

"I've just been doing some thinking, that's all."

"You know Pete's partner at the law firm is single."

"Mama, please."

"I mean only that he's going to be the best man, and there's not a thing wrong with two single young people having a good time."

"You're right, Mama. It will be a wonderful wedding."

"It's not the wedding I'm trying to discuss, *Mija.*"

"*I know. We'll talk later, okay?*"

Thirty-Eight

Friday, June 22, 6:45 p.m.

"I sure fixed her little red wagon." Nan stood outside the family room watching her father watch a war movie. His head was stained blue by the light of the television, which for some reason made her feel almost like breaking into tears. He didn't look real in that light; he looked like a dead man.

"What'd you say?"

"Corina Vasquez," she said, trying to shout above the noise of the film. "She'll never dare to come snooping around here again. You can't teach those people any respect, but we won't have to worry about it much longer."

"Fucking A."

She walked over and kissed his cheek. "Got to get to the meeting, Daddy." When he started to protest, she shushed him and patted his shoulder. "I need the support of these people. Just remember, it's for us, for everything you've worked for. We'll be able to regain all that was lost."

"Fucking A," he said again, intent on the violence on the screen.

She started to say more, but knew it wouldn't do

any good. "I'll try to get back early so we can discuss the next step. I know we can do it, Daddy. We're so close."

She heard a noise at the door and turned. Danny stood there in a short-sleeved shirt and a pair of tan pants.

"The car's ready," he said.

"Put on a tie and a jacket and meet me there."

"A jacket? In this heat?" He brushed back already wilting thin hair. One look from her and he nodded. "Okay," he said. "I'll be down in a minute."

Nan glanced over at the movie on the television set. Her father turned his head, and in the blue stream of light, their gazes met and locked. Nan saw the love in his eyes, felt it in her own. "Fucking men," she said. "They just can't get it right."

The company station wagon Corina and Henderson had checked out smelled faintly of gas and pizza. Henderson parked it on the side of the road, and they walked the rest of the way to the house. Although it was close to seven-thirty, the evening still carried the leftover heat and scent of day. The dusty, desiccated air, devoid of life, reminded Corina of summers in the San Joaquin Valley right before the harvest.

She left her purse in Henderson's car and carried her notebook in the pocket of her denim jacket. She felt clammy all over but kept the jacket on. Henderson was wearing jeans, along with a pair of odd brown shoes, without socks, that looked as if they were constructed more for sailors than reporters.

"Let's hope Eugene's really alone," he said.

"He will be. I talked to Gloria this afternoon. She knows you're coming with me."

He flashed her an expression of disdain. His shoes made squishing sounds as he walked. "How do you know you can trust her?"

Corina had already been over that scenario in her mind. "I know what she'll say and what she won't. She won't tell any more than she has to."

"What makes you so sure?"

"You wouldn't understand."

Being on foot made Corina feel smaller and more vulnerable. She pulled her jacket tighter as they approached the house and its double-door entry.

Spot lighting illuminated the silhouettes of the trees in front. The porch was lit from above.

"So?" Henderson said. "Do we just walk right up and ring the bell?"

Corina recalled what had happened the last time. "She'll be watching for us."

He gave her a questioning smile. "Yeah? Will that be before or after they arrest us?"

He had a point. They certainly would look suspicious to anyone passing by, standing in front of the house, to the side of the front light. Corina felt her breath quicken. "Maybe we ought to go around to the back."

"Why don't I go? You wait here." Henderson moved into the shadows.

"No," she said. "We'd better stick together."

At that moment, the front door opened, and Gloria stepped stiffly into the light.

Corina exhaled with relief and heard Henderson do the same. "Let me go first," he said. "In case—"

Before he could finish, Corina stepped in front of him and walked toward the door. Gloria saw her, then shifted her gaze to Henderson. She put her fingers to her lips and stood aside as they entered.

The furnishings did nothing to add warmth to the cavernous room. The fireplace looked as if it had never been used. A scent reminiscent of old bananas filled the air. Furniture polish, she guessed. A mahogany buffet stood against one wall, and a long table stretched behind each side of a floral-print sectional. Two rust-colored love seats on wooden rockers faced each other, separated by a round maple table on three legs.

She introduced Henderson in a whisper, and Gloria responded in the same way. "I talked to someone at City Hall," she told Corina. "You didn't say your friend was the mayor. I have a job, starting Monday."

Bless you, Wes, Corina thought.

"And Eugene? He's alone?"

Gloria moved her head in the direction of the hall. "She comes back about ten, never earlier. I am supposed to go home then."

"Perhaps you should leave right now." After all the whispering, Henderson's normal tone sounded like a shout. "You don't need to stick around here."

"But I can't." Gloria's voice trailed off. She looked steadily at Henderson. "You'll see."

In spite of the overworked air conditioner, the musty, banana smell grew faint as they stepped into the hall. This must be where the Belmonts really lived, Corina thought. The room with the sofa seemed forgotten.

The sound of a television blared from one of the

doors. Explosions and climactic music thundered through the yellow-blue light of the room. Eugene Belmont must be deaf.

Gloria stopped. "He's in there."

Corina touched her arm. "Thank you."

Their eyes met. "Thank *you*," Gloria repeated, emotion finally breaking through the polite veneer of her voice. *"Gracias."* She turned in the direction they had come and disappeared.

Corina hesitated. Henderson stepped in front of her and approached the doorway as if he belonged there. He looked inside and rapped gently on the door frame.

"Hey, Eugene? You have a few minutes?"

No answer, only the cracking of rifles.

Corina joined him, wondering briefly if he might be right, and if Nan would step out of the shadows at any minute. No, Gloria had been too sincere, too grateful. She'd be out of this dead refrigerator of a house in moments. They all would.

A large-screen television, complete with noisy battle scene, dominated the far wall. Two smaller televisions on either side of the large one flicked with changing programs. A weight lifter, a football game, a tour of Greece. Their sounds blended into a low hum, over which the movie of choice blasted its weapons. On the large easy chair before it, a figure leaned forward, a remote-control switch clutched in his bony hand.

Henderson cleared his throat. "Eugene?" he said, raising his voice.

The figure in the chair slowly turned from the screen. He wore a brown sweater, several sizes too big for his scrawny arms. Corina was struck by how stooped he was. The light from the screen tangled in his hair. His eyes looked hollow and disoriented. He reached clawlike fingers to scratch the sagging flesh of his cheek, like a man waking up from a long nap. His eyes narrowed on her then returned to the screen.

"Kill them Japs," he muttered.

"Mr. Belmont," Corina said, stepping forward. "You remember Matthew Henderson, don't you?" God, she thought. He didn't remember, did he? His mouth hadn't closed since they'd entered the room. It hung open, like a door, slightly ajar. She wondered if he'd had a stroke, if his speech had been impaired, but then his eyes filled with fire.

"I said kill them fucking Japs," he shouted, looking directly at her. "Get the fuck out of my store." He reached out for the cane leaning against the chair. "Get," he said, waving it at her.

"Eugene," Henderson repeated.

The old man reached down, picked up a small glass lamp from the table and hurled it at Corina. Henderson jerked her out of the way. The lamp grazed her shoulder. Eugene hooted with delight.

"Fucking Japs."

As the movie behind him flashed into another battle scene, he waved a fist, continuing to swear at the screen. Henderson turned to Corina, his eyes full of questions. But he knew the answer. They both did. Eugene Belmont, one of the most powerful men in the Valley, was absolutely out of his mind.

She backed out of the room as Eugene limped to the table on his cane and picked up a large ashtray.

"Come on," she whispered.

Henderson slammed the door as they left the

room, just as the heavy smashing of glass sounded from the other side. Eugene's high-pitched laughter followed them down the hall.

They walked without speaking. Corina's shoulders felt stiff and heavy. She continued to see the monster Belmont had become. The living room looked as dead as it had when they'd arrived. There was no sign of Gloria, thank God. At least she'd gotten out in time.

Henderson opened the front door and stepped aside as Corina ran to safety. Once he closed it firmly behind him, they turned to each other. Shock had wiped Henderson's face clean.

"Son of a bitch," he said. "Do you realize?" The porch light washed over him. His ears looked as if they'd been scalded.

"We'd better get out of here." She moved closer, as if to nudge him.

"Yeah, you're right. How long you think he's been like this? Months, years?"

She tried to think as they hurried down the gravel-covered path. The night of Craig Menlo's speech? Before that? The station wagon sat before them, a bulky, beige haven.

"I don't know," she said, wanting to burst into a run, to get inside the car and close the doors, lock them, and drive like hell. "He's nuts. That's all I know for sure."

The moment he unlocked the car, Corina scrambled inside. Henderson lit a cigarette and got in behind the wheel. The leather-and-smoke scent smelled almost comforting after the mausoleum of banana peels and the crazy man who ran it.

No, she thought. Not running it at all. "You know who's in charge, don't you?" she said slowly.

"You read my mind." Henderson sat with his key poised in the ignition. "Nan's been at the helm for a long time, hasn't she?"

"That's my guess. Some of the people Eugene does business with probably don't like taking orders from a woman, either, senator or not." She thought of Menlo and his obvious contempt for her and all females. "Bet the governor doesn't know."

Henderson cracked the window, and blew the smoke out. "Bet none of that trio of theirs does."

"You think she's managed to keep it from them?"

"She managed to keep it from us."

"True," she said. "That night of Menlo's speech she made sure no one got close to him."

He smashed the cigarette in the ashtray then shoved it through the cracked window. "You think Skin Burke knew?"

"Betsy said he had lunch with her. Maybe he did know. Maybe that's why he wanted out."

"Because he thought she couldn't run it on her own?"

"Or Tina did. Maybe Tina found out."

"Maybe."

She sighed, pressed her forehead against the cool glass of the window. "I'm glad we can be honest with each other now. I couldn't tell you much at first. I wasn't sure you'd believe me."

"Because of the Wes Shaw connection?"

"Hardly." She hated this guilty feeling that shot through her. "I know you don't like him."

"Quite the contrary. I do like Wes Shaw. Hell,

everybody likes Wes Shaw. He's like television or vitamins."

"Stop it," she said.

He lowered his voice and turned to look at her. "Just be careful how much you tell him."

"Why do you always say that? How do you think I got Eugene's maid to let us in tonight? Where do you think she'll be working starting Monday?"

"I can guess."

The traffic signal before them turned red. Henderson put on his brakes, then said in a voice that was almost too kind, "Look, I know how you feel about him, but the fewer people who know what we're finding out, the better."

"I know," she said, "but you have to trust someone, don't you?"

The light washed his face an ethereal white. "Do you?"

"Come on, Matthew. Don't you ever feel like talking to someone, away from work, kind of thinking aloud?"

"No."

"And you never discuss anything you're working on with—" She paused, groping for the right word. "The people in your personal life."

"There's only one person in my personal life, as you call it. She's six years old. We talk about bears."

"I didn't mean to pry," she said.

"And I didn't mean to lecture. I'm probably just paranoid."

"That did occur to me," she replied.

"Well, I got that way with years of practice."

"Maybe I'll be luckier."

"I hope so. In the meantime, just be careful, okay?"

The light turned green, and he hit the gas, as if glad to be in motion.

"You think Nan will call Chenault again?" she asked.

"Why would she? Eugene's not going to remember we were there. I don't think he even recognized us."

Corina thought of his gaping mouth and menacing, hollow stare. The chilly, creepy feeling returned, spreading through her body.

"He recognized me," she said.

Thirty-Nine

Monday, June 25, 9:40 a.m.

Peter Case shouted into Geri's headphones, vibrating more than singing, but it was all the same to her.

Something out of the corner of her visual path moved or changed color in the shifting light. Geri looked up to see Corina leaning over her desk. She wore slim black pants that tapered at the ankles, a cropped black top about the same color as her hair. And she looked confused. Only one source of confusion in this room, folks, and that was yours truly.

How long had she been standing there? What had she said?

Geri ripped off the headphones, waved them like the excuse they were and looked up into Corina's frown.

"I asked if you'd found it yet."

"Found what?"

"The information on Bertram Electric. Have you located an address yet?" Corina gave her a curious look. "Are you all right?"

How do you tell someone you almost think of as a friend that your head feels as if your dog's been kicking it in? How do you say you're a liar, worse than a liar? How do you tell someone you kind of know but not really that you're scared?

Easy. None of the above. You grab the closest excuse you have.

"Just distracted. Looks like this is going to be another badass week. They canned Sam, the printer. You must have heard."

Corina stepped back from her desk, as if from a blow. "What happened? How could they possibly get rid of Sam?"

"They're calling it early retirement."

"That's ridiculous." Corina's eyes shone with emotions that ran deeper than the polite concern Geri expected. "He's the best. Everyone knows it. He's always taken such pride in his work, his craft."

"It's wrong what the company's doing," Geri said. "He'll fight back."

"I hope so."

She'd been right about the eyes. Corina blinked back tears. Geri had to turn away. She'd done something mean, thoughtless. Hell's bells, she should have known. Sam always boasted that he trained Corina. Called her, "Kid," to her face. She'd blundered in without a thought for anyone's feelings. As usual.

Geri pushed back her glasses and stared up at Corina. "Sorry. I didn't mean to spring it on you. I just figured you'd heard. You still haven't located Bertram Electric, either, I take it."

"No."

"I was just leaving, but I'll postpone my appointment. If the sucker is anywhere on earth, I'll find it for you."

"You mean it?"

"You better believe it."

Corina wiped her eyes, lifted her chin. "Thanks."

Just that. One word. *Thanks*. It hit her in the heart. Geri shrugged. "No problem. It's my job."

"No, it's not. You know that, and I know that. Thank you, okay?"

"Okay," Geri said. "Cool beans. Now, let me get to work."

She rode the computer all afternoon trying to trace the company. The phone wasn't just disconnected; it didn't exist. The mail drop didn't, either. Geri started to e-mail Corina and let her know she'd run out of places to search, but realized that something more personal was in order. Instead she braved the phone on her desk.

"Thanks for trying," Corina said through the static. "And thanks for postponing your meeting, Geri."

"No problem, and don't feel bad about Sam. I hear he's going to file a grievance."

"I hope he does."

It wasn't a lie. She'd helped Sam write his statement. Although she shouldn't have told anyone yet, she owed Corina one. Of course she hadn't told her that the meeting she'd put off was with the group, or that she was on her way to join them right now.

It would probably be the last time. Corina was right. The dirty tricks weren't mature, and they hadn't uncovered anything to help their cause. She'd take part in this one last attempt to scare the crap out of management, but after that, she was finished.

Verna and Wally, the fired photographer, met her in the underground parking garage. Verna wore her security guard uniform. The photographer was dressed in similar attire.

"Where'd you get that?" Geri asked him.

Verna flashed her a smile. "Where do you think? If we're right about this, we'll get rid of Chenault and Dieser."

"And then what?" Geri asked. "More new managers?"

"But maybe better ones this time. They won't dare let something like this happen twice. Wally here will cover your back. You go in first. He'll be right behind you."

"I've never been in the corporate suite before."

"Chenault sure has. He reserved it every day last week and this one, too. And we don't have no one from corporate staying here."

"So what do you think they're doing?"

Verna grinned. "We can only hope, but whatever it is, you can bet it's something management don't know about. Wally here's going to take photos if there's anything good. You write down what they say."

Yeah, right. That's the job for me. "What if they don't say anything?" she asked, grappling to come up with a plausible reason, any reason, for backing out at the last moment.

"Oh, they will. We got the light switched jammed, so you'll be able to see everything they do, too."

Thank goodness for that. "Awesome possum," she said. *If you only knew,* she thought.

The corporate suite, located on the eleventh floor, rested directly below the hotel's rooftop bar. Geri and Wally entered through the back, the way the maids did. A long conference room, complete with refrigerator, portable bar and large-screen television, occupied most of it. The bedroom was tacked on like an afterthought, with its own bathroom. A locked linen closet in the conference room provided towels and sheets for the maids. That was where Geri and Wally were to hide.

Lights blazed in the room as they entered the closet. She looked through the louvered doors, taking in every detail of the room. What had she gotten herself into this time? If Chenault found her here, it would be her job. The old guy beside her had nothing to lose.

She turned to make out his figure in the darkness. No talking. That was the rule. He smelled of some supermarket aftershave. She felt sorry for him, standing here in this closet, holding on to the camera that had made his living for years. His wife was dying, and nobody cared. She'd do this one thing, for his sake, and for Sam the printer, and for the rest of the people who, like her former boss, Millie, were too old to find another employer.

The photographer nudged her. She felt him stiffen. They were there, in the room, someone was. She could feel their presence, felt the vibration of music. Someone had turned on music. Nobody she could really pick up like Peter Case, Van Morrison, or lord knows, Delbert McClinton. This felt more like Neil Diamond or one of the British one-hit wonder groups out of the sixties. Meaningful music for the masses.

A shape approached the closet where they stood. Geri watched the knob turn. She stood completely still, willing herself not to breathe. *Please,* she thought. The shape moved away. For several minutes, she could see nothing but the conference table with its perfectly arranged chairs, embossed with the *Valley Voice* logo, and its brass bowl of silk flowers.

Then someone came into view, stopping directly in front of the conference table. Geri drew in a breath. It was Ivy Dieser, buck-ass naked.

Forty

The photo, blown up to an eight by ten, was posted to the editorial bulletin board that Tuesday morning. Ivy Dieser, naked on the table in the corporate suite. Corina hadn't seen it, but the news was all over. A tearful Ivy had already torn it down by the time Corina arrived at work that day. She'd rushed from the building, and the staff speculated that she wouldn't return. Whoever had taken the photo had certainly sent a copy to the San Francisco office. Poison Ivy's career was over.

The news shocked Corina, but she had no time to engage in office gossip, not even something of this magnitude. A DEA source of Henderson's was flying in from Sacramento to meet with them that morning.

They caught up with Victor Martinez in the luggage-claim area of the airport. He looked older than his haircut and sunglasses, younger than his conservative navy slacks and white shirt. His face lit when he saw Henderson.

"It's been too long, man. How've you been? I was sorry as hell to hear about you and Sheila."

"I'm doing all right."

So this was more than a purely business relationship. Henderson introduced her to Martinez, and the three of them walked the length of the building together.

"Get you some coffee?" Henderson asked.

"Don't think I can stand another cup. Let's go outside. I have an appointment in a couple of hours."

"About this stuff?" Henderson asked.

"No." He adjusted his sunglasses, opaque-blue glass with sleek black frames. Corina guessed they cost more than everything else he was wearing.

"Are they trying to find the two agents?" she asked.

He gave her a sharp look. "I can't discuss our actions with you or anybody else. This is war."

"Looks like it's heading that way," Henderson said.

They stood outside, where the sound of the wind swallowed their words. Even in the shaded area, the heat hammered down.

"Airports," Martinez said. "I used to love them." They said nothing, letting him get used to their presence. Finally he spoke again. "I'm trusting you on this, Matthew."

"I know," Henderson said.

He looked at Corina. "I'm trusting you because he says I can."

She cut a look at Henderson. "That's one thing he told you that you can believe."

"I'm not making light of what's happened to those agents. Roxene Waite's a friend of mine. I've met Flannigan a few times."

"Do you think they're dead?" Corina asked.

He shook his head. "Not yet."

"Why do you say that?"

"Because we'd have heard about it. Whatever this is all about—it's bigger than just Roxene and Flannigan. They're part of something else."

"What's your guess, Victor?" Henderson asked.

"You're the guesser. I'm the facts-and-figures man. Here are the facts. Roxene and Flannigan disappeared three weeks ago in Ensenada. The same week two nuns disappeared from Santa Maria."

"Could be a coincidence," Henderson said.

"We don't think so." He leaned against the rail and removed his glasses. Lines of weariness outlined his eyes. "When Baja nationalized and threw out the Americans, those people didn't all come home. In fact, some of them haven't turned up yet. That's too many coincidences for me."

Henderson shifted, looked at her. "Corina and I have been working on a story about a builder who was killed. She found something in his files about your two agents."

"Just their names," she put in before Martinez could ask. "And a date. July 4. And a place. San Quintin."

Martinez's face froze.

"There's something else," Henderson said. "The builder who was killed was partners with a guy who may be sending large sums of money to a white-rights group. We ran into a dead end trying to trace the group. Our leads said Alabama and San Quintin."

Martinez shook his head. "It's worth a try," he

said, then broke into his first smile since he'd arrived. "You two are a hell of a team."

Henderson gave Corina a conspiratorial look. "I'll have to tell you that story one of these days," he said.

"Think they'll go to San Quintin?" Corina asked, after they had dropped Victor Martinez at his hotel.

"Probably. They treat cases like this individually. The agents are looked at as military personnel. In this case, it's more than a matter of taking care of their own. These other Americans who are missing—what do you think it means?"

"Something big," she said. "Something happening with Mexico."

Henderson glanced over at her. "War?"

The word chilled her with its truth. "If enough Americans were killed on the Fourth of July, would that be sufficient cause to push the president into action against Mexico?"

Henderson frowned. "It might, especially if Menlo keeps escalating the pressure on him."

"How much does it cost to charter a plane?"

He jerked his head toward her. "It's too dangerous. J.T. would never allow it."

"Who said anything about J.T.?"

"So you're suggesting we sneak down to Mexico, without telling anyone?"

"Just to go look around," she said. "Call in sick, take vacation time, whatever."

"I still think it's too dangerous. If anything, I should go alone."

"Do you even know where San Quintin is?"

"Baja, of course."

"But where in Baja? Do you know your way around down there?"

He jutted out his chin, but the confidence in his voice dropped a decibel. "Sure."

"And you can speak the language, of course?"

He shrugged. *"Poquito."*

"That's probably the only word you know, that and *cerveza*." The look on his face told her he knew she was only half kidding.

"Just in case you're keeping score, I got As in Spanish."

"How many years ago? Come on, Matthew. You know we have to do this. At least we have to try."

He sighed. "Without any backups?"

She hadn't thought that far ahead. This whole plan was hatching as they spoke. He pulled into the *Voice* parking lot, the car silent, waiting for her answer. "We'll have backups," she said.

He parked the car, turned to her, expectantly, his bloodshot eyes skeptical. "Oh?"

"You'll call Victor Martinez, tell him what we're doing. And I'll tell Geri LaRue."

"Geri LaRue? Why the hell would you tell her anything?"

"Because I trust her," she said.

"You're sure throwing your trust around these days, lady."

She met his gaze. "Yes," she said. "I am."

Forty-One

Geri sat facing her computer, clutching her mouse ball. In the past, Corina had considered only the part of Geri's job that affected herself—retrieving information. How many hours did it take to sit here and copy the pages of the newspaper into the electronic archives each day? In the old days, the editorial archives, then called the morgue, were compiled by librarians who cut out articles and put them in appropriately labeled envelopes. Geri wouldn't have fit in that world, where she might have to talk to somebody now and then.

Geri looked up with a start. "Hey you." Her smile was sheepish.

"Mind if I sit down for a minute? I need to talk to you."

Geri watched Corina's face intently as she told her what they were going to do. "Ultimately," she said, "we're not breaking company policy. And by not asking permission, we won't give management a chance to come up with any new rules."

"And you trust me with this?" Geri reached into

the Altoids tin on her desk, popped a mint in her mouth, and then another.

"Yes."

"I won't let you down," she said. "If you can get to those people in time, you might be able to turn it around."

"First we have to find out if there's anything going on in San Quintin. I just want you to know, in case something happens."

The meaning of her words registered in Geri's eyes. She seemed in a battle with herself, then she sighed and said, "Shit."

"What?"

"I know something that might help you, something I found out that night in the closet."

"What closet?"

"Up in the executive suite."

"Oh, no." She should have known. "Were you part of that?"

"For the last time, but, yeah, I was part of it. I could make you understand my reasons if you listened to my side of it. Want an Altoids?" She pronounced the word carefully, as if it were the first time she'd said it. Something was wrong, but Corina didn't have time to figure out what.

"What did you find in the closet?"

"Not find, saw. I saw Ivy Dieser."

"Apparently."

"This was way after that. She was saying how it would never work out, how she thought she should leave the newspaper."

"Was she talking to Chénault?"

"Yeah, although I couldn't see him very clearly. Ivy had a lot to say about you. Said at first she just thought you were a cost-cutting measure." Geri ducked her head, looked back up through the rectangular glasses with an apologetic smile.

Corina cringed. Geri shoved her wilted bangs from her forehead, as if what she'd just revealed had drained the life from them.

"I know, but just listen to me. She had her clothes on by then, and this was a serious conversation."

"Spare me the crass details."

"Just let me talk, will you? Ivy said she thinks you have the makings of an excellent reporter, that you're on to something with your idea about Eugene Belmont killing Tina Kellogg and Skin. Said you'd shared a lot of your ideas with her about the case, and she was going to back you all the way." Geri's eyes grew wide. "After what I helped them do to her, it won't happen now, will it?"

"No. Do you know what she's going to do?"

"She told someone she has a possible job in Oregon, that she's leaving right away."

"I'd like to see her before she goes." Corina stood. "Do you know where she lives?"

"I can find out." Geri turned to the computer as she spoke. "All editors have to have their addresses and telephone numbers listed now. Prepress will have it on their database."

Corina started to leave, then turned to Geri's desk. Her back was turned away from the computer, as she waited for a document to print. "There's something I want to know," Corina said.

Geri continued working.

"Geri," Corina said. Nothing.

She walked around the computer so that Geri could see her.

"What?" Geri asked, holding the piece of paper she'd just removed from the printer.

"How'd you lose your hearing?"

Her face flushed. She bit her lip. "An infection, when I was a kid."

"You read lips?"

She nodded. "Boy howdy, do I learn a lot that way."

"Why don't you tell anyone?"

Geri gazed at her through the rectangular glasses. "I think you know."

She didn't want to be treated differently, would rather be thought of as just a weird kid with purple hair who communicated via e-mail.

"Yes, I think I do."

"Deaf community doesn't accept me, either," Geri said, "on account of I have partial hearing. Now, that's a tight little world."

"Can you hear me right now?"

"Not too well, and when the radio's on, forget it. They gave me a hearing aid once, and I nearly went nuts tuning into all this stuff for the first time. The clock would tick, and I'd go out of my skull." She looked down on the papers on her desk, then up at Corina. "How long've you known? Did you see the equipment on my phone at home?"

"It was gradual. When I like someone, I want to understand them. It was the only thing that made sense."

"I don't mind if you know. I was going to tell you, anyway. I get a lot of my information that way, reading people's lips."

"You know that if you tell the company, they'll provide you with a special phone," Corina said.

"One area they are strong is recruiting employees with disabilities. You'd probably get a promotion out of it."

Geri's smile stiffened. "Would you want to get a promotion that way?"

"No, I guess not. Maybe I shouldn't have said anything, but I didn't want it standing between us."

"Neither did I. And I'm glad you came back." Geri handed her the paper she'd just taken from the printer. "Ivy Dieser's home address and phone number. I threw in the e-mail, too, free of charge."

"Think I got us a plane," Henderson said as Corina came into the office. "Hey, what's wrong?"

"Nothing, I hope. But I want to talk to Ivy Dieser before we leave."

He made a face. "Leave me out. As far as I'm concerned, the lady got exactly what she deserved."

"Matthew." She meant it as a plea. It came out a demand. "I need to go by her house. I told her a lot about this story. I want to be sure she doesn't share it with the wrong people."

"You didn't let her know we're going to Mexico?"

"Of course not." One step forward and two back. That was what working with Henderson was like. She'd about run out of patience. "When in the hell are you going to learn that you can trust me, Matthew?"

His expression didn't concede an inch. "About the same time you learn to trust me, I guess."

They glared at each other for a moment. "Damn, you're hardheaded," she said.

"There are two sides to that story." He stood and

began shoving notes into a folder. "If you want to stop by Ivy's, we'll stop by Ivy's. Just know that this woman's goal in life was to see me fired."

"She couldn't, though, could she?"

He shrugged and picked up the folder. "They don't want a lawsuit. If they're dead set on getting rid of me, there are easier ways."

"Like giving you a new assistant, for instance?"

His unhappy smile was the only answer she needed. "Exactly. On the other hand, it's been good for me."

"Good how?" she asked.

"I had a prof at J-school I'll never forget. If you were any good at all, he said, you had to edit with your hat on. It's a lesson I almost forgot, but not quite."

"Edit with your hat on? Does that mean cop out if things don't go your way?"

"It means to remember your values," he said, "and lately I've been doing just that. If it gets too crazy, I'd leave before I change who I am."

They didn't speak until they reached the parking lot. Henderson stood next to his dusty Honda, its surface radiating the heat it had soaked up in just a few hours. "You should remember it, too. Edit with your hat on. Write the same way."

"I hope you stay," she said, amazed to hear the words come out of her lips. "I could learn a lot from you."

His throat tightened as he swallowed. For a moment, he poised, his keys in his hands. "Let's go to Ivy's," he said.

Forty-Two

Ivy Dieser had never felt so sexless in her life. She knew now what her mother meant when she said she hoped she died before she lost her looks. Mom had done it, too, thanks to all the sun and cigarettes she'd soaked up back before anyone suspected that the trappings of glamour could also be deadly. Ivy hadn't been so lucky.

"My mother was a beautiful woman." She held the photo for Brandon to see before she placed it in the suitcase. "She was on the original *Perry Mason* show once, a small part, but if you saw the show, you'd remember her. White-blond hair swept to one side, almost over one eye."

"How did she die?"

"On the show or real life?"

"Both."

"Suicide, I guess. There are different types of suicide, you know."

Why did she feel so morbid? Because she was dealing with a death, she knew, the death of love. Regardless of what Brandon promised, he wouldn't follow her to Oregon. She had to just be grateful for the job he'd arranged for her and forget the rest. Learn to forget. Learn to stop hoping. That or end up like her mother.

She returned to the closet and pulled out a dress, the tags still on it. "I was going to wear this with you," she said.

"When?"

A tailored dress of winter-white. When the hell did he think?

"If we ever had a special occasion, a party or something." She zipped it into a garment bag and lay it on the outstretched suitcase.

"It's beautiful," he said. "Why didn't you ever show it to me?"

She looked down, humiliated by the hope she'd once felt. "I don't know. Maybe I was waiting for the right time."

"Maybe we'll still find that time."

"I don't think so, but that's okay." She tossed her head, trying to mimic her mother's laugh, her screw-you-all attitude. "I'll be fine, I really will."

She was happy for the distraction, any distraction but talk of love, talk of losing.

"It's not as if we're finished," he said. "I go to Portland all the time. I don't want to stay here after what's happened. I'm sick about it, sick about what's happening to you. They aren't all that happy about the publisher at the paper up there. I was born in Oregon, and I love it."

"Raised by your uncle," she said. "He looked just like you, your uncle Joseph."

"No, *I* look just like *him*." He got up, helped her carry another load.

"Might as well give this to you now." She went

to the closet and pulled out a box. "This was going to be your Christmas present. I know it's a bad omen, buying presents this far in advance, especially with a new relationship. So now it's a goodbye gift."

He opened the box. She watched his gray eyes fill with unreadable emotion as he studied the framed enlargement she'd made of his uncle and him, he on a bench, his uncle behind him. She'd tucked the original photo in the back of the frame. He lifted it out.

"Where'd you get this?" he asked.

"From that little box in your sock drawer where you keep the polaroids of us. I wanted to do something really special for you, Brandon. It never occurred to me that we would end like this."

"We're not ending." He pressed the frame against his chest.

"Do you like it?"

"Of course. I'm touched. You're one of the few people who know how much he meant to me."

"You mean a lot to me, too." Her voice caught. No, this wasn't the time to go mushy on him. "I need to finish packing," she said.

"Goodbye then, for now." He took her into his arms, pulled her to him so violently she could barely breathe. "I didn't realize how much I'm going to miss you. You added a new dimension to my life, something I didn't think I needed anymore."

So wistful and full of longing were his eyes that Ivy thought he might not be speaking to her at all. The look on his face broke her heart. "Don't, Brandon. Just go." He nodded, touched her cheek. "Go," she said, then turned so that he couldn't see the tears in her eyes. She heard the door close behind him, then finally let herself collapse into sobs.

She had just gotten up and washed her face when she heard the taxi driver's knock on the door. Now that was refreshing, she thought, an omen perhaps, for her new life. She'd expected an idiot, honking his horn from the curb. She opened the door ready to compliment the man on his manners. What she saw knocked the wind from her. A repulsive creature, skin albino pale, his neck so thick with scars that his head listed to one side, stood there lighting a cigarette.

"I'm sorry. You have the wrong place. I thought you were the taxi driver."

She started to close the door, but he reached it before she did. He put his foot in. The rest of him followed. "Oh, no, Miss Ivy Dieser," he said, his voice a husky whisper. "I got the right place, all right."

"What do you want?"

Before the question was out of her mouth, something sharp hit her in the stomach. She reached up to try to ease the splintering pain, but she couldn't find its source. She could see only the five round lightbulbs and the whirling ceiling fan around them. How had she ended up the on floor? Why was she covered with this sticky sweat? And this face floating above her, this fetid cigarette breath in her nostrils? What was going on?

"You have the wrong person," she said.

She heard the click of his lighter, saw the flare. No cigarette, though. What was burning? What was that nauseating smell? With great effort, she lifted her arm, reached up for her hair and screamed.

* * *

Wes started to drive home from the cemetery through the old part of town instead of taking the freeway. His father had told him to do so at least once a month. "It's the only way you'll really see the city changing," he had said.

Another promise he had trouble keeping.

The city had changed all right. Deteriorated was more like it. Old Victorians had evolved into apartment buildings. Prostitutes of both sexes stalked the road beside the railroad tracks like hungry dogs. Downtown sat rotting, waiting for a miracle that didn't seem likely given the current economy and the predators and unfortunates who had taken up residence there when the city had moved north.

It must have been even more difficult for his father to witness this decline. He'd helped build this town, had been raised in one of these neighborhoods it wasn't safe to walk now. Maybe that was what he wanted Wes to see, how improper planning can ruin a city, how rapidly poverty and crime can take over when too much focus is put on growth and not enough on preservation.

Usually visiting his parents' graves made him feel better, connected to the past and the future. Tonight, he just felt lonely. Corina was part of it, of course, most of it, if he were honest about it. She'd always been determined but now she was unreasonable, especially where her own safety was concerned. Or maybe he was just too close to understand why her job had become so important to her.

His cell phone rang beside him. He picked it up, and for some reason thought of Melissa Henson and the stupid tune her phone always played. He wished

there were something he could do to make up for
the way he had treated her.

Betsy Webster's sobs drowned out the rest of his
thoughts.

"Oh, Wes. God, I'm so scared."

"What's happened?" he asked. "Are you at
home? I'll be right there."

She continued to sob, barely able to speak. "A
man called me up, said if I wanted to live I better
get back that tape Skin sent your friend at the paper.
Said if I didn't, he'd burn me up, starting with my
hair."

"She doesn't even have the tape," Wes said.

"That's what she told you, but he sent it to her.
I know. Skin told me that last day we were together
that what he had on it could destroy all of The
Trio."

"Sounds as if they need to be destroyed."

"You might not agree on that one." She coughed,
then said. "I don't want to see good people get hurt,
Wes."

Ivy Dieser lived in one of those gated communi-
ties that used safety as one of its selling points, a
dicey proposition considering the current crime rate,
Corina had always thought. The security consisted
of a gate that gaped open when a card was passed
through a detector on the driver's side of the car.

"Some security," she told Henderson. "We could
crawl over that thing."

"We won't have to." He pulled aside as a car
approached the gate. The driver held out a small
object the size of a credit card, and the gate swayed

out before them. Henderson pulled in behind. The car in front of them went left. They headed right.

The ground-floor apartment had a security door with a decorative floral motif designed to let the tenant observe visitors from within. It stood open, as did the wooden door behind it. Corina jumped from the car as soon as Henderson stopped it.

"Wait," he said. "You don't know what's in there." But she could smell it, even from the parking space before the unit. An oily, combustible odor. The odor of something burning. Her stomach twisted. She knew who was involved in this, who had been here before them. She went ahead, although every instinct told her she was too late.

Ivy lay on the floor directly inside, two suitcases on either side of her. Her body, dressed in a pair of jeans and a shirt, was ablaze, reduced to a pyre. She was the kindling which was supposed to ignite the rest of this unit. How many people would she have taken with her? Was there a chance, even now, to save her, to drag her out of this smoky stench into fresh air, away from the flames? Gagging on fumes, Corina moved forward. Henderson grabbed her arm.

"There's nothing we can do."

"We've got to try." She looked at the inanimate form before her and knew he was right.

She pulled away from him and turned toward the door that still stood ajar. Her eyes stung, but she fought to keep her voice steady. "We'd better call someone," she said.

Forty-Three

The flag in the parking lot was already at half-mast when Corina arrived at work that day. It was the traditional way to observe the death of an employee, and the diverse, often fractious newspaper staff, from credit union to circulation, came together at such times.

The chairman of the board of directors and two other members had arrived from San Francisco that morning on the corporate plane. Brandon Chenault was nowhere to be seen. Rumor was he had not come in. Finally corporate would be forced to deal with the problem they'd created in hiring him in the first place.

Already, meetings were being set up with department managers. The consensus was the appointment of J. T. Malone to managing editor would boost morale and rally the spirits of the team in the newsroom. Corina spoke with J.T. briefly, and she and Henderson put together the story of Ivy's murder.

"You've talked to the cops?" J.T. asked.

"Yes," Henderson said with a grim smile. "Listen, man, we need to get out of here early tomorrow.

We think we're getting close on the Skin Burke murder.''

"Then go," J.T. said. "Take as much time as you need. I appreciate the way the two of you are working as a team now."

They glanced at each other. Neither of them told him where they were going, knowing that especially now, he'd have to demand that they cancel their plans. No chance of that. They were taking the only possible action. And as Henderson pointed out, they had backup. A DEA agent and a research librarian, who had at least enough circumstantial evidence to link Eugene Belmont's operation with a white-rights group.

They stood together in the parking lot, looking up at the flag.

"Poor woman," Corina said. "Why did they have to kill her?"

Henderson shook his head. "Just be glad they think you have something they want."

She'd been thinking the same thing, but to hear it spoken chilled her. She turned away from the flag and started for her car. "I'm going to go home, get something to eat and call my mom." She paused, not wanting to admit the rest of it—that she had to talk to Wes. "I have a couple of other things I need to take care of before we leave tomorrow."

"Don't bother coming back this afternoon." He reached for his pack of cigarettes. Damn it. He'd guessed.

"Wes left messages for me here and on my cell," she said, defending herself from his unspoken accusation. "I've got to call him. I should have sooner."

He nodded. "Just be careful what you say."

Didn't he have any confidence in her? "You be careful what you say, too," she fired back, then stormed toward her car before she could tell him what a paranoid asshole he was.

Parental Guilt Call 926

"You're going where, *Mija?*"

"To Baja, on business, leaving tomorrow morning. I won't be gone long, and I'll call you as soon as I get back."

"You're not going with this divorced man, this boss of yours, are you?"

"Don't worry, Mama. This trip's very important to the story I'm working on. It's important, period."

"My daughter is going to Mexico with a man, and I'm not supposed to worry. Tell me, then, how is that possible?"

Gee, Mama, I don't know. I'm a little worried, too, but not about traveling with Henderson.

"You need to trust me."

"You shouldn't be going down there now with all the trouble."

"It's for a couple of days, that's all."

"I just sent you some fabric samples for the wedding."

"I'll get them when I come back. By the way, I have a new condo address now. It's 1236 instead of 1234, but I'll still be able to get my mail."

"A new address? Why?"

I'll have to tell you about that one sometime, Mama.

"I moved, but I'm still in the same complex. This place is just nicer, that's all."

"You need to settle down, *Mija,* have your own home. I'm still getting mail for you here. I sent a bunch of it along with the samples, since I didn't know the next time you would come to visit."

"I'll come just as soon as I get back, okay?"

"Okay, then."

"Bye, Mama."

"*¿Mija?* This divorced man, this boss of yours. Does he respect you?"

"*Does he respect me?*"

"*Sí,* that's what I said."

"Yes, Mama. Yes, I guess he does."

"That's some comfort, then. Goodbye, *Mija.*"

"Goodbye, Mama."

The conversation had made Corina jumpy. Must have been Mama's off-the-wall question about whether Henderson respected her. No, that wasn't it. She had just started packing when it hit her. She reached for the phone, her skin crawling.

Her mother sounded surprised to hear her. "Are you all right, *Mija?*" she asked. "Your voice sounds funny."

"I wanted to ask you about what you sent me," she began. "What exactly was it?"

"The fabric samples for your bridesmaid's dress. You won't like the color at first, but you'll get used to it, and you'll get to choose your own headpiece."

"No, not that. You said you had a bunch of mail."

"Well, not a big bunch." She paused, trying to remember the items the bridesmaid fabric obviously overshadowed in her mind. "Just that builder magazine you pay so much for, and some other letters, and a little package that came to you here a couple of weeks ago.''

She could barely breathe. Skin had used her parents' address, where she had lived when she first met him. He had known no one would think to check there. "Mama," she said, trying to keep her voice from trembling. "That package. Was it a tape of some kind?"

"Could have been." Her voice grew defensive. "You know I would never read your personal mail, *Mija.*"

Corina called Henderson and told him.

"Holy shit," he said. "What are you going to do?"

She couldn't stay here waiting for her mail. That was for sure. "I'm going back down to the paper right now and give Geri LaRue the key to my old condo," she said. "As soon as the tape arrives, she can turn it over to the police."

And, she thought, whether Henderson liked it or not, she was going to call Wes and tell him she was okay and that she was leaving town. She couldn't let him worry any longer. On the way to the newspaper, she tried his cell phone, but got no answer. His secretary at City Hall said he was attending the opening of the Hmong Cultural Center. She had time to catch him if she hurried.

First, she stopped at the newspaper and went straight to the editorial library.

Geri sat at her desk, headphones on, holding half a tuna sandwich. When she saw Corina, she shoved the sandwich in her lunch bag and took off the headphones. The glasses she wore couldn't hide her swollen eyes.

"I still can't believe it," she said. "I've been kicking my ass since I heard the news, hating myself for what I did to hurt that woman."

"Don't blame yourself." Corina sat in front of her so that Geri could watch her lips. "Having an affair with the publisher wasn't enough to get her murdered."

"Why?"

"Because of the way she was murdered." Corina remembered the oily smoke again, and almost gagged. "That man, Whiplash. He's into fire, a pyro. He's probably the one who killed Skin and Mayor Kellogg. Ivy's death is connected to theirs, not to her affair with Chenault."

"That makes me feel better, but not much." She nodded toward the bag. "You had lunch yet?"

"I'm fine," Corina said. "I came because I have a major favor to ask."

"Ask it, and you've got it."

"I knew you'd say that. The tape everyone's been trying to find is going to be dropped through the mail slot of my old condo in a day or two."

Geri squinted at her lips. "Come again?"

"Skin sent the tape to my folks' home," Corina said. "My mom mailed it to my old condo."

"No shit." Geri ran both hands through her purple spikes.

"Here's the tricky part. Henderson and I are flying to Mexico tomorrow." She reached into her wallet and took out the key. "This unlocks the condo. The mail comes through a drop in the front door."

"You trust me to handle this?" Geri watched her lips carefully.

"You're the *only* one I trust. It could be dangerous, though. That tape is what Whiplash and whoever hired him are after. They'd kill for it in a heartbeat."

"But they trashed your place once. They won't think to trash it twice."

"That's what I'm hoping."

Geri took the key from her. "Cool beans. I'll take care of that tape for you. Might take care of something else, too, while I'm at it."

"Like what?" Corina asked.

Geri shook her head. Put on her headphones again. Reached into the bag for her sandwich. "Nice thing about my disability," she said. "When you're through listening, you don't have to anymore. Good luck in Mexico, okay?"

That's all she was going to get from Geri, and it was more than enough. Corina nodded, mouthed a "Thank you," and got out of her space.

The Cultural Center was only a few blocks from the newspaper. Women in vivid dresses displayed their embroidered handiwork, while their male counterparts smoked cigarettes and visited among themselves.

The Hmong had settled in the Valley in the late seventies because of its resemblance to their homeland and because the welfare laws allowed them to collect aid.

People like Eugene Belmont, who wanted them out pointed to the problems many of their young people caused with gangs and car jackings. They called them Vietcong and said they paid no taxes and lived like cockroaches. Those, like Wes, who felt they should stay, reiterated that they had been uprooted by the Vietnam War, or as they called it, the American War, stripped of the only homes they knew.

Corina spotted Wes at once. He wore the white linen shirt and unstructured spice-colored jacket he'd had on the first night they'd made love in the new condo, the night Whiplash had destroyed her home.

"Where have you been?" he demanded when he saw her. "I tried to call you all night. My God. What happened?"

"I was at the paper most of the time. It was horrible, Wes. We found Ivy's body, Matthew and I."

He put his arm around her, pulled her close to him, almost angrily. "When are you going to realize your life's more important than a newspaper article?"

Ivy's death had unnerved him. Corina pulled away, trying to reason with him. "It's not just an article," she said. "It's much, much bigger. But I didn't come here to discuss that. I came to let you know I'm okay."

He paused before a display of jackets embroidered in emerald and red. "The Hmong believe a story is sewn into each design," he said. "When you buy the jacket, you buy the story, as well." He lifted a silken sleeve. "Would you really want to buy anyone else's story?"

Something was wrong. Something more immediate than Ivy's murder. "Wes? What is it?"

He dropped the sleeve. "People are getting killed right and left. Please listen to me, just this once."

"If we don't find out what's going on, there's going to be a war with Mexico," she said. "It's that simple."

"That's going to happen, anyway. Menlo's already gearing up for it. He's planned a big press conference for next week, a direct challenge to the president."

"Menlo can be stopped," she said, keeping her voice low and controlled.

"You're wrong." He turned, gave her what she used to think of as the love look. Only the look had changed, or maybe she had. "How long are you going to keep this up? Until you find that tape?"

They stepped through the front door of the center into the blazing sun. But her body was cold all over. "I've found it."

"You can't have. Where?"

She started to tell him, but something kept her from it. "I can't reveal that right now, and I don't have the tape in my possession yet."

"Don't risk your safety for it." He stood beside her, looking out at the parking lot, his eyes so full of sorrow that for a moment she thought he might weep. Guilt. That's what she saw in his face. She knew it now, had seen it before. A nauseating feeling hit her in the gut, the way it had the first time she realized he'd betrayed her. She looked at his pained expression and took a breath. Let her be wrong. Let her be right. Let her find out the truth, damn it, now.

"Wes," she said, "what do you know about all this?"

"Not much." His eyes, once his best feature, looked dead. "I talked to Betsy, though. Skin told her about the tape, called it their insurance. She's convinced he sent it to you.''

She nodded, not wanting to explain that Betsy was right. "What else did she say?''

He took her arm again. "How much do you love me?''

Corina shook herself free. "What else did she say, Wes? What the hell's on that tape?''

"According to Betsy, some pretty nasty stuff.''

"About you?''

"No, of course not.''

She stood facing him, trying to make sense of what could upset and distract him this much, even more than his concern about her safety. Only one thing, only one person.

"Oh,'' she said. "Nasty stuff but not about you. About your dad.''

He didn't have to answer. She could see it in his face. "You have to understand about him. He was the finest man I ever knew, and in some ways, the most flawed.''

"Was he involved with any of this, Wes?''

"Of course not.''

Good. That would be a tough call. "I have to go now,'' she said. "We'll talk when I get back.''

"Get back? Where are you going?''

Before he could stop her or ask more questions, she got into her car. There was no way now she could tell Wes she was going to Mexico.

Skin
Sunday, June 3, 7:10 a.m.

A man has to protect himself, his woman. No, don't think about women, not now. Just get this stuff down, make the bastards pay. It's a beauty, this thing, no bigger than a pencil and shorter. No way they'd guess. Only turns on when there's activity in the room, and I'll bet the natives were active last night. Got it all down. Let's see how bad it is, if it's enough to nail those maniacs, enough to save my ass.

"The Treaty of Guadalupe Hidalgo," Craig Menlo looks directly into the camera. "We signed it back in 1848, and we gave away the store."

"We'd captured Mexico City." Nan Belmont paces in and out of range, carrying a tumbler of what looks like bourbon. Her husband, Danny, follows her, hands at his back, handsome face set with its usual inquisitive expression. "The treaty provided for fifteen million dollars in damages," Nan says, "and they had to cede fifty-five percent of the territory including California. Those pussies under Polk could have had the whole thing. As a result, we have out-of-control drug traffic, everything from auto parts to kids being sold at the border." She stops, takes a breath.

"And our grandchildren are all going to grow up speaking Mexican," Menlo says.

"Spanish."

"No, Mexican. It's not just a language. It's a culture. This is the only way we can take our land back."

Nan steps in front of the camera again, sips from her glass. "I detest bloodshed, you know that. Daddy does, too."

"With all due respect, your dad's the one who started all this. If he hadn't gone to jail for Joe Congdon way back when, he wouldn't have had the money to put the right people in office and get the ball rolling."

"Don't you dare blame him. If it hadn't been for his hearing, he would have fought in World War II. He knows the realities of war, and so do Danny and I. But we abhor senseless killing."

"Like it or not, it's part of war," Menlo says.

Nan turns to face him. "You're scaring me, Craig. I get the feeling you enjoy this. Tina Kellogg, for instance. We could have bought her off."

"I told you I don't know what happened to Tina Kellogg."

"And I told you I don't believe you."

"Ask Whiplash."

"I'd rather not. We both know who gives his orders."

"That jellyfish." Menlo gets up from the sofa. For a moment, only the sounds of liquid on ice activate the tape. "What about Burke?"

"He's a problem," Nan says, and to her husband, "don't you think, Danny?"

"A problem," Danny repeats. His blank expression hasn't changed since the camera has been on him.

"Skin's been losing it since Tina disappeared, thinks we're a bunch of murderers."

"See what I mean?" Menlo says. "Skin was on our side all the way before. He helped put as many people in office as we did. Then we get close to something big, and he decides to start a new life. He's as much a turncoat as old Wes Shaw."

"Don't even talk about that bastard." Nan's face hardens in a look of pure hatred. "Nothing I hate more than a fucking hypocrite. Wes Senior was the biggest."

Menlo laughs. "At least he died of natural causes."

"But not before he convinced little Wessie that my father was the nasty bigot. Anyone can change his ways when he's staring cancer in the face. Before then, he was happy as a clam to support the cause."

"Wes Senior wasn't a bad guy," Danny says.

Nan glares at her husband. "He was a bastard. He made it look as though my father were some kind of monster, when old Wes himself was the biggest bigot of all."

"Bias aside." Craig Menlo moves past Nan, then returns with a full glass. "I'm going to raise hell about the events that will soon take place in Mexico. Come July Fourth—" He crosses his arms across his chest and squeezes his chin between his thumb and forefinger. "I see no other way but execution."

"Innocent people," Danny murmurs. "It's not right, honey."

"Shh," Nan says. Then to Menlo, "How many?"

"Enough to get the president to move. Enough to take back Mexico."

"Meaning, what? Five? Ten? One hundred? I want specifics, Craig."

"As many as it takes. The DEA agents, the nuns, the American property holders. Come July Fourth, they die. The Mexican government is implicated, and the president has no choice."

"Which brings us back to Burke." Nan sighs, as if the question is too complicated for her.

Menlo rattles the ice in his glass and nods. "Poor Skin. I don't trust him anymore. Do you?"

"That doesn't mean we have to do anything drastic. We have enough on him that we can let him go quietly and start that new life he keeps talking about."

"Our associate doesn't agree with you."

"Of course not. Our associate is the one who found Whiplash in the first place. Our associate is probably the one behind Tina's disappearance." She gave Menlo a speculative look and took a sip from her still-full glass. "Unless my first guess is right, and you're the guilty party."

"Your first guess is wrong," he says. "And you're wrong about Skin Burke, too. He doesn't want just a happy little life away from us anymore. He wants to avenge whatever he thinks happened to Tina."

"Bullshit." Nan's tone doesn't ring true.

"He does, and he will. Your father will be his first target, Madame Senator. You ready for that?"

Forty-Four

Thursday, June 28, 12:30 p.m.

Corina no longer doubted Henderson. She had to tell someone what Wes had shared with her about his dad. Henderson was the likely candidate.

"I'm not surprised," he said, as they drove to the airport. "Everyone loved Wes Senior, yet he was involved in too much to be as clean as he appeared. What do you think is on that tape? What does Wes think is on it?"

"He isn't concerned about himself." She felt compelled to say that. "He's just worried about how his dad's going to come across."

"But Wes Senior was dead when Skin made the tape, wasn't he?" Henderson dug in his shirt jacket for his pack of cigarettes.

"Yes." She opened her window a crack. "So, I'm not sure how badly his reputation would be hurt by the tape."

"Maybe the Webster woman was overreacting. She seems the type."

"Maybe," Corina said. "We'll just have to find out when we get back. In the meantime, what's this flight going to cost us?"

"It's not cheap, but I phoned six charter services and got the best rate I could on short notice."

"They'll have to reimburse us, regardless of the outcome," Corina said, then laughed. "I just realized that I no longer know who *they* are anymore."

"That's why God invented American Express," Henderson said. "No matter how you figure it, the pilot alone will run us about a grand a day, but it beats the hell out of driving. We'll be there in a few hours."

"Sold," she said.

"I didn't even know you could fly into San Quintin," Henderson shouted above the roar of the plane.

They sat facing each other in the five-passenger Beech Bonanza. It had been a high, smooth flight, and as the aircraft begin to dip out of the sky, she could see they were nearing their destination. "It's down there," she said, pointing.

She looked down and saw it below them, a brown brushstroke between the blues of the ocean. It was the last of the tourist towns on the coast before the highway went down and over to the Sea of Cortez, its bays one of the largest on the west coast of Baja.

"You spend much time here?" he asked, raising his voice above the din of the engine.

"Just passed through a few times. It's mostly agricultural. A lot of fishing, clamming."

"Good place to get lost in."

"People do it all the time."

From the border, it would have been a four-hour drive, shorter if she were driving. Soon it would be developed as a tourist area, complete with waterfront homes, a golf course, a marina, and those who

wanted to keep a low profile would have to head
farther south.

They sat back in their seats as the plane landed
and came to a halt in front of the small airport ter-
minal. Regular airline service was not a part of the
San Quintin airport, but the facilities could support
a number of private and corporate jets. Corina hoped
Martinez had gotten here ahead of them.

The odor of burning asphalt stung her nostrils,
reminding her of the stench at Ivy's still fresh in her
memory. Corina followed Henderson off the wing
step and onto the ground.

Even in late afternoon, the sun was relentless.

"Where do we start?" Henderson asked.

"We need a car, and my guess is we'll find one
in that direction. The Baja Highway is over there,
and it kind of divides the town. We need to get to
Bahia San Quintin. That's the inner bay, past the
military camp. If we don't turn up anything there,
we'll try Bahia Falsa."

"False Bay?"

"Very good. You did study your Spanish. It's the
outer bay. Not as deep as the inner bay but wide.
Just a few gringo homes on the peninsula. Unless
they're in one of those, I don't think they'll be on
that side."

She shifted into her Mexico gear, but the slow
pace of the country battled her need to find what had
happened to the agents. Henderson was worse. He
must have thought he could dash into the nearest
Avis and snap his fingers.

He surprised her with Spanish far better than she'd
expected. He wasn't afraid to use it, either, even
when he had to struggle for a word or phrase. Mo-

mentarily she wondered why he'd never before used it around her. Probably something to do with political correctness. She let him handle the car-rental details, complete with the exchange of money and the compliments about his *señora muy bonita*.

"At least maybe we'll get some service," he said, after the two men were out of earshot. "Those two were damn near salivating over you."

"Probably haven't seen a woman in years," she said.

"Yeah, that must be it."

A long wait, and the car had yet to materialize.

"Maybe they didn't think you were so good-looking, after all," he said.

"Get used to it. If you think this is a long wait, try going into a restaurant and ordering something to eat."

Henderson lit his umpteenth cigarette of the day. "Food's the last thing on my mind. I feel like I've drunk a gallon of coffee."

"You have." She stretched on the wooden bench, smelled the ocean, looked up at a sky so blue and innocent it was difficult to believe it could be witness to the evil occurring beneath it.

He took another deliberate drag, his skin lobster red beneath the sun, the stubble of whiskers starting to show against it, a burnished shadow. "So have you."

In another twenty minutes, they had their rental, an old Jeep with more miles on it than Henderson had on him. After a momentary dispute as to who would drive, he got behind the wheel and headed through town and past the military camp, west of the highway. The road reached a dead end at the Old

Mill Motel launch ramp on the long inner bay. Miles south, it would open into the main bay. They got out of the car and went into the nearby restaurant.

A stern woman in an ill-fitting dark apron informed them that they were too late for lunch, too early for dinner. Corina tried to ask if she'd seen other Americans in the area, but the woman told her she could not be bothered with foolish questions and headed back to her kitchen before Corina could ask another.

Farther along the bay, a second restaurant stood with its door open. They walked inside, and the screen door rattled shut behind them. It had only a single latch, the sign of someone with great faith or little to steal.

Inside, a long gray cat strolled across the tops of the wooden picnic tables, all unoccupied. She breathed in the blended aromas of seafood and long-simmered herbs.

"Pescado," Henderson said.

"You trying to impress me, Matthew?" She walked ahead of him toward the only other person in the restaurant and approached the lone inhabitant, a well-fed man with a bald head and a jovial manner that reminded her of her father when he was in a good mood.

Did she and the Americano wish to try the lobster quesadillas? he inquired. The lobster was fresh. The crab, too.

No wonder the cat looked so pleased with itself.

She thanked him and explained that they would return later. What they needed to know was whether he had seen other Americanos in the area.

His face darkened, and he stepped back, taking a

better look at her. Such a beautiful woman, he said, to be so full of questions. He hoped that she was not here to cause trouble in their peaceful community.

"No trouble," she said in Spanish. "I'm looking for my friends."

"The only Americans I have seen here would not be friends of yours," he replied.

"A man and a woman?"

"Not many couples have stopped here recently."

"I have a photograph of them." She took the snapshots of Waite and Flannigan from her purse.

He shook his head. "I would remember them. Since the trouble started, few Americans stay here long except the gringos with homes up there." He nodded in the direction of the peninsula. "And the ones who stay out on their boats. Fishermen."

Or those involved in the traffic of drugs. No need for him to say that. They all understood. He was, indeed, like her dad, a decent man, but a restaurateur, who knew how to play to a crowd regardless of its size. A master of understatement. She could feel Henderson's anxiety building, just as it had as they waited for the Jeep.

"The Americans left after the trouble began?" she asked.

"Yes, yes. No one here right now, except people who should not be. They come on the plane." He made a face. "Rude Americans who drink too much and complain about the service." He studied Henderson as if trying to decide if he might qualify.

"Ask him about Whiplash," Henderson said, but Corina had already began describing the man with the deep scars on his neck.

The man narrowed his eyes. "You DEA?"

"Newspaper reporters," Corina said. "We're trying to stop the man you saw."

"Go back to your newspaper. He and the other are no good."

"Are they here now?"

"No, not for a week, maybe more."

"Where do they stay?"

He shrugged. "I don't know. La Pinta, maybe. Perhaps one of the gringo houses."

"And this other man? Can you describe him?"

"Tall." He looked at Henderson. "Taller than he is and bigger. I knew they were bringing trouble here. The other Americanos were getting out, and they were coming in. Like rats. Now you should go, too, before they come back."

"First we have to find these people," Corina said, lifting the photos once more.

"Try La Pinta. That's the biggest hotel. Now go, please."

Corina thanked him and said, "We'll see you for dinner, if we're still here."

"No, no dinner," he said. "I knew those rats were bringing trouble."

As she and Henderson walked down the wooden steps, she saw the Closed sign appear in the window.

They drove the dirt road, the Jeep bucking in spite of Henderson's newfound skill. At least he had figured out how to drive down here.

The road ended abruptly, and they turned onto a real, honest-to-god street. Ragged trees on each side met in the middle, forming an archway and dimming the harsh sunlight.

"Tamaracks," Henderson said.

"How do you know that?"

"We had them on the ranch where I grew up."
She wouldn't have guessed him for a farm kid and
gave him a look that must have told him so. "We're
not all bigots," he said.

"I know. I'm just surprised. Tamaracks. They're
lovely."

It was like driving into a telescope bordered in
green. The trees at the other end looked too narrow
to pass through, but they did.

The hotel stood before them, alone on the beach.

"La Pinta," Henderson said. He reached for his
backpack, where she knew he kept a gun.

"You think we'll need that?"

"If they're inside, they aren't alone."

And to that, she had no answer.

The desk clerk was a handsome kid in his early
twenties with striking green eyes. His abrupt manner
underscored his words, spoken in a lilting, lisping
language that had its origins in Spain.

"I have no time to talk to you."

She reached for her photographs. "We're looking
for these Americans. It's very important that we find
them."

"It's very important that I find some customers."
He gave her a forced smile, revealing even teeth.
This was no poor laborer scratching for his next
meal. More like a rich kid on summer break.

"Do you own this hotel?"

His smile grew wider. "I am the manager. Without customers, I lose my job." He hadn't bothered
to glance at the photos. Beside her, she felt Henderson reach into his jeans.

"Would you like some customers?" The harsh
sound of his voice, combined with the sound of En-

glish, exploded off the tile and dark walls. He placed his wallet on the counter.

"But, of course." The answer came in English, as well.

"We'll be paying cash." Henderson began to count out bills.

"Cash is always nice."

"Two rooms. That okay with you?"

He nodded, catching on. "But you'd like me to show you the hotel, perhaps? Take a look around?"

"Right," Henderson said, "assuming you can leave your desk right now."

"Are you kidding?" He glanced at the lobby with disdain. "No one wants to stay here with all this shit coming down with the Americanos." He looked at Corina and tried to regain a modicum of his earlier attitude. *"Perdón."*

She nodded and let Henderson continue. "Have you ever seen the folks in these photographs?"

"Sure have, but it's been a while. Separate rooms, upstairs. The lady likes to run on the beach early in the morning. The man is *mucho Americano*. Bacon and eggs, prime rib, that kind of thing. I can't remember their names." Corina looked down. Somewhere in the course of the conversation, the bills disappeared from the counter, but the antiquated cash register remained silent.

"Roxene Waite and Norm Flannigan," she said.

"DEA, right?"

"Posible." She spoke it in Spanish before she remembered, then corrected herself. "It's possible."

"Doesn't matter to me, lady. I can usually spot them, is all. Let me show you those rooms now."

They walked the entire length of the hotel, which

felt vacuous, no, more than that. Abandoned. On the second floor, he stopped and reached for his oversize key chain.

"Here's the room she liked. Flannigan usually stayed down the hall. Now, if it had been me—" He turned around to look at Henderson. "And before you ask, no, I don't think they're a couple. I'm not even sure they like each other."

"Why's that?" Henderson asked.

"I don't know. She's a looker, into fitness, asking what the fuck oil her breaded clams were fried in." This time he didn't apologize, unaware of what he'd said, just chatting with buddies. Corina remembered what a professor of hers had once said about investigative reporting. "Make the source your new best friend."

"And Flannigan is different than that?"

"Way different. Older, I think. Likes his booze, likes the sound of his own voice. But the times they were here, they always seemed to work together okay, you know what I mean?"

Corina glanced back at Henderson. "Sounds like an odd couple to me."

Henderson responded with an ironic smile. Then he said, "Let's see this pleasure palace."

The room, although large, was something from a Mexican monster movie. Crude panes of colored glass surrounded the mirror, the lamps and the lights behind the bed. It was as if the artisan had attempted to reproduce an extraordinary sunset using the most ordinary of objects.

"Is this original art?" Corina asked.

"Matter of fact it is. We get it cheap down here. Bathroom's this way. I've got to warn you. Don't be surprised if there isn't any hot water. It goes out a lot.''

The tiled shower was as large as another room. They walked to the balcony and looked down. The beach stretched in both directions as far as Corina could see. There was absolutely no one on it, not a soul. She shivered inside her flimsy top.

''Cold?'' Henderson asked.

She turned from the balcony and its deceptively peaceful view. ''No. There's just something about this place.''

Henderson turned to the clerk and put out his hand. ''I'm Matthew, by the way. This is Corina.''

''Juan.'' His hand reached for hers. It felt like a soggy paper towel.

''Look, friend,'' Henderson said. ''We want to find these people. It's worth a lot of money to us.''

''I wish I could help.'' He grinned. ''And, to tell you the truth, I could use some cash. My old man wants a p-and-l statement for every peso he doles out.''

Henderson touched his pocket where the wallet rode. ''Can't you tell us anything at all?''

''Maybe tomorrow, my friend.''

Corina stepped between them. ''Why not now? He paid you, didn't he?''

''It's just that it's late. My father will be here at any moment. My apologies, but I cannot talk to you any longer.'' He smiled at Corina, then stretched the smile to Henderson. ''These are probably the safest rooms in the area. Be glad that you can sleep without fear, my friends.''

Forty-Five

She didn't sleep without fear. She didn't sleep at all, even knowing that Henderson was in the room next to hers. After a cold, restless night, they stood at the front desk, ready to hold Juan to his promise. He looked alert and relaxed. Corina guessed his father had left him alone with the hotel again, and that he was eager to return to his newest money-making scheme. Them.

"We need to know more about those people we were discussing," she said. "Norm Flannigan and Roxene Waite."

Juan took a swig from a glass of something the color of orange juice. "I was down in Cabo in May. I don't know when they were here last, but I can check the register for you. That ought to be worth something."

Henderson nodded. "Ever see a guy with scars around his neck, his head tilted over to one side?"

Juan stopped in the act of reaching for the twenty Henderson extended to him. "You know that crazy bastard?"

"We're just interested in what he's doing here."

"Getting drunk, for one. I saw him at a bar a couple of nights ago. He's a wild man." He tried to laugh, but it came out more of a dry cough. "Dude takes out his lighter and burns this chick on the arm, just 'cause she won't dance with him. Can you believe it?"

"Does he stay here when he's in town?"

"No way. My dad would kill me if I let him in the place." He grinned. "No, Whiplash used to stay at the Old Mill Hotel, but they closed it last year for repairs and haven't opened up yet. Don't know where he is, except maybe one of the haciendas."

"You saw him at a bar here?" Corina asked. The mention of his name made the hotel feel even colder.

"Sure did. Even the Mexicans know what Whiplash means. His neck's really messed up, but let me tell you, don't ever ask him about it. He's touchy, to say the least. Threatened to burn that chick's legs off."

"Thanks," Corina said. "But, you see, we can't leave until we find him or until we can locate these two people."

He seemed to sniff the air, anticipating greater rewards. "Check back with me, and I'll let you know what comes down."

"This is serious." Henderson's voice left no doubt as to the fact. "Do you know where they are or not?"

"Hey, man. I just work here. But if I were you—" He eyed the twenty. "I'd try the Old Mill. After that, I'd go to Costa Azul in town. They still have disco on Sundays."

"Disco?" Corina asked.

"Yeah." He shrugged and took the money. "Whiplash likes to dance."

Forty-Six

The coast was wicked cool. Hard to believe it was less than three hours from the San Joaquin. It felt older, more relaxed, less angry than the tightly knotted city Geri had just left. Pismo Beach, said the sign. She remembered something she'd read about the name. Pismu, the tarlike substance the Native Americans found along the beach.

Nathan rode with his golden head out the window, drinking in the ocean air. They'd made good time, even though she'd waited to leave until after Corina's mail arrived. Still nothing from her mother. It would probably arrive Monday, and by then Corina would be back. She hoped.

"We'll get you out on the beach in a minute," she said. "Maybe if you like it here, we'll get out of the Valley, I'll find a job at the *Pismo Gazette* or whatever."

He paid no attention, just panted out of the window. Even her piddly salary was higher than what the coastal papers paid, and she wanted to stay in newspaper. At least she thought she did.

Lawrence waited for her down by the pier, his

board leaning against a row of benches. He had
dressed in cutoffs and a khaki shirt the color of his
eyes. For a moment she was glad she'd worn the
one pair of decent shorts she owned, then chided
herself for the thought.

"Right on time," he said. Nathan tore off into the
surf, biting at the waves. He'd been that way the
first time he'd ever seen water, as if born already
knowing what it was and how to navigate it.

"Nathan, back," she called.

"Classy name for a dog," he said.

"Mutt City. The name's good for his self-
esteem." She looked him over, trying to decide if
he'd just gelled his hair back or actually been out
on his board. "You surf?"

He glanced down at the board. "All the time."

"You any good at it?"

"Not really. What about you?"

She shook her head. "Never saw the ocean until
I was twenty years old. I can't even swim."

"Where the hell were you raised?"

She turned away, watching Nathan bounding back
across the sand. "Fosters."

"Fosters?"

"Homes. Foster homes. Didn't have a hell of a
lot more fun than you probably did living with your
grandmother in Morro Bay, pissed off you didn't
have parents of your own."

He stepped back as if her words had knocked him
off balance. "You're not really one of Betsy Webster's neighbors, are you?"

She patted Nathan's wet head and released him to
romp toward the ocean once again. "I'm afraid that
was a fib I made up the night I met you. It was the

only way I could think of to get into Betsy's. I work for the *Valley Voice*."

"Reporter?"

"Editorial librarian."

"Chick from there came to see me. She knew I'd been to Betsy's."

"She didn't find out from me. I haven't told anyone I was there."

"Why were you there?"

Her rat-fuck group sounded too petty compared to what had happened since that visit where she and Lawrence had met. "Guess you could say I didn't trust Corina. Wanted to see what she was up to."

"I didn't tell her you were there."

"Doesn't matter now. We're friends."

"Then why are you here? I told her everything I know."

"No, you didn't." She stared him down while her ears roared, and she swallowed her fear. The worst he could do was tell her to go to hell, and it wouldn't be the first time someone had done that.

Finally he spoke. "What makes you so sure?"

The misty air whipped her hair across her face. She brushed it back, her eyes never leaving his face. "Because I think we're alike."

"Oh, you do?"

She nodded, realizing this wasn't just a gimmick she'd concocted. "I know what it's like not to have parents, Lawrence. I know how it feels to have a secret like you do."

His lips puffed into a pout, and he rose up straighter as if to look down on her, which wasn't necessary, considering he already had her beat by three, maybe four inches. "And why the hell should

I tell you, of all people, someone I met one other time in my life, someone I don't know anything about? Why should I tell you about my fucking secret?''

"You want to find out who killed your mother?"

"Of course."

"That's why."

Forty-Seven

Friday, June 29, 5:30 p.m.

The Old Mill Motel sat where the road dead-ended, the bay behind it. A wooden sign outside read *Cerrado.* Closed.

Henderson tried to phone Martinez again, as he had all day. Costa Azul had been closed, as well, along with both of the restaurants they had visited earlier. The whole town had shut its doors, at least to them. Not even the shopkeepers would talk to them.

They decided to wait at the Old Mill until the disco at Costa Azul opened.

"You think we should try to get in?" Corina asked.

"Still too light," he said.

"We don't have time to wait. I'm going around the restaurant, try to get in through the back."

"I'll go with you."

"No, wait here. We're safer if we're separated."

She moved through the brush until she reached the back. A barn-style door the color of weathered teak was bordered on each side by two small windows, their screens torn out.

Corina dashed for the door, tried it, wasn't surprised to find it locked. She cupped her hands around her eyes and tried to see through the glass. A dusty light reflected the deserted restaurant's dining room. Corina struggled with the glass. It slid open. She managed to pull herself up and dropped onto the floor inside.

The air was stale as old newspapers. A musty stillness had settled over the room. If Whiplash had stayed here, he hadn't done so recently.

Corina walked through each room to confirm for herself the accuracy of her instincts. Stark tables. Empty chairs. Empty, except— Something bright caught her eye. She reached down, untangled it from the dowels on the back of the chair. It stuck to her hand. Tape, cut in a harsh, zigzag line. Something had been taped to this chair. Someone. The other two chairs at the table were smooth and free of dust, as if someone had sat in them recently.

Corina turned. At the table directly behind this one, sat another chair, chunks of tape dangling from it. On it was a plate holding a partially eaten hamburger, an empty Tecate can. A crumbled napkin beside the plate was stained and stiff. Corina picked it up. Blood. She dropped it and rushed through the building and out the front door.

"Someone was held in there," she told Henderson. "Two of them. There was blood, but not much. From the placement of the tape, it looks like their hands were probably secured behind them."

"The agents." The phrase came out soft, yet harsh, an oath.

"They could still be alive." She said it as much to convince herself as him.

"The guy at the hotel said he thought Whiplash might be staying at the haciendas."

"Just drive the peninsula. There can't be that many."

Either nightfall came rapidly, or the lack of lights from the haciendas made it appear so. Home after lonely home stretched along the peninsula separated by sand, bordered by the ocean. The local government had ousted the homeowners overnight, turning a sanctuary into a graveyard.

"Mexican localities rule their own principalities." She turned her head to avoid the sand that the wind and their rental threw up into her face.

"Yeah? You think this might be more local than national?"

"Local governments have been known to take bribes. Part of that money was being sent down here."

"Laundering?"

"That and payoffs, maybe."

The homes sat like sad, shadowed testaments to a fantasy gone bad. Oceanfront property in Mexico. Vacation home in Baja. Phrases so romantic, so hopeful she could almost hear the voices that spoke them. Now, some of these homeowners were missing, the rest disenfranchised.

War didn't brew, she thought. It was nothing like the cliché. Coffee brewed; storms perhaps. War sat solid and deceptive as a stone. It bore down until one day the pressure exploded, and nothing was ever again the same.

Except for the sound of the ocean, it was a soundless night, Mexico quiet, nothing like the Valley with its birds, insects and constant conflict of man

and woman against nature and each other. It was
getting to Henderson, she could tell. For a moment,
she thought of how she and Wes used to count the
sounds of the night. But there were no sounds to
count here. No bird calls, no insects chirping, no
implements of the civilized to click, buzz or hum.
Baja, where people went to run away, to soak up sun
and anonymity, had closed its doors, and no one was
home.

"Over there."

She followed Henderson's pointing finger to the
large structure farther up the road and across the
dunes. A soft glow the color of moonlight shimmered in back. "A light," she said.

"Maybe the owners forgot to turn it off when they
left."

"Or maybe—" They exchanged glances. "I'm
going to drive past it," he said. "We can walk
back."

They hid the Jeep in the driveway of an abandoned hacienda and made their way down the road
in the dim light. Henderson called in a hurried message for Martinez. This time he left his backpack in
the Jeep. The gun was now tucked inside his jeans.
She prayed he wouldn't have to use it.

"What kind of people live here?" he asked.

"Rich ones. People who want to fish, drink and
whatever it is rich people do in their off hours.
They're gone now, though."

As they neared the home, the light was no longer
visible. A gated courtyard guarded an L-shaped
structure pale as the sand. Upon closer inspection, it
was smaller than it appeared from a distance. The

expanse of sand on three of its sides and the endless ocean behind the building dwarfed it even more.

"Where the hell's Martinez?" she said.

"He'll be here any minute. He doesn't dare trust the local and national police at this point. He's probably working with the Mexican army, INS, too. He knows this area sideways."

Corina looked at the house. "We can't wait, though."

"No."

They moved slowly forward. "The lights are in back." Henderson whispered, although no one could hear them over the sound of the sea. "We can try to get in the front."

The mailbox stood out from the house on the main road.

"They get mail out here?"

"Same as we do. It's just not as reliable. Most of my friends use Mailboxes, Etc."

"There's a sign above it," he said. "Maybe—"

A weathered wooden slab was printed with the word *Congdon.* And below that in small black letters, *Bertram Electric.* The words just sat there, like the punch line of a bad joke.

"Bertram Electric," she finally said.

"This is it." Henderson looked at her, his eyes dark with shock. They were still standing there, staring at the sign, Corina's heart pounding, when they heard the scream.

Forty-Eight

Friday, June 29, 6:40 p.m.

A large stone wall with just one small fireplace covered one entire side of the room. In the time they'd been held here, Roxene must have counted every rock in it. She lay against it now, pain radiating from the back of her head.

"That will teach you." The guard rubbed his cheek, still a deep scarlet where she had slapped him.

She pulled her torn blouse around her, fumbled with the buttons. "I told you to keep your hands off me."

"You don't make the rules. Keep it up and you'll end up taped like him." The guard jerked his head toward Flannigan. Above the silver strip over his mouth, his blue eyes pleaded with her to keep talking. Parched as she was, she tried.

"Please. We'll give you money."

The man's eyes glittered. "How much money?"

"All of it. Everything I have."

"You think I won't take your money, anyway? You'll have to do better than that." His gaze surveyed her torn jeans, the curve of her leg.

"We'll help you."

"Don't need your help." He watched her, slowly squeezing her thigh. "You're a good-looking woman."

She shuddered. Play this guy. It was the only way. "I could look a hell of a lot better with a shower and some food."

He jerked his head in Flannigan's direction once more. "And this pig?"

"The same for him as for me. Food, water."

"And for that?" He watched her closely now, his eyes darkening with something she didn't want to contemplate. "What will you give me?"

"Anything you want."

His lips puffed into a smile. "Don't try anything. If you got away, I'd be a dead son of a bitch."

"Water," she said, "first. Water for both of us."

He watched her for a moment then turned abruptly and went outside. Flannigan leaned against the wall, rolling his head from side to side as if to tell her no, please no.

"At least we'll live a little longer," she said.

Again he rolled his head, more vigorously now.

"I know," she said. "They're going to kill us, aren't they?"

He stopped rolling, nodded.

"But maybe they won't. We can't do anything without food or water. At least he can give us that. At least—" She couldn't finish the sentence, as before her, Flannigan's eyes filled with sadness and tears.

Roxene felt tears of her own. The bastard would fuck her then kill them without thinking twice. He might not even bring them any water at all. She closed her eyes, wishing she could die, just evaporate from this room that had soaked the life from her.

No, she had to fight, no matter what. She looked around the room. Intended once as a kitchen, it had been a headquarters of some type. The kitchen table, a cheap plastic laminate, had been gray and yellow once. Two other tables stood facing the stone wall, where only a fire hydrant and a large wooden cross hung side by side. Tools covered the table. What had they made here? Explosives? Or had this really been an electrical company?

The man had not yet returned. Had he changed his mind? Was this part of his game? She glanced out the sliding glass door, that small rectangle of hope that carried light to her each day. What she saw made her almost scream. Flannigan sensed it, jerked his head toward her.

The face of a young woman.

"What?" Roxene began.

Quickly, the woman put her finger to her lips, then disappeared.

Corina stepped back from the glass door and flattened herself against the wall. Even in the dark, the building was so hot it seemed to breathe against her skin, sucking out the moisture.

"They're in there," she whispered.

"I'll go around the front." Henderson whispered, as well. "Wait here. Don't do anything. Martinez will be here any minute."

Their eyes met in the darkness. She was as aware as he what a risk they were taking. The woman screamed again. Corina sneaked another look. The wiry Mexican was taking his time kissing her. She moved closer to the door, as Henderson took off toward the front.

The burly Mexican lifted the woman's short, blond hair, tossed it up with the fingers of both hands.

The woman—it had to be Roxene Waite—backed off and spat. He grabbed her shoulder, calling her a tease, a bitch, a *puta*. Roxene's gaze darted to the glass then back to him. She knew Corina was out here, watching, listening.

"Why'd you change your mind, bitch?"

"Why bother? You're gong to kill us." She spoke clearly, making certain she was heard. "The Fourth of July, isn't that correct?"

"Not you," he said. "Not if you be nice."

"No." She took another hasty glance at where Corina stood. "You have the two nuns, the property owners, the retired cop and his wife. We'll all be killed July Fourth, and Governor Menlo will demand that the U.S. go to war against Mexico. How can you do this to your own people?"

He turned to the taller man stretched out on a wooden chair, his feet propped in another. A gun rested on the table before him. "What's she saying?"

"That you're a prick." The man took a slug of Tecate. "But by this time next week, we'll be a couple of rich pricks."

"You mean they haven't paid you yet?" The woman's laugh cut through the stillness of the night. "That means they're going to kill you, too. Bad news, gentlemen."

A heated exchange of Spanish followed. Her suggestion had unnerved them. Without having ever met her, Corina knew this woman, Roxene Waite. She'd fight beyond the moment of hopelessness when most would cave in. Even if they killed her, she'd have to see her own death warrant to believe it. This was what a woman could be, what she, by God, had better try to be, if she were to survive this.

The Mexican grabbed the woman's arm again. Where the hell was Henderson? Had he gone through the front wing, or was he on the other side of this room, waiting for the right moment, waiting for Victor Martinez?

"We work for them. You'll be the dead one," the Mexican said.

"Let us go, and you might be able to escape. Do you think they'll start a war and leave you two geniuses with a chunk of money so you can share the story with everyone at the local cantina?"

"*¿Qué?*" He dropped her arm, turned to his friend, who'd stopped drinking the beer and taken his legs down from the chair.

The tall man did a fair job of translating, adding a few concerns of his own.

"She's full of shit," the short man said.

Roxene Waite faced him head-on.

"No, I'm not, and you'll be just as dead as the rest of us unless you help us get out of here."

The two men engaged in a heated exchange muffled by the crashing of waves.

Roxene's clear voice rang above theirs, interrupting. "That's what you'd like to believe, boys, but it just isn't true. These fuckers haven't given you a dime, have they? Just this rattrap no one's used as anything but a mail drop for forty years. A mail drop owned by an old KKK-er who needed a place to hide after he killed the son of a black activist.''

God, she was smart, articulating all this for Corina, confirming what she and Henderson already guessed.

"You don't know what you're talking about," the wiry man said.

"Wait." His friend stopped him with a hand on his shoulder. "She might be telling the truth. Why would they pay us when they can kill us like the rest of them?"

"And why should they trust you?" Roxene moved closer to the tall one, the one who'd started to understand. "Why?"

The two men looked at each other. Corina held her breath. Yes, please let these people out of here. Run like hell.

"If we help you," the taller man said. "What would your government do for us?"

Corina allowed herself to exhale. Finally!

She heard a noise behind her, started to turn. A form came out of nowhere. Fingers grabbed her arm, yanked her away from the door.

She tried to recover, to fight back but lost her footing. She fell forward, but the fingers ripped at her shoulders, slammed her against the wall. Her knees buckled, and again, she almost went down. He yanked her up, pressed her back with greater force.

Corina fought for air, trying to scream, but she couldn't catch her breath. Nothing left. She felt herself slide down the wall, yet his hands held on to her. She opened her eyes, forced herself to focus on the face of her attacker.

Pale as talcum in the night, his lopsided head giving him a curious look, he studied her with eyes the color of moonstones, as if she were an insect he'd captured. Thin wisps rose from his scalp as if a breeze were blowing them. She heard birds flapping their wings close to her ears. She began to slip into unconsciousness. Whiplash. Birds. He laughed, and she saw a flame in his hand. Smelled something burning. Hair.

Forty-Nine

Friday, June 29, 6:45 p.m.

The acrid odor revived her. Corina tried to pull herself to her feet, but her arms wouldn't move. He'd dragged her inside. She sat facing the door from which she'd watched what happened earlier. The wall of stone stretched to her left with a black hole of a fireplace. A wooden cross and fire extinguisher hung from the wall. A large sandy-haired man, tape over his mouth, sat in a chair facing her.

The rank-smelling man behind her, pulling her shoulders to the chair, had to be the tall one. The beefy one, a vertical streak of hair dividing his chin, stood in front of her, between Roxene and Whiplash. God, he was worse than she remembered. He flipped the lid of the lighter, scrunched the small black wheel, and the lighter burst into flame.

"Flint," he said in a whispery voice. He snapped the lid over the flame, then flipped it open and started all over, smiling at her, his head askew. She reached for her hair, felt brittle ends, still warm. That was the smell.

"Flint makes fire," he said. "Bet you've never seen one of these old Zippos, have you?" He shoved it too close to her face. Corina drew back, but not before she felt the bite of the flame. She started to cry out but held back her pain. "You say something?" he asked.

"Let us go." Roxene moved between Corina and him, challenging him in a sure voice. "Hear that noise? You don't have much time to get away."

Night noises. Corina heard the rotor sounds growing louder now, raging overhead. Some kind of plane, a helicopter, large judging by the sounds, trying to land. Whiplash lifted and dropped his head, making a hooting sound that must have been his version of laughter.

"That 'copter's waiting for me. Got a good Mexican pilot who flew in 'Nam like I did. We'll get out just fine."

"You won't," Corina said. "Too many people know."

"I knew you had that tape." He cast his pale gaze over her body. "Been wanting to get you close up, see how gutsy you really are. Where the hell'd you have it hidden?"

Roxene gave a look of encouragement. *Keep talking,* it seemed to say. Then Corina saw why. Flannigan had moved imperceptibly closer to Whiplash. Somehow Roxene had freed his hands.

The glass door slid open, and the Mexican went to investigate. Henderson, she thought. Please. "We have copies of the tapes," she said, standing. "They know where we are. They'll be here any minute."

"She's right." The door before her slid wider, and Corina could not believe what she saw. Brandon Chenault strode through the opening, into the room. "DEA and Mexico City are working together." He brushed past the Mexican and walked closer to her, his black jeans and T-shirt as free of lint and wrinkles as his suits always were at work.

What the hell was Chenault doing here?

Whiplash raked twiglike fingers through his hair. "It's about time you got here," he said.

"Something unexpected came up. Had to revise the schedule." He studied Corina, gray eyes cold and flat as the surface of a pond. She was trying to make sense of it, of why he was here, of how he knew these men. Tried to make him a hero in her brain, a hero come to rescue them. But that wasn't the case. No amount of hoping could put Brandon Chenault and them on the same side now.

"Hello, Corina."

"What are you doing here?"

"You mean you haven't figured that out? You would have, of course."

"The Trio," she said. "You didn't let Belmont buy you?"

"Hardly. Gene Belmont and my family go way back."

"But why would you be involved with someone like Belmont?"

"Money, Corina. Uncle Joe Congdon was a fine man. I didn't necessarily believe as he did, but I respected him. Then later, I saw the profit in his way of thinking, his connections."

"Money? That's all?"

He nodded, a large man, she thought. Why had she never noticed how large he was? "You could have had a career," he said. "Henderson's job. Better than that if you wanted it."

"If I didn't probe too deeply into what was happening?'' She watched his placid expression as he glanced from Whiplash to her as if trying to decide how to tidy up this mess. ''You thought I was stupid,'' she said over the drone of the idling helicopter. ''That's why you had Ivy promote me. You were afraid Henderson would figure it out.''

Oh, Henderson, please be okay. Please figure something out.

''I don't have time to argue with you.'' Chenault took the gun from the table and motioned toward the stone wall. ''Over there, all of you. We can't wait for the Fourth. DEA will be all over the place any minute.''

''You killed Ivy, too, didn't you?''

''I said move. I couldn't trust her. She knew too much about me. And she was underrated as a manager. She told me you were smart.'' He jerked his head to the creature flicking his lighter. ''Whiplash, get over here.'' The burly Mexican and his friend came as if they had been summoned. ''You, two. Against the wall.''

''I told you,'' Roxene said to the Mexican. ''They aren't letting you go, either.''

''Now,'' Chenault demanded.

The Mexicans moved slowly, looking at each other in bewilderment. Corina didn't move. Whiplash shoved her against the rocks, then turned to Roxene, who moved to Corina's right. The two men stood to her left.

The lanky one wailed. ''We won't tell nobody. We won't say nothing. Please believe me.''

The gun exploded, and the man crumbled, holding the place that used to be his stomach. His partner dived at Chenault. Two more blasts, and he lay in a bloody heap.

Something moved in the shadows behind Chenault. "Don't fucking move." Henderson's voice.

Chenault whirled, diving for the shape behind the door. Another shot. Corina screamed.

Chenault ran down the long hall toward the other wing of the house, dripping blood, Henderson not far behind.

Whiplash lunged for her, slamming her against the stone, hitting her head on the wooden cross. The cross. She reached up for it, found the fire extinguisher, instead. A long-ago lesson flashed in her mind. *Just pull the tab.* In two quick motions, she grabbed the solid hose and yanked it out and pulled the tab as hard as she could.

A white blast of chemical foam shot Whiplash in the face. He shrieked and turned from her, hands moving over his eyes as if trying to gouge them out. She kept shooting until the back of his shirt was soaked, and he ran as if the blast of foam had catapulted him from the room.

Roxene lay propped against the wall like a doll, a bloody hole torn into her arm. She looked up at Corina with glazed eyes. "Get him."

Corina hesitated. What if Roxene were dying? What if there were something she should do? "Your arm?"

"Get him, damn it."

Corina turned from the bleeding woman, let the gutsy, guttural voice propel her down the dark hall where Henderson had chased Chenault. A door stood open. She burst through it, out onto the beach where the helicopter sat, loud and ferocious. It was almost alive, its large rotor blades swishing eight, maybe ten feet above, its red and green navigation lights illuminating the sand.

Corina looked down. At her feet, in that eerie light, as if it had been placed there, lay a gun. Henderson's. Damn. No.

The oval-shaped cabin rested beneath the black, rotor blades. The sliding door was open, waiting.

She could see the dark-haired pilot and behind him, the slanted silhouette of Whiplash beside the 'copter's open door.

"Corina. Over here." Henderson, thank God.

Two ghost shapes struggled just beyond the helicopter. Corina grabbed the gun and ran to them.

Chenault had Henderson pinned to the sand. His fingers ground into Henderson's throat, choking the movement from him, the life. Her hand took on a will of its own, steady as she pointed the gun and pulled the trigger. Steady still as she heard the shot, as if from somewhere else, and waited to see if she should fire again.

The helicopter's lights tangled in the noise of the accelerating rotors. The noise increased; they were preparing to escape. She felt dizzy suddenly, guilty, holding in her right hand, the proof of what she'd wanted, of what she wanted still. And she waited a second too long.

Chenault fled to the shadows. Henderson doubled over in the sand, gagging. She had wanted to kill Chenault, had longed to fill his black, moon-stained back with bullets. She still did. Pointing the gun through the flashing lights, she tried to find him.

A sudden, angry grip from behind shot pain through her arm and shook the gun loose. Chenault had circled and returned for her. She fought back without hesitation, kicking at him, shouting for help. The propellers out-shouted her. She looked wildly across the beach, seeing flashes of Henderson, still kneeling in shock in the flickering lights.

"Help me," she screamed at the top of her lungs. The sound of her words bounced back at her, like the roar of the sea, the keening of an animal.

Chenault grunted and dragged her through the sand. They struggled within a few feet of the helicopter. Corina could feel the hungry breath of the frenzied tail rotor in her face. For every slowly increasing beat of the main rotor blades overhead, the rear rotors were flying ten times faster.

Then she knew why Chenault was taking this chance with the few remaining minutes he could allow himself. He wasn't trying to pull her into the plane. He wanted to kill her on this abandoned beach.

She kicked, tried to claw at his face. He'd turned into a warrior, unable to see or hear her, she knew, concentrating on slowly working her into position to squeeze the breath out of her throat, or twist her neck until it snapped.

Beat beat beat. Flap flap flap.

The wind in her face gave her the idea for their only chance for escape. She couldn't overpower this mass of muscle, and she didn't have a weapon. At least not one in hand.

And then, in that hopeless mixture of biting sand, pain and limited sight, came something else, a sound—limited, at first—but no, real, not just in her mind. The official siren of authority, of help.

Chenault paused. He heard them, too. She hadn't

imagined it. He stood deathly still for a moment, a Miró painting, black on black, a squiggle of crimson where a bullet had grazed his shoulder. Then he came to life. The wail grew more insistent, closer. Chenault threw her away from him. She skidded into the sand, breaking her fall with her hands. Her palms were bleeding; she could feel that much, but the pain was on a different, less-important level than Chenault and his frantic run for the front of the helicopter.

Henderson barreled out of nowhere. He grabbed Chenault from behind, slung him around. Chenault took a swing but barely connected. The bullet must have weakened him more than she'd realized.

"They've got you," Henderson gasped. "It's over. There's still time for you to help us stop this thing."

"Fuck you." Chenault grabbed him with both hands, tried to shove him away, into the whirling blades.

Shouts in Spanish and English exploded out onto the beach. At least a dozen men rushed onto the sand, their guns flashing in the aircraft's reflected lights.

Chenault held Henderson against his chest, gun to his throat. "This is it," he shouted. "Up to you, fuckers. I'm getting on this plane now, with or without him."

A dark shape streaked past Corina, past all of them, an angry form, short, blond hair scrambled in the wind of the helicopter. One arm limp at her side, the other holding a gun, Roxene rushed straight toward Brandon Chenault, with a shout that made the hair on Corina's arms stand on end.

Roxene hit Chenault as if she'd been shot from a

gun. Henderson fell to the sand and rolled away, close to where Corina was crouching. "My God," he said.

It was as if Henderson knew what would happen next—Roxene's savage, fearless shouts, Corina's reaching out, Chenault's backward step, the push. Did Roxene push him, did Corina trip him up, or did he stumble, trying to regain his balance?

The back rotor, spinning blades now invisible knives, took him, headfirst, his screech of anguish drowned in the pulpy, meat-cutter sound of the chopping blades. And for a moment, he stood there in a halo of blood and brains, his mutilated body reflected in the light of the helicopter. Then what was left of him pitched forward into the sand.

Henderson reached out for Corina's arm. "Don't look."

But she couldn't take her eyes from the carnage before her. Besides, there was something else the rest of them seemed to have forgotten. "Whiplash," she said.

As she spoke, there was yet another increase in the noise level, the man-made sand storm became blinding, and the helicopter began to rise.

"Stop them," Henderson shouted. Gunfire filled the air.

"Tail rotor's damaged," someone said. "They won't make it." Corina shuddered, knowing that the reason for that damage lay just a few feet from her. Still she couldn't turn away. The shots continued as the helicopter continued its wobbly climb into the sky.

Roxene stood beside them now, her eyes wild, her gun limp at her side. "He's getting away," she said.

The gunshots sounded fruitless against the finality of her tone.

"Maybe not," Corina said, looking up.

"He's getting away. The sick bastard's getting away." Roxene threw down her gun and began to weep.

Victor Martinez stepped out of the crowd.

"She needs a doctor," Henderson said.

Martinez frowned. "You all do."

They took Roxene and Flannigan out on stretchers. Roxene's assault on Chenault seemed to have drained every bit of energy she'd been able to conserve.

Corina and Henderson walked out with Victor Martinez. Corina couldn't erase the image of Chenault's bloody head from her mind.

At Victor's car, she turned to Henderson, and said what she must because she could no longer contain it. "I would have killed him, Matthew."

His usually ruddy face was drained and dead. "I know. Me, too."

"But he would have killed us. He wanted to."

Henderson touched her arm, motioned toward the open car door. "I don't know what to tell you," he said, his voice flat and devoid of emotions. "I don't have any answers right now."

Fifty

Corina and Henderson made their way through the media tent, both of them refusing the trays of fresh orange and grapefruit juice shoved into their faces. They'd both talked to J.T. late the night before, and he'd told them they didn't have to cover this, that the authorities had enough to nail Menlo.

"Are you kidding?" Corina said. "After all this, we have to be there. We need to be."

J.T. had paused only a moment. "Then I'll send photographers."

The names of the bodies had not been released. All that had appeared on television was that three people were killed in a shoot-out in San Quintin. Corina glanced to her right and spotted Wally Lorenzo, who lifted his camera in greeting. Apparently he had resumed his old job. Maybe Sam, the printer, and the rest of those whose termination Chenault had engineered, would, as well.

Henderson grunted a greeting to Wally. "Will they all get their jobs back?" she asked.

"Who knows? Cutting fat is one thing. Chenault cut muscle, and now we know why."

"Because he was afraid of the old-timers. Because he thought people like Geri and I were stupid."

Henderson started to speak, then stopped. "I think Menlo's ready. Come on."

Governor Craig Menlo must have rehearsed for this moment, the proper gleam in the eyes, the grim, unsmiling expression. Against the pale white of his face, the navy suit and red-striped tie sent a not-so-subtle message.

Behind him at the podium, Nan Belmont shone like the jeweled American flag pin on the lapel of her white suit. Her husband, Danny, stood just off the makeshift stage, watching.

"Greetings and God Bless America." Menlo's voice boomed through the microphone.

Corina wasn't surprised by the minimal applause. This was a press conference. Menlo was talking to those who received the news, not those who transmitted it, but only the latter shared this muggy tent with him.

"We're here because we love our country," he said. "We're here because of the atrocities going on in Mexico, once a peaceful neighbor to the south of us, now—" He paused with a shudder. "I just got word that Brandon Chenault, a respected California newspaper publisher, was one of those murdered in San Quintin, in Baja, last night. Other Americans, including two Drug Enforcement Agency officials, are still missing. As governor, I can and will summon the National Guard to defend our boundaries. I challenge the rest of our country, and our president, to do the same."

He continued in the same vein, blaming Mexico

for the transgressions that Corina now knew he himself, with the help of his network, had brought on.

Nan Belmont shifted from one foot to the other as he spoke, her movements almost imperceptible. Something was wrong here. Nan was wrong here. She kept looking to her left, toward her dorky husband, as if for reassurance. That was a first.

The press hammered Menlo with questions.

"What makes you think the Mexican government kidnapped the people who disappeared?" asked a reporter for the *Sacramento Bee*.

"I'm not saying they did it, only that they're not controlling it. Next question?"

"If the president doesn't send troops into Mexico, what will you do?"

"I have the authority to command the National Guard, and I am certain our president won't allow acts of this magnitude to continue."

Corina stepped forward. "Why did you accept money from a white-rights group to run for office?"

He seemed to stumble, almost as Chenault had into the blades of that rotor she couldn't erase from her mind. "I accepted nothing from any group such as the one you're describing, and we're not here today to discuss political campaigns."

"But you did, Governor. You have. That's how you got elected, how you stayed in office."

"Incorrect. And I don't appreciate the allegation." He looked up at the cameras, Wally's included. They reminded her of the night before, the entanglement of light and sound. She tried to ignore every level of her pain and just listen to Menlo. He spoke slowly, his voice full of conviction. "This meeting is about our right to take back Mexico, to reclaim what belongs to us, to send in our National Guard and take back what was taken from us in the Treaty of Guadalupe Hidalgo in 1848. It was wrong then, and it's wrong now.''

"It was wrong for you to try to have me killed,'' Corina said. "It was wrong for you to arrange the murder of Skin Burke and Tina Kellogg.''

Menlo paled even more, then jerked his head toward Nan Belmont. "Get her out of here,'' he said. And to the crowd, "National security is of the utmost concern at this time. I challenge the president to follow our lead, to overcome these killers who threaten our country.''

"What killers?'' Corina demanded. "The murders you planned for July Fourth aren't going to happen. The two nuns whose murders you ordered are already free. You wanted various Mexican property owners, Americans, executed, but my colleague and I just heard that they're safe, as well. The DEA agents were freed last night. They're saying they heard the people who held them captive talking on the phone to you these past few weeks.''

"That's a lie, and this is preposterous.''

The lights grew brighter around her. The soft buzz of conversation rose to a roar. Corina realized how weak she felt. And she thought of Roxene, out of danger now, sleeping off what she'd endured in a San Diego hospital bed, Norm Flannigan hanging on in ICU.

"It's not a lie. We have witnesses.''

"Then bring them forward.'' Nan Belmont stood before the microphone under the starred-and-striped canopy. "Governor, can you explain these charges?''

"You know I can.'' Menlo turned on Nan Belmont, shouting into her face. "Don't go two-faced on me. Either you're on the side of this country, or you're not, and you'd better decide right now, Senator."

Nan Belmont stepped back from him, severing her allegiance forever, as cameras flashed.

Her husband, Danny, stepped forward, put his arm across her shoulder. She turned to face the crowd. "There's something wrong here. Can someone please help us?"

The men in uniform approached the platform. Menlo turned, wild-eyed, still talking about justice, about freedom. "You're the one with the crazy coot of a father who doesn't know his own name," he said, directing his rage toward Nan Belmont now. "You helped them, didn't you, helped them set me up."

They got every word of it, even after he was forcefully removed from the stage. Excitement and commotion still buzzed around them and would for a long time, but it was over, finally over. Corina looked up at Henderson, drained and dry as the emotional ditch that she was. "I need to get out of here," she said.

Henderson flipped shut his notebook. "Me, too."

They arrived in Pleasant View that afternoon. When J.T. met them at the airport, he hugged Corina.

"Can't remember the last time you did that," she said.

"Nor I. Maybe it's because you look so bad."

"She has a right to," Henderson said.

As J.T. drove to the office, they filled him in on Nan's attack on Menlo.

"She's off the hook," J.T. said.

"Whiplash, too," Henderson said from the back seat. "I can't believe that psycho is out there somewhere." Corina shuddered. Henderson reached forward, brushed her shoulder. "Sorry."

"It's all right. Though I don't know if I can ever sleep again."

"For Chenault, it was about money," Henderson said. "But Whiplash just did it for fun. Ivy, Skin Burke, Tina Kellogg."

"Not Tina Kellogg," she said.

"No?" Before she could answer, Henderson went on. "There's something wrong about that, isn't there?"

"I think so," she said. "It just doesn't track." The questions had been nagging her since they'd left Mexico. Before that, maybe. She should have known he'd be bothered, as well.

"It doesn't make sense to me, either," Henderson said. "If Whiplash did it, why wasn't he bragging about it the way he did about Skin and Ivy?"

"And why did he crush in her skull?" With numb horror, Corina realized that she'd started figuring out how the mind of this madman worked. "He'd want something showier and more public, not a body tossed in a canal."

J.T. turned toward her, unsmiling. "You two are something else."

"What do you mean?" Henderson said.

"Geri LaRue called a little while ago. She knows who killed Tina Kellogg and why."

Corina sank back in the seat, unable to take anymore. She backed up the tape recorder of her mind, let the various conversations play through it. "The oldest motive in the world," she said.

Fifty-One

Something beyond good sense propelled Geri toward the curving drive. She couldn't help herself, not now. The obsessive mind she'd always hated had nagged her into a discovery that would at the very least right a wrong. A wrong? Lord, it was murder, any way you looked at it, and she'd been doing nothing but look at it. She just hadn't known what she was seeing.

The late afternoon sun reflected off the golf course in blinding green that forced Geri to look away. Colors were brighter, the house clearly outlined as if it had been cut into the setting. Fear, making her senses go crazy. Because she couldn't sharpen her hearing, her vision took the brunt of it, as if she were looking at this house she approached through a pair of binoculars adjusted to the nth degree.

Betsy didn't answer the front door. Geri found her in the back, slamming her club into a golf ball. Geri cringed at the impact. Titlest balls, no doubt. Her brain hadn't let her rest until she'd translated the word on Betsy's bumper sticker.

Betsy turned and spotted her. "What's the matter?" she asked. "Locked out of your house again?"

Geri felt herself squirm. This was more difficult than she'd expected. "Could we, like go inside for a minute?"

Betsy looked out over the artificial-looking grass. Why did perfection have to look so artificial? Why was she worrying about it right now when she ought to be thinking of what to say next?

Betsy came across the patio, looking more impatient than pissed. "Do you need something? You okay?"

"I have to talk to you," she said. "It's important."

Betsy squinted and pursed her lips as if pulling on an invisible cigarette. "You're not on something, are you?"

"Like drugs?" That did it. "Do I look high to you? Do you think that's what I am?"

"Hey, take it easy."

"I talked to Lawrence Kellogg," she said. "You want to hear more?"

Betsy's face froze. Maybe this wasn't the right approach, after all. "Come on. Let's hear it." She led the way in through the back, stepping over the newly tiled mudroom on her way to the kitchen. Mud would never see this room. Several pots of violets sat on a white-tiled counter. Geri bet they'd come with the house. Next to the large glass window with a view of the Sierra range, sat the one item in the room that Betsy probably did use, a monster of an exercise bike, a bottle of water still in its holder, a book opened in the slot before it.

"Is this where you killed her?" The words slipped

out, the impact more damning once she'd spoken them. Geri forced herself to stop, to wait, just breathing. Betsy turned, her face the same, except for the color—pure chalk. "What'd you say?"

"Asked. I asked you a question. Is this room where you killed Tina Kellogg?"

"Are you crazy?"

"With all due respect, I know what you did, and I think you did it here."

"How can you know anything about anything?" She looked around as if for witnesses. Geri prayed that Lieutenant Wise would hurry. "Tina's kid's nothing but a punk."

"He's Skin Burke's kid, too."

She took a step back, then steadied herself, leaning on her club for support. "That's not true."

"You know it is, and so does Skin's mother. I started thinking about it when I read his obit, and I called her. Lawrence "Skin" Burke. The man had a name other than his nickname. And he gave it to his son."

The fingers around her club turned as white as her face. "If I kept anything secret, it was because Skin asked me to, because he didn't want his dirty laundry aired in public."

"That's not what Tina told his son. She and Skin had worked out their differences and were going to get married as soon as he got out of that weird group that owns this development. Skin was in too deep with you, the same way he was the Vineyard Estate guys. What happened? Did Tina come to see you?"

"She was a bitch."

"She loved Skin in spite of their problems. She was ready to settle down with him. She wouldn't have wanted him to just dump you. She would have tried to soften it.''

"Soften it? By stealing someone else's man?'' She stepped back, closed her eyes, her skin an unnatural gray beneath the tan. "I wouldn't even know how to plan a murder, let alone commit one.''

"You probably didn't plan it. I think Tina came here, maybe talked to you out back there. You came inside. Maybe you were still carrying your club. She told her son she had something important to do—the decent thing, she'd said. She came here to explain herself to you, to tell you about Skin and her, to ask your forgiveness. Didn't she?''

Betsy reached into her shirt pocket for a cigarette but didn't light it. "You and the kid cooked this up, didn't you? You're his girlfriend, right? What do you really want? Money?''

"You probably did it here. That's why you're having the floor redone. Then you dragged her through that door into the garage. That's the real reason you sold your van.'' She turned to gesture toward the garage door. In that fraction of a second, she felt more than heard the danger. She moved just as she felt the pain smash into her shoulder. She whirled around, her left side numb, as Betsy brought the golf club down again over her head.

Geri grabbed it with both hands, feeling it graze her cheek. The world had gone black and white, pain draining it of color. Betsy grunted as she tried to wrest away the club. Geri held on, fighting to remain conscious. She had to hang on to the club. With a quick yank, she pulled it from Betsy's hands.

Betsy charged, her face a fierce mask. Geri threw the club from her and grabbed Betsy by each arm.

Pushed her hard, away from her, into the exercise bike. The large machine hit the window with a smash. Betsy screamed as she fell backward. Geri grabbed the club, holding it like a baseball bat.

Betsy lay splayed in the toppled bike. Blood trickled down the corner of her mouth. She struggled to get up.

Two police officers hurried down the back path toward the door.

"Police," Geri told her.

She pulled herself to her feet. "No one will take a punk kid's word over mine."

"They will." Geri relaxed her grip on the golf club. It was all over now. She could give herself up to the pain.

The Asian officer was the first one through the door.

"This kid broke into my house," Betsy said.

He ignored her remark, addressing Geri. "You the editor from the *Voice*?"

"Research librarian." She watched the shock register on Betsy's face.

"You?"

Geri turned to the cop. "Her name's Betsy Webster. She killed Tina Kellogg."

Fifty-Two

Geri LaRue's car blocked the entrance of Betsy Webster's home. Police cars waited on either side.

The double doors stood open. They followed the circular driveway to it.

The decor was mail-order tasteful, both expensive and uninspired. The furnishings looked as if they had been purchased from a catalogue with little regard for who actually lived in these rooms and how. Blue-and-white slipcovers draped every sitting surface, even the straight-backed chairs in the adjoining dining room. The slipcovers gave the room an ephemeral, almost ghostly air, as if someone had neither quite moved in nor out. Turnkey mansion, Corina remembered. Turnkey nightmare.

They went to the back of the house, following the sound of officers' radios. They were in the mudroom, cops trying to tape off the area. The large, black exercise bike lay smashed into the window, ruining one of the best views in the Valley with a spider web of broken glass.

Betsy sat drooped and faded on the rattan sofa, her hands cuffed, her visor askew. Geri stood before her like a person in shock. She'd retreated to wherever she went when real life got too scary, leaving just the compressed lips and the birdlike gaze. She lifted her hand, almost apologetically, as if trying to cover her bleeding shoulder. Her purple hair looked like a Halloween costume.

"Are you all right?" Corina asked.

"Ambulance is on its way." Mel Wise closed his notebook and motioned to his partner, Officer Chinn.

"Don't touch anything," Chinn told Corina. "No statements."

Geri either didn't hear him or didn't care. "It was all about jealousy," she said. "This lady bashed Tina Kellogg's head in with a golf club." She glanced over at the crashed bike and the object sticking from it. "Tried to do the same thing to me."

Betsy looked as if someone had beaten her from the inside out. "She didn't love him." She lifted her head, pleading to some unseen entity for mercy. "She used the kid to try to get him back. Then she used what was going on at Vineyard Estates. Claimed they were trying to take over the world or something."

"When I was checking out Tina for you, I found out that her husband died before Lawrence, Tina's son, was born," Geri told Corina. "Like a year before."

"She was taking him away from me." Betsy's sobs filled the room. Corina tried to conjure sympathy but felt nothing.

To Geri, she said, "How'd you figure this out?"

"The son." Geri tightened her lips as if forcing out the words in the right shape. "I remembered from my research that Skin's real name was L. "Skin" Burke, *L* for Lawrence."

"Why didn't you tell us?" Corina asked.

"You were in Mexico. I went to talk to the son and told him what I'd found out."

"He's a monster, that kid," Betsy shouted through her tears. "He's laid a guilt trip on Skin all his life."

"Not what he says." Geri was loving this. "According to Lawrence, his folks never stopped loving each other. Skin got way too deep into the white-rights group, and when Tina found out from Wes Shaw Senior what was going on, she tried to get Skin out."

"That bastard Wes." Betsy lifted her tear-streaked face, glaring at Geri. "That old bigot was worse than any of them. Kept Wes Junior from marrying *her*." She shifted her hateful gaze to Corina. "And he was all for the plans, whatever they were, until the cancer got him, and he decided he wanted to cool his sorry old ass in heaven."

Corina felt sick. She couldn't run away from it. Wes's father had made his son promise not to marry her. And Wes had agreed. She was too drained of emotion to respond or even try to make sense of it.

Mel Wise and Officer Chin exchanged looks. Thanks to Geri, they had a confession. She could almost hear their silent conversation. Give her time, and she'd know the whole force the way Henderson did. This was how it happened, of course. Shared experiences built trust, and trust led to sources.

"Excuse us," Chinn said. "We need to talk to Mrs. Webster now."

"You might as well show us the golf club," Geri

said. "No matter how clean you may think it is, you can't ever remove the traces of her blood."

Betsy rose to her feet. "Oh, you think so. Where'd you hear that?"

Geri pushed up her rectangular glasses and recited, as if from memory. "Discovery Channel. The proper tools and light will prove the presence of blood on an object, maybe enough for a DNA match, maybe not. You want to gamble on it?"

Betsy looked up at the officers. "Just get me away from her." As she moved toward them, she looked at Corina, her skin the texture of wilted rose petals. "Don't judge me," she said, "just don't any of you judge me until you've been where I am."

She tossed her head, and the visor flew off it. Corina's hands went out, caught the visor. A simple sweep of plastic, it was lined in terry cloth stained with dark makeup. Corina didn't want to hold it but couldn't let go of it, either. It clung to her fingers as Betsy went out the door, tears running down her weathered face, head held defiantly high.

"*Mija*, what a surprise!"

"I've been meaning to call, Mama. How are you?"

"Much better now that I can hear your sweet voice. The last few times we talked, you didn't sound good."

"I was working on a story that kind of did me in."

"It's over now then, this story?"

"Pretty much. I'll tell you about it when I see you. That's why I'm calling."

"Have you thought any more about the wedding?"

"Actually I have. The first minute I can get away, I'll drive down for a fitting."

"Really?"

"Yes. This week, if possible. I could come for the Fourth, stay a few days."

"Are you serious?"

"Absolutely. Mama, do you think I should wear my hair up or curl it?"

"Well, I— Give me a chance to think about it a little."

"You do that. I've got to run now. Mama?"

"Yes?"

"I love you."

"I love you, too, *Mija*."

Epilogue

Tragedy generates its own heroes. Circumstance starts the process, and the media do the rest. Nan Belmont denied involvement, claiming, through her attorney, and a one-on-one with Larry King, that she pretended to go along with the group only to expose Menlo's crazy plan. She would not be seeking his office, however, Nan said. She was stepping down from politics, at least for now, in order to spend more time with her husband and her ailing father.

Menlo got stuck with the role of the obsessed king, whose ego and need for power pushed him over the edge. The villain, Brandon Chenault, had paid a gruesome price. The play was over. Justice had been done.

But this was not Shakespeare, not Ibsen. Somewhere Whiplash still lived, hating Corina, if someone like Whiplash cared enough to hate, taking money for other people's dirty work.

The newspaper was wounded, its credibility challenged. But newspaper people thrived on challenge. Corporate was sending a new publisher from the Santa Rosa paper, a highly respected manager, by all reports, to heal, they said, to bring the staff together once more.

Corina could already feel it happening. Sam was back at work, in the imaging department, where he was needed again. She and Henderson had worked around the clock, repeating their stories to those in charge of the case. The tape Skin had sent her arrived. She and Henderson watched it that afternoon, speechless. Roxene Waite and Norm Flannigan were well enough to expose the plot and help the authorities free the other captives.

J.T. told them to take as much time as they needed, but adrenaline still surged through Corina. She doubted that she'd be able to sleep, let alone think, until she and the terrible movie flashing through her brain, ran down.

Her shirt felt glued to her. She needed a shower. She needed a drink. She needed to cry.

As she and Henderson walked down the hall that night, Geri LaRue caught up with them. In one hand she carried her ceramic coffee mug, a giant tin of Altoids sticking out of it. In the other, she held the only photo she kept on her desk, one of her dog.

"You have a visitor at the front guard station," she told Corina.

"You're not leaving?" Henderson said. Geri turned to watch his lips as he spoke, and now Corina understood why.

"Yep."

"It will get better here now," Corina said. "Don't quit."

"It's not that." Geri adjusted her rectangular glasses. "I know now that I can do more than interact with a computer all day. The company's agreed to give me a chance at our San Francisco paper." Her fair skin flushed. "As a reporter."

"They'll train you?" Henderson asked.

"My degree's in journalism. I just never could get up the nerve." She looked at Corina, and swallowed hard. "You had a part in it, you know. Twenty-five years old, and you're the first friend I ever made."

"That won't change when you move."

"That's why God invented e-mail. I'll watch for your byline."

Corina tried to find her voice. "Cool beans," she said, and put out her arms. The hug, orchestrated without regard for the coffee mug and framed photograph, made her feel alive and something close to sane.

At the rear guard station, just outside the café, they hugged again. Then they took their separate paths—Geri and Henderson to the back parking lot, Corina backtracking to the front desk. Even before she got there, she saw the reason for her summons.

Wes Shaw sat on one of the black-leather chairs. His blue eyes were riveted on her. Every hair was in place, even the ones that were supposed to be in casual disarray. He wore jeans and a soft buckskin-colored shirt that brought out the peach-colored tones of his tanned skin. For just that moment, she took in the image of him, a man whose mismatched features elevated him beyond handsome. God, he was something.

He jumped to his feet when he spotted her. "I was here until after nine last night," he said as she approached him. "When you still didn't come out, I thought I'd better wait another day. You look exhausted."

"I am exhausted." She'd almost killed a man, almost been killed herself. Yes, she was exhausted, confused, and on the brink of tears. "You look wonderful, by the way."

"It's all an act. I feel as if my heart's been torn out."

"I wish I could tell you it will get better. I saw the tape this afternoon, and Betsy was right. Your dad doesn't come across as a criminal, but he is portrayed as a bigot."

"They didn't understand him."

"Neither did I."

Wes turned, his eyes hollow. "He was dying. He asked me one favor. And even then, the moment I promised, I knew I couldn't keep it, vowed to make it right with you once he was gone."

All the nights she'd wondered why, why, why. The agony she'd spent recounting their every moment spent together, wondering what she'd done wrong, why she wasn't enough for him. And all this time, Wes had left her because his father didn't want his son to marry a Mexican. And he didn't have the nerve to tell her the truth.

"I need to go now. I can barely stand up." She started for the door.

He opened it for her, followed her out onto the steps. "That's why I'm here. I want to take care of you."

"I'll be okay."

"We need to start fresh, put all of this trouble behind us."

"No, Wes." The words came from her heart. She didn't have to think about them.

"Please," he said. "You love me, and I love you, damn it."

"You don't love me enough. You never have."

His eyes deepened and grew desperate. "Because I tried to save my father's reputation? Is that the reason?"

"Only part of it." She looked up into the face she knew so well she could draw it from memory, every line of the high forehead, every curve of the enigmatic smile. "You left me and didn't tell me why. Left me to go through hell for almost a year." She paused, gritting her teeth to keep the tears at bay.

For the first time since they'd met, Wes looked shaky. "He was my father. You don't understand."

"That's the problem. I do understand." She turned and began to walk away.

"It's that goddamn pride of yours again," he said from behind her, his voice raised. "That's all it is. Are you really going to let something like that stand in our way?"

Something like pride?

She turned wearily. "Yes," she said. "I am."

He, too, was proud. He wouldn't follow her, wouldn't call, and finally that was a good thing. But, oh, it wouldn't be easy to face her car, her condo, her memories and her life tonight. She stepped past the security guard, refusing his offer of an escort the few short steps to her car.

Henderson's Honda was just pulling out of the parking lot. She ran toward it, mouthing only one word. "Stop."

He rolled down his window. "What's wrong?"

"Everything," she said. "Absolutely everything."

Her voice came out shaky. If she weren't so exhausted, she'd be crying, shedding tears all over this dusty car.

"Need a ride home?"

"No," she said, "but I could use some coffee. I'll even buy."

His expression didn't change, his face as battered as she felt. Only his arm moved, over toward the handle of the passenger door. "Guess I'd be a fool to turn down free coffee."

She walked around the car and climbed in. As they reached the Stop sign at the entrance to the lot, she saw the Saab in front of them. It turned left, and they turned right, and the frenetic beating of her heart finally began to slow down.

"They're gone," she said. "They all are."

"For now, at least," Henderson said.

She leaned against the seat and watched the lights of the city pass by, glad that someone else was driving for a change, grateful to be a passenger in a car driven by someone she trusted.

"Yes," she said, more to herself than to him. "At least ̶ ̶ ̶ ̶ ̶ ̶ ."

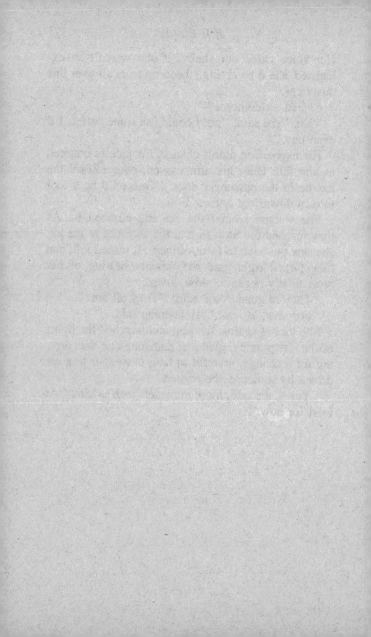

One

The Fat Lady

The cropping determines everything. Every newspaper person knows that.

CUTLINE: Golden Gate Park. Dawn. A shower of silver-green trees against a black, back-lit sky. So solid that sky, so stable, in spite of its carefree life by day. You can trust it with anything, and so does the couple, leaning like two trees behind the shelter of the building. Oh, yes, there are structures in this open place. They are not the first lovers here. Earlier they dreamed themselves one within the walls of that small sanctuary. They breathed earth and each other. They laughed. But now, outside, he's changed, trying to go back to his other life, although she knows he wants only to be with her.

"We shouldn't have." His voice diffuses into the air, the words difficult to differentiate. Remorse drips like rain.

"Don't talk like that. You know you love me."

"Listen to me. You must listen." He puts out his hand, his sleeve draping darkness. "Why can't you hear me? I told you. I made a mistake."

The words tinkle like bells. Something's wrong. Someone's making him lie.

"Don't try to fool me, not after what we just did."

"I'm sorry. I really am."

He's afraid to look up, even in the dark. She notices the soft, pale spot of his head. She loves him in spite of it. Bald doesn't matter when two people love each other.

"You wanted it as much as I did. Can't you feel it, even now?"

He moves away, and she knows how difficult it must be for him. She reaches out so that he knows it's okay. "I never meant to hurt you," he says. "I didn't know what was happening until it was too late."

His features fade. What is wrong? Why does everything desert her, dim at her touch, lose its appeal the moment she begins to love it?

No, push those thoughts away. Just look at this man. Even in the darkness, his eyes are coals of desire.

"You knew everything," she says. "You wanted everything. We did everything."

"I can't live with it. I've requested a transfer, confessed to someone I trust."

"Don't be silly, darling."

"I'm never going to see you again."

"Of course you are. Right here tomorrow night."

"No." She hates that word. "No." This time he stretches it out. Nooo.

He lifts his hand, then a flash of silver blinds her. Silver so bright she cannot hide from it, slashing the night with its vicious blade.

Her lover topples at her feet. For one disoriented

moment, she wonders what happened to him, then she looks down at the hideous slash on his throat, the thin red line, his twisted shadow, and remembers. Oh, no. Not this, not to this wonderful man, their wonderful love. She'd better do something about the razor.

CUTLINE: The body of San Francisco priest David McCaffrey was discovered today in Golden Gate Park.

Crop out everything but the body. The cropping is everything.

Father, forgive me.

NEW YORK TIMES BESTSELLING AUTHOR
CHRISTIANE HEGGAN

Grace McKenzie is shocked when she receives word that
her ex-fiancé has been murdered. She's equally shocked
when she discovers that he left her his art gallery in
New Hope, Pennsylvania.

She isn't the only person drawn to the small town.
FBI agent Matt Baxter has returned to his hometown
to clear his father of a bogus murder charge. But beneath
the surface of this charming, peaceful town lies an old
secret that Grace and Matt are dangerously close to
discovering—or being buried with.

WHERE TRUTH LIES

"Heggan dishes up an addictive read."
—*Publishers Weekly* on *Blind Faith*

*Available the first week of September 2006,
wherever paperbacks are sold!*

BONNIE
HEARN HILL

32001 INTERN   ___ $6.50 U.S.   ___ $7.99 CAN.
32145 DOUBLE EXPOSURE   ___ $6.99 U.S.   ___ $8.50 CAN.

(limited quantities available)

TOTAL AMOUNT $ _____
POSTAGE & HANDLING $ _____
($1.00 FOR 1 BOOK, 50¢ for each additional)
APPLICABLE TAXES* $ _____
TOTAL PAYABLE $ _____
(check or money order—please do not send cash)

To order, complete this form and send it, along with a check or money order for the total above, payable to MIRA Books, to: **In the U.S.:** 3010 Walden Avenue, P.O. Box 9077, Buffalo, NY 14269-9077; **In Canada:** P.O. Box 636, Fort Erie, Ontario, L2A 5X3.

Name: _____
Address: _____ City: _____
State/Prov.: _____ Zip/Postal Code: _____
Account Number (if applicable): _____

075 CSAS

*New York residents remit applicable sales taxes.
*Canadian residents remit applicable GST and provincial taxes.

MIRA®